Worth a Thousand Words

by

Doreen Alsen

The Lobster Cove Series

Worth a Thousand Words

Cover Art by *Tina Lynn Stout*

The Wild Rose Press, Inc.
PO Box 708
Adams Basin, NY 14410-0708
Visit us at www.thewildrosepress.com

Publishing History
First Champagne Rose Edition, 2016
Print ISBN 978-1-5092-0975-0
Digital ISBN 978-1-5092-0976-7

The Lobster Cove Series
Published in the United States of America

Dedications

To the Provincetown High School, Class of 1975!
"We are the Fishermen, Mighty, mighty Fishermen!
Everywhere we go, people want to know,
who we are, so we tell them!
We are the Fishermen!"
Didn't we have us a time?
Yes, we did!
~*~

To Rhonda Penders,
the best publisher in the world.
Your support has been invaluable.
~*~

And, as always,
to Eberhard, Emilia, and Louisa.

Prologue

Angelique Durand huddled on the edge of a cold metal bench in the middle of a holding cell in a Parisian jail. She shivered, even though she wasn't cold. In fact, the air was heavy and hot, full of the scents of cheap perfume, funky old sweat, and stale cigarette smoke.

The plugged up toilet in the back of the cell didn't help matters.

Surrounded by hookers, drug dealers, and crack-heads, she was totally out of her element. No place could be further away from the world of high fashion, where she'd lived for the past year and a half. She wrapped her arms around her middle.

She'd thought the other models were her friends. She couldn't believe they thought she was a thief.

Angelique was done with the fashion scene, which ended up being all flash and glitter, with nothing substantial. Once, if, she got out of this nightmare she swore she would start a brand new life, far, far away from the shiny, glossy designer runways of Paris.

"Mademoiselle Durand, you must come with me," the police officer said to Angelique as she unlocked the door of the jail cell.

Angelique closed her eyes hoping to quell the dizziness that washed over her. She'd been in this cell in a Parisian *maison d'arrêt* since her arrest four days ago.

1

Arrested for a crime she didn't commit.

She opened her eyes and lifted her chin. Whoever planted the fortune in diamond jewelry in her purse wanted to see Angelique humiliated and she was not going to give that person the satisfaction. As she shuffled to the door of her cell, she held out her wrists for the handcuffs.

"No need for that," her jailer told her.

Just like that, in the time it would take to snap her fingers, hope flicked on in her breast. The officer led her up the stairs and into an office.

"Here she is, sir. Do you need me for anything else?"

The man seated behind the big desk in the center of the room shook his head. "*Non, merci.* You may go."

The other man in the room stood and turned. "Angelique."

And, *le bon Dieu*, it was Jacques Leblanc, her brother Lucien's attorney here in Paris. Her knees buckled and Jacques caught her and led her to a chair and dropped her into it with great care. "Breathe," he said, his voice soothing and kind.

"We are dropping all charges against you. You're free to go," pontificated the man behind the desk.

Angelique shook her head to clear her hearing. "The charges are dropped?"

"Yes. Someone who was in the models' dressing room and saw someone put the jewels in your bag has come forward."

Jacques lifted a box that held her things, her Chanel tote and her calfskin Louboutin heels. "May I change my shoes?" The sooner she got the ugly sneakers they'd made her put on when she'd first been arrested, the better.

He handed her the expensive stiletto heels as she toed off the offending footwear. She sighed as she slipped her feet into her own shoes.

"I've got orders from your brother to take you to his flat here in town. He's unable to come right now due to problems with his London restaurant, so he wants you to stay put."

"For how long?" For once she'd do what Lucien told her. If he wanted her to stay put, that's exactly what she'd do. She grabbed her tote and hung it over her right shoulder. She fought the urge to make a quick trip to the ladies room to fix her make-up, even though she knew she must look a fright.

"I don't know. We'll find out when he calls. He pulled quite a few strings to get this mess smoothed over."

Of course, he had. Lucien was the King of the String Pullers. Right that moment she wanted a shower, a glass of wine, and a soft bed to sleep in. She hadn't slept since before her arrest. "I'm ready. Let's go."

Jacques nodded. "I've got a car waiting out front."

Tears welled and prickled against her eyelids as relief flooded through her. Even though her future was uncertain, to say the least, she felt better than she had in a long time.

They walked through the doors to the outside and a burst of sunlight blinded her. She shielded her eyes against the onslaught. She gasped and her knees threatened to crumble underneath her again.

Cameras, there must have been hundreds of them, flashed brighter than a million suns along with clicking and whirring noises. Over it all, reporters and paparazzi shouted her name and waved their hands in the air, trying to get her attention.

Overwhelmed, she hung back as Jacques grabbed her arm and tried to plow through the restless throng. "Please stand aside. Mademoiselle Durand has no comment."

"Over here, Angelique," yelled the reporter closest to her. "Give us a smile, *cherie*!"

"No," she shook her head and whispered as the world started to swoop and swirl around her.

"Hold on," Jacque commanded and held her elbow tighter as he pushed his way through the camera-snapping crowd to the waiting limo.

She had to duck and bob to avoid flailing elbows, jutting camera lenses, and feet that threatened to trip her. Police officers jumped into the fray and tried to clear a path to the car.

The photographers wouldn't stop coming, pushing toward her, all of them trying to get her attention.

Angelique couldn't speak. She felt like she was the bait in a zombie movie, with the press of bodies against her and Jacques, the grasping hands pounding out a random, heavy beat; the clicks and whirrs of their cameras all made it impossible to think and made it impossible to get away.

A paparazzo stepped on her foot as another pressed against her legs from behind. Her legs, still none too steady, almost gave out as she twisted away from the camera lens in her face.

She wrenched her ankle and cried out as she fell. At the same moment, a camera lens the size of a small elephant crashed into her right cheek.

She raised her arms to protect herself from being

crushed as tears exploded out of her eyes in a hot rush. Kicked in the ribs a couple of times, she heard people screaming obscenities and being shoved around.

Then it all stopped. For one terrifying second all she could hear was the clicking of cameras around her and her own weeping. Wetness spattered her face, wetness she assumed was her tears. She cracked her eyes open and found it wasn't tears after all.

It was blood. Her face was covered in it as it gushed out of her cheek.

She screamed and that was the last thing she remembered.

Chapter One

"I now pronounce you man and wife! You may now kiss your bride."

Tim Baldwin watched his best friend, Jeff Myers, wrap his arms around his brand, spankin' new wife, Beth, and plant a lip lock worthy of the record books.

Jeff and Beth deserved all the happiness in the world. After years apart, they finally found each other. Tim knew better than anyone how much Jeff suffered after Beth disappeared. His buddy deserved his happily ever after.

As for himself, Tim thought, not so much.

Good thing Jeff had asked him to be his best man instead of asking him to be the wedding photographer, because who-da-thunk internationally acclaimed, Pulitzer Prize winning photojournalist T.L. Baldwin had lost his gift?

He couldn't take a picture to save his soul. Life as he knew it was over.

Cut it out, he told himself. He needed to get a grip. His best friend was finally married to the woman he'd loved forever. Add on to it, he had a kick ass son with Beth.

He glanced over to where Jeff high-fived his son Danny. Twin grins spread over both their faces. Who knew someone could be so happy?

"Tim."

He turned to see the bride smiling up at him. "Hey, gorgeous."

The word didn't even begin to describe Beth. Radiant maybe. She glowed. Being Beth, both traditional and lovely, she wore a white lace dress and a crown of blush roses in her hair.

"Thank you for being here today." She hugged him.

"Wouldn't think of being anywhere else." He bent to give a quick peck to her cheek.

"Hey, get your own woman. This one's all mine," Jeff teased as he pulled Beth out of Tim's arms.

"You're a lucky man." Tim held his hand out to shake, but Jeff grabbed him and gave him a one-armed bro hug.

"Don't I know it? We've been waiting for this moment a long time."

The photographer came up to them. "Let's head over for some pictures." The wedding reception was taking place in the ballroom of the Spinnaker Yacht and Sail Club.

Despair and jealousy stabbed Tim in the heart at the thought of this photographer. He probably had a day job at Sears taking portraits of wiggly, drooling babies and snot-nosed kids, and could take pictures while Tim couldn't anymore.

Jeff and Beth couldn't have asked for a prettier day to get married. The sky was robin's egg blue and dotted with high fluffy clouds. The sun shone brightly, while a light breeze kept the day cool. Gulls swooped and squawked as they dive-bombed to snap some food.

Tim looked over the docks of sailboats and wished he were on his own boat. The longing grew with every ping and pang of halyards knocking against their masts. Whitecaps raced to the shore on top of the deep blue ocean.

That's when he saw her and his world turned upside down.

A solitary woman walked along the beach. Barefoot, wearing a flowered sarong and bikini top, she meandered along the foam of the waves as they broke on the shore. Her long black hair cascaded down her back as the wind toyed with it.

She wore sunglasses, but he imagined that her eyes were dark and maybe a little mysterious.

She was the most beautiful thing he'd ever seen.

Just as Tim was about to jump down to the beach and run after her, Jeff called for him. "Hey, Tim! Get over here. We need you for the pictures!"

Oh, right. Those damned photos. He shot one last glance at the woman, but she was off in the distance now.

"Coming," Tim said as he tore his gaze away from her. "I'll be right there."

What if he never saw her again? He had to find out who she was and where she lived.

****

Angelique Durand strolled in the surf. The water was so cold here in Maine. As she was born and bred in Louisiana, she wasn't prepared for how chilly the ocean was.

She walked away from the surf, sat on the stony beach, and looked out to sea. She'd come to Lobster Cove to hide and to find redemption.

The small seaside town, well, more like a village, had seemed the perfect place to do both those things.

Her brother had arranged everything for her and she was grateful. One look around the town told her that she had found her home, a quiet life as a recluse where nobody knew her name.

Where nobody cared if she was the notorious, disgraced, super-model Angelique.

The few people she'd met knew her as Angie, and she wanted to keep it that way.

She glanced over to the Yacht Club, where a wedding party posed for pictures. She shuddered. She never wanted another photo taken of her again.

Never.

The wedding people laughed and the wind carried the sound so she could hear them from where she sat. She envied them. She didn't have a lot to laugh about.

Angelique missed her brother's wedding because she'd been over in Europe, the French Riviera no less, and had been too busy to make the trip back to Addington, Massachusetts, where Lucien and his wife, Hope, lived.

How foolish and selfish she'd been.

Such a brat.

As she watched, a man in a tuxedo pulled away from the crowd and walked to the end of one of the docks where the boats were moored. He stuffed his hands into his pockets and stared out over the water.

In her previous life, all she'd see was how hot he was. Now, all she could see was sadness. Deep, soul-crushing sadness.

He mourned. He grieved deeply. She didn't know how she knew that, she just did.

He carried burdens, she imagined, heavy ones.

Then he turned his head and zeroed in on her, like

she was his true north.

She felt caught. She couldn't look away if she tried. This man was a kindred spirit united with hers by bone-shattering loss.

She looked away from this singular man, this lonely man, and walked the long way back to her cottage, where safety and sanity lived.

She looked back, but the man had left, most likely to celebrate with his friends. Or maybe he was the groom and needed a break from the crowd.

Angelique had known a lot of married men who didn't give a flying fig about their wives. She hated each and every one of them.

She rubbed her hand over her heart and hoped that her lonely guy wasn't a cheater.

Affairs with married men? Totally made of so much no.

****

"Thanks again, man, for doing all the best man stuff."

Tim nodded and shook the hand Jeff extended. "I was happy to do it. Are you taking off soon?"

"As soon as Beth is ready." He rolled his shoulders. "I still can't believe I found her after all these years. When are you going to find someone and settle down?"

Tim thought of the goddess on the beach. "My job keeps me moving around. That doesn't make for a good marriage."

"Are you going back to Iraq?"

His stomach rolled over. "Maybe. I don't know where the magazine's going to send me. I've got a whole lot of leave still." Which he intended to use to get better.

"Well, here comes my bride." Jeff's mouth quirked up into a goofy grin. "Off to Paris."

"Have a good trip."

"I plan to." Jeff slapped Tim on the back as he went to catch up with Beth.

Tim wandered back to the pier, thinking about the woman he'd seen. He had to meet her. Lobster Cove was a small town. She shouldn't be hard to find.

Chapter Two

"Okay, good Chester," Tim crooned to his one-hundred-pound Doberman. "Want to go for a run on the beach?"

Chester gave a loud woof, turned around in a circle, and licked the stump that stood for his tail.

Tim hated that, all this cropping of tails and ears, but he'd rescued this amazing dog so he couldn't be outraged.

Well, he couldn't be outraged much.

"I'm going to get some poop bags and then we can go."

More seismic barking.

God, he loved this dog. He'd rescued him when he first came home from Iraq and having him around had saved whatever sanity Tim had left.

"Come on, buddy. Let's go."

They made it down to the beach and started to run. Well, he ran. Chester trotted along next to him. He'd do three miles one way and three miles back.

Then when the wind picked up, he'd go for a long sail.

After that, he would try to take some pictures, during sunset.

If a sunset over the Atlantic Ocean couldn't inspire him to drag out the camera, nothing would.

He pushed himself to the point of exhaustion these

days. Even so, he still had trouble sleeping.

But the dreams, those damn nightmares, were always just a heartbeat away. In the desert, a foul-smelling bag over his head, the sudden darkness of being dragged away.

The beatings were the easy part. The worst thing was having that horrendous torrent of water poured over his head, again and again.

He stepped up the pace of his run, hoping the miles would take all the ugly away.

****

Angelique had just finished going through her Yoga routine. She took a deep breath of the fresh, salty air, turned off her music, and grabbed a glass of cucumber water.

Brrrrrrrrr. How could these people stand the cold?

That was the least of her problems.

A job. She had to get a job.

Her brother Lucien told her to take her time and get well before she put herself out in the world again, but the thought of continuing to let him pay her way after she walked all over him for years made her nauseous.

She wasn't trained for anything but wearing designer clothes, Louboutin skyscraper heels, and just being all around beautiful.

She didn't know what else to do.

Angelique knew clothes, hair, and make-up. Maybe she could go into business for herself.

Unfortunately, she'd need cash for that and she didn't have any. Lucien would float her a loan, but that made her stomach knot up worse.

Okay. She did know the restaurant business, at least the front of the house. She knew how to greet people and show them to their seats.

She'd been an ornament, nothing more.

Angelique turned to go back to her beach house when something caught her attention, a man running with his dog. They looked hell bent to nowhere.

She slipped inside before they noticed her. The last thing she needed was any attention. What she needed was an unremarkable job where she made enough money to support herself, but didn't have to go into the public, where someone might recognize her.

****

"Well, look what the cat dragged in?"

"Hey, Mrs. Troy. How's my best girl?" Tim smiled at the proprietor of the Lobster Cove Grocery Mart.

"Don't you try to sweet talk me, young man." She shook a finger at him.

"I'll try to behave. I just got in from sailing, and I need a six of Thunder Hole Stout."

"I hope you're going to get some food to go with that beer."

"Do Doritos count?"

"Pfffffffffft. Don't be fresh."

The bell above the entrance jingled as another customer came in.

Tim high-tailed it to the beer section. He'd just get the beer, leave, and order a pizza from Lobster Lanes delivery. He'd love to order Chinese, but that came from Bar Harbor and they didn't deliver.

As he bent over to grab his six-pack, a woman wandered down the aisle. From his position, he only could see her lower half, clad in skinny jeans and very high heels.

The front bell rang again and Birdie McCorkle

from the Sea Crest Inn walked into the store. As he didn't want to talk to her for any number of reasons, number one being that she never stopped talking, he decided to beat a hasty retreat.

And wasn't that a damn shame. He wanted to see more of the woman in the stiletto heels.

****

Angelique wandered through the Lobster Cove Grocery Mart, grabbing a pint of blueberries, several low fat, plain Greek yogurts, some granola, and finally, a copy of the Lobster Cove Anchor, the local newspaper, so she could start her job hunt right away.

On impulse, she picked up a couple of bottles of mineral water. Pricey, but she missed what the Germans called *Sprüdel*.

She went to pay for her groceries. There were two women at the checkout, one at the register, the other leafing through the latest *Soap Opera Digest*.

A bit on the plumper side of things, Helen Troy looked more than a little grumpy. The Soap Opera Lady, on the other hand, sported hair a virulent shade of red, one nature had never intended. She did all the talking. Mrs. Troy just nodded with a long-suffering smile on her face.

"Hello!" Angelique put her items on the conveyor belt.

"Angie! Hello!" Mrs. Troy had the look of a gladiator who really didn't want to go into the ring and had just gotten a last minute reprieve.

Angelique loved that they called her Angie around here. Angie was so far away from the screwed up Angelique Durand.

"And who might you be?" Soap Opera Lady turned

her attention to Angelique. The magic of Ireland tinged her voice.

Angelique's new sister-in-law, Hope Monahan-Durand had grown up in Ireland. Angelique crossed her fingers, wishing that Hope would one day forgive her for all the crap she'd doled out.

Angelique opened her mouth to answer but Mrs. Troy cut her off. "Angie is spending the summer in her brother's cottage on the northern beach." She lasered a glance at Soap Opera Lady. "Mind your own business."

Soap Opera Lady threw Mrs. Troy a very sour look. "And now, Helen! Don't I always?" She turned to Angelique. "I'm Birdie McCorkle, head housekeeper at the Sea Crest Inn. It's glad I am to meet you."

"I'm glad to meet you, too."

"Oh my God, Helen." Birdie slapped a hand over her ample bosom. "She's got an adorable accent."

Mrs. Troy rolled her eyes. "People from Iowa have an accent, according to you."

"Well, they do! They waltz around in their cornfields emphasizing their 'r's." She shook her head. "So sad."

Angelique rolled her eyes. Like people around here didn't have an accent.

"Dear Lord, Birdie. We're not in Kansas anymore."

"As if I don't know where we are. We both know Kansas is in the back of beyond."

Mrs. Troy chuckled. "So true. Everyone here knows that the mid-west begins at Buffalo, NY. Let me check you out."

"Thank you." The thought occurred to her that Mrs. Troy might know of some job openings. "May I ask you a question?"

"Ask away," Mrs. Troy said as she bagged Angelique's groceries.

"I'm wondering if you know of any job openings in town."

"Oh, I don't think so. All the summer jobs are filled with college students back from school."

"Not so fast," Birdie interrupted, tossing her hair. "It just so happens that we just lost a waitress/chambermaid at the Sea Crest Inn. Have you any restaurant experience lurking about in your past?"

Angelique's heart pounded. "Yes, I do. Lots of experience."

Okay, she'd only ever been a hostess at L'Enfer, her brother Lucien's restaurant, and rarely ventured back to the kitchen, but how hard could it be?

She'd also never been a chambermaid or cleaned a bathroom in her life, unless you counted the bathroom at Lucien's beach home here in Lobster Cove. Well, she'd just have to suck it up until she could find something better to do.

"I'll have to check with Betts Quinn, as she's the owner, you see. And we'll need to get a reference from one of your past employers, of course."

Her insides cringed. The only person who could give her a reference was Lucien. He'd be reluctant, but she'd get him to do it. "I can arrange that."

Birdie beamed. "Why don't you come with me now, I'll introduce you to Betts and we can go from there."

"Um, I'm not really dressed for a job interview." As a former runway model, she knew that the right outfit made all the difference. Dressed as she was in skinny jeans, a tight blue crop top, and her favorite stiletto heel Marc Jacobs sandals, she didn't think she'd make a good impression.

"You look fine. You'll have to wear a uniform, anyway. Let's go, dearie. No time like the present." Birdie pulled her out of the store.

"Wait! My groceries!"

Mrs. Troy waved her away. "I'll keep them here and you can come back for them."

Angelique shrugged and let Birdie McCorkle drag her to her car. She might as well go along for the ride.

Chapter Three

Tim sat on his deck, camera by his side, drinking a beer. Early June could still be a little cold in the evening, but after Iraq, he welcomed the cool air. The sun would set soon over a still, serene sea, waves lapping at the shore. He'd spent the afternoon taking photos but deleted each one after he looked at it.

He might as well take Chester for a walk on the beach. As he stood to get the leash, some movement caught his eye.

His pulse spiked. The goddess from the yacht club on the day of Jeff and Beth's wedding strolled down to the water.

She sat near the water's edge and shook out her mass of long silky-looking hair. The slight breeze tangled with the dancing strands she'd freed. She wrapped her arms around her knees as she stared into the distance.

His mind went blank and his mouth got a little dry. Without realizing what he was doing, he grabbed his camera and started snapping photos.

Chester had other plans. Before Tim could react, the dog took off on his own, down to the sand where the woman sat, barking for all he was worth.

"Chester!" Tim put down the camera and ran to catch him.

The woman screamed, jumped to her feet, and ran

up the stairs to her patio. Chester barked happily and crouched down into play-with-me position, front paws down, back haunches up, his stump of a tail wagging for all it was worth.

"Chester!" He grabbed him by the collar. "I'm so sorry! He got away from me. You don't have to be afraid of him. He's harmless."

"I'll be the judge of that." She looked at him, dark eyes wide, her left hand over her left cheek. "Is he a dog or a pony?"

Tim laughed. "He's big enough to be a pony. His name is Chester, and he's totally harmless."

"Uh-huh." She crossed her arms across her stomach, just underneath her breasts, plumping them up and making it very apparent that her nipples were erect against the material of her shirt.

He blinked, let go of Chester's collar, and extended his hand. "Hi. Tim Baldwin at your service. Welcome to the neighborhood."

She cocked her head to one side. "Angie." He noticed she didn't offer a last name, nor did she offer her hand. "Thank you for the welcome." She walked down her stairs to the beach

She was even more gorgeous up close. Her hair tangled into an impossible mess around her shoulders. She didn't seem to notice. And those eyes. Dark and exotic, slightly tilted up at the outer corners, just like he'd imagined them. That sexy mole next to her mouth. The spice of the south in her voice completed the package.

Then she moved her hand away from her face. A fierce red scar curved down her cheek. It did not take a single thing away from her beauty, not to him.

She eyed him with defiance, obviously waiting for him to say something about it or to react with disgust. Well, she could just keep waiting for that.

"Are you staying here long?"

Her eyes clouded over. "I don't know."

"Well, would you like to come back to my house for a drink or something?"

She shook her head and looked back to her cottage. "No, thank you. I don't think so. I've got to get back."

"Maybe some other time." *Sound desperate much?*

"Perhaps." She turned to go.

"I'm sorry I destroyed your evening."

"You didn't. Chester did."

The dog's stump of a tail wagged wildly at the sound of his name. "I'm apologizing in his stead."

"Then Chester is forgiven." She threw one last smile over her shoulder. "Good evening."

He watched her walk back to her cottage before he headed back to his own house to take a look at the shots he'd taken.

****

Angelique turned on the heat under a teakettle and thought about the man, Tim, and his huge dog. He was certainly a very handsome man.

He sported more than a little five o'clock shadow, the scruff making his face more chiseled, more angular. His eyes were an odd shade of gray and fringed with lashes thick enough to make any woman weep with envy. Broad of shoulder, slim of hips, he was truly a fine hunk of a man.

She had turned around after he'd started to go back to his beach house because she had to check out his behind. It was worth the effort because his butt was

F.I.N.E.—fine.

She considered herself a connoisseur of that part of the male anatomy, and she'd seen some excellent ones in her day. Shane Baker, her last boyfriend, had possessed an extremely fine one.

The thought of Shane filled her with regret. She'd treated him awfully, and he was such a good man.

Lucien reminded her of that often. How odd was it, her brother becoming besties with her ex-boyfriend, a boyfriend he'd hated at the time.

All she had seen was what she wanted and what she had to do to get it. In doing so, she'd hurt people, not the least Shane, but also Lucien and his wife, Hope.

Once she'd resented her brother, but he had really come through for her when she'd been arrested. She'd been so horrible to him, yet he'd dropped everything to go to Europe and help her.

He didn't want her to get a damn job, but she'd gotten one anyway, and he would laugh when he heard what kind of job. Birdie had come through, and so Angelique had to show up at the Sea Crest Inn, bright and early to train.

The kettle whistled and she poured the boiling water into a real china cup, over a teabag of Constant Comment. She added a couple of allspice balls and a cinnamon stick. The spicy, orange, cinnamon scent wafted up from the cup.

She'd always preferred the chicory coffee of New Orleans. A huge sense of longing flooded every molecule of her being. Tea was such a poor substitute.

She almost told Tim her real name. She knew better than that.

Something about him pulled to her, but never

mind. She needed, more than the breath in her lungs, to stay away from men.

Any men.

Men were just not on the menu.

No matter how sexy they were.

Of which, Mr. Tim had sexy in spades.

She probably should get some sleep. Her interview went well, she supposed, and she was getting a try-out day tomorrow.

Following a busboy around cleaning and setting up tables, hokying floors, she wrinkled her nose before taking a slow, careful sip of tea.

She was so ready for this nightmare to be over, so done with it all. When would she get her life back?

****

Tim sat at his kitchen table, reviewing the shots he'd taken of Angie No Last Name. He shook his head in wonder as he went over each photo.

The composition, the light, the texture, everything added up to a pretty damn good picture. He'd caught her profile, every graceful line running from her neck down to her back, and the hair.

He'd captured that gorgeous hair but not the scar. If she knew he was taking her picture, she may very well be too self-conscious for him to get any good shots.

Okay, he'd never done portraits. He'd taken pictures by the seat of his pants, dodging explosions, bullets, and whatever fresh hell the opposition threw at all those innocent civilians to get the best shot, the one shot that would tell the story he felt needed telling.

The story the world needed to know.

The pictures he took tonight were very different.

Somehow he caught the aura of sadness he'd sensed from the first time he saw her. The colors of the sky had begun to turn into magnificent magentas, fuchsias, and apricots streaks. The gentle waves broke on the shore as the ocean took on a very intense, saturated blue.

They told a story of a beautiful woman, as the day moved into twilight on the beach. They were lyrical and filled with music.

They didn't tell an ugly, hopeless, sensational story. They spoke to peace and yearning.

He'd never taken pictures like this before.

Tim got up and walked around his kitchen, while he ran his fingers through his hair. He should be jumping up and down, having the ability to see the truth through a camera lens again.

He wondered if she'd pose for him. She had to pose for him. It wasn't an option.

He'd have to keep trying to capture moments when she was unself-conscious and at ease. He'd worry about getting a written, legal release if and when he ever did anything with the magic of Angie.

Chapter Four

Angelique stared at the green T-shirt Birdie McCorkle held up for her. "Now, this is the top, you see. You'll need to tuck it in." She looked askance at Angelique's black, cropped skinny jeans and the tortoise shell patent leather flats Angelique wore.

Angelique looked down at the shoes, filled with delight. They were from last year's Michael Kors' fall collection and he'd given her a pair. She thought them adorable, with their pointed toes and shiny surfaces, and, of course, they went with everything.

"Now here's the shirt, so go in the staff room and try it on." Birdie pressed her lips together. "Might you have any more sturdy or comfortable shoes to wear, dear?"

Angelique smiled. "Oh, these are very comfy. I'll be fine."

"They're your feet I suppose. Now go get changed and I'll take you around and introduce you to the crew, especially Patricia who you'll be following today."

"Great," Angelique replied, pasting a sunny smile on her face as she took the dreadful green shirt. She checked out the tag and groaned. There was some cotton in there, as in traces, but she wondered how many polyesters had died to make that shirt.

She'd taken an antihistamine so she wouldn't break out in hives. Little itchy, red spots were hardly

25

attractive, to say the least. She thought she still had enough of her Temple Spa skin regime products left, but if she didn't?

Disaster. Total and complete disaster.

She had more to worry about than skin care products. She pushed the heavy, dark framed hipster glasses she wore as a disguise up her nose, where they were more comfortable.

After settling the shirt around her and tucking it in so it looked kind of flattering, she stepped out, ready to begin her new career.

"Let me have a look at you," Ms. McCorkle ordered. She sighed. "I guess you'll do. Go on now with you to the kitchen."

"Okay." Angelique took a couple of steps and looked back just in time to see Ms. McCorkle make the sign of the cross.

****

Tim squinted as he looked to the wind direction indicator on top of the mast then pulled the genoa sheet to eke out just a little more speed from his sailboat, *Fantasy*. A Melges 24, this honey of a boat was one of the hottest racing boats around.

Actually, it was the fastest boat he could buy.

These days he lived for pushing the limits, to go as fast as he possibly could. The limitless horizon, the slap of the waves as *Fantasy* cut through them, the salt spray stinging his face all went a long way to keep away the demons.

He'd been sailing for as long as he could remember. As a matter of fact, it was a near miss that his mother hadn't given birth to him right in the middle of Nahant Bay, where his hometown of Addington,

Massachusetts bordered. His parents had to call the Coast Guard to get her off the boat and to the hospital. Tim chuckled at the story. His mother and father loved to tell it to anyone who would listen. Again and again.

Right now, the two of them navigated their dream trip, to make it from the St. Lawrence Seaway all the way down to Key West. Retirement hadn't slowed either of them down. Just one more item checked off their bucket list.

The wind shifted a bit and he re-trimmed the genoa and the mainsail so he'd hit Sheep Porcupine Island sooner if the wind held.

He pondered how he could get the lovely Angie to come on a sail with him. He probably should find out what her last name was before he took her sailing.

She intrigued him more than any other woman, ever. There was a story there in that scar and he itched to hear it, especially since she seemed to have given him back his ability to take pictures.

Tim hoped the shots he took last night weren't a fluke. He needed his gift back, and she might be the key to unblock him.

He'd just have to walk Chester again tonight and see what Angie was up to. Sometimes it was good to own a dog.

He grinned. Okay. It was good to own a dog all the time.

****

Angelique didn't think she could hoist another tray of dirty dishes. Her arms, shoulders, and upper back ached underneath the weight of the food encrusted plates and bowls, and the filmy glasses still partially filled with liquid.

Her oh-so-cute shoes cut into her skin, creating blisters, the patent leather got a few cracks, and she'd stepped into something slippery and definitely unsavory.

She'd never get the smell of grease out of her hair.

Worst of all? She'd broken a nail and who knew where you could get a quality manicure here.

Thank heaven the lunch rush looked to be about over.

She hauled the heavy tray into the kitchen to the dishwasher. Groaning, she leaned it on the edge of the stainless steel counter and unloaded the dishes.

Birdie McCorkle came up behind her. "Angie! Just who I'm after finding."

Angelique turned. "Is everything okay?"

"Aye. We just need you to the office and fill out some forms so we can pay you. I also want to make sure you see the patio area around back. Sometimes people have cocktails out there and you need to know where it is."

"Okay. Just let me wash my hands." She winced as she took a step.

Birdie clucked her tongue as she looked at Angelique's shoes. "They look a little worse for wear, don't they?"

She sighed. "I guess you were right."

"Sure and I was. I always am. Let's go."

Angelique limped along behind her.

They walked through the elaborate gardens and paths behind the inn. Gorgeous Adirondack style benches lined the way to the patio.

"Here we are," Birdie said. "Isn't the view spectacular?"

The patio was a small lookout area that sat over the rocks, like a shelf. An ornate iron fence bordered the natural rock floor. It jutted out over the water like it was suspended into space. The wind picked up the closer they got to the edge, creating a bit of instability. Angelique felt her stomach turn over and her breath caught in her throat.

She was terrified of heights.

"Go on, go look over the fence. The cove is beautiful from here."

Angelique reached out and braced herself against an iron chair some ways from the edge. A wave of dizziness made her ears buzz. "No, it's okay. I'm good."

Birdie gave her a quizzical look. "Well then, let me show you the lanai."

Angelique nodded, ready to go anywhere away from the patio edge and followed her.

The lanai was quite lovely, with a fire pit and padded furniture and a little bit further away from the cliffs. *Thank God.*

At the end of the tour, Birdie took Angelique to her office. She picked up a packet of papers and handed them to her. "Here, take these home, fill them out, and bring them back tomorrow. I've scheduled you for breakfast and lunch again." Birdie flashed her a grim smile. "And, for the love of sweet baby Jesus, lass, get a sensible, sturdy pair of shoes."

"So, does this mean I have a job?"

"That it does, me girl, that it does. Oh, and I almost forgot." She pulled a wad of single dollar bills out of her pocket. "This is your share of the tips today."

"Tips?" Didn't only wait staff get tips?

"The waiters are expected to give the bussers fifteen percent of their tips. You worked hard. So, here. Good job today."

Angelique's hands shook a little as she took the money from her. "Thank you."

"You're welcome. Now get on home and soak those poor feet of yours."

Angelique smiled at her as she slid out of the office as fast as her injured little tootsies could take her.

Chapter Five

Tim sat on his deck, kicking back, and scowled at his camera, willing it to work with him and start taking the kinds of pictures he used to take.

He picked up the ice cold, condensation beaded bottle of Thunder Hole Stout and drank deep, the bubbles prickling down his throat. He welcomed the discomfort. The sea was mirror still and a placid shade of blue. If he kept his gaze trained out to the horizon, he might catch a glimpse of a herd of whales or dolphins.

He heard some commotion from Angie's patio. Glancing over, he saw her limping and carrying a beach chair down her steps. She also muttered some terse French words that sounded like curses.

She put her chair down where the waves broke against the beach and lowered herself onto the chair, wincing as she did. Kicking her feet into the surf, she let her head drop against the seat back.

Tim didn't even think. He just picked up his camera and started clicking away. The ethereal light created a perfect backdrop for this goddess kicking in the foamy water then burying her feet in the ocean-cooled sand.

Clad in a pair of shorts and a red bikini top, Angie practically vibrated against the perfect blue of the water. Of course, he was photographing her from the back but that dark hair of hers flew in the light wind.

Standing up, Chester padded over to Tim and put his head on Tim's thigh, pitiful brown eyes begging for permission to go out and say hello to his new friend.

Well, it was only the neighborly thing to do, right?

Tim would find out.

****

Angelique sat on her beach chair, inhaling the June breeze that always carried the taste of salt. Of course that salt wasn't doing her hair and complexion any favors.

Her feet felt a lot better than they had when she'd hobbled out of the Sea Crest Inn. Still, a good soak in the ocean and some of the foot balm she had for after a long day walking the runway should do the trick.

"Hey!"

Oh, look. Her handsome neighbor, Tim, with his very large dog.

They stood at the bottom of their stairs watching her with matching grins. Well, not quite matching. The dog's tongue stuck out of his mouth while Tim kept his in his mouth.

"Hey," she called back. She stood, only wincing a little bit. "Out for a walk?"

He held up the leash. "Yep. Want to come along?"

She hid a grimace that threatened to spread all over her face. "Uh, no thank you. I'm happy to stay right here for now. It's a pretty and restful view."

"That it is." He looked out to the distance. "So, Miss Angie No Last Name, what did you do today?" He smiled at her. "Or maybe you can let me know your last name."

Angelique's breath hitched. She'd give him the name she'd put on those tax forms she had to fill out.

"Doucette. Angie Doucette."

He raised his brows. "Doosit? Angie Doosit? That's not a name you hear around these parts. But then, your accent is a big clue that you're from somewhere warmer."

"That's true." She looked out over the water. "But I like it here. Lobster Cove is very charming and low key. The people are friendly."

He put the hand she'd released into his cargo shorts pocket. "Low key is good. People pretty much leave you alone if you don't want to socialize."

"It's definitely a plus." She wrapped her arms around her middle.

He bent down and picked up a sizeable piece of driftwood. "Hey! Chester!" He threw the stick. "Fetch!"

The dog woofed and galloped after it.

"He's not as scary when he's not running at top speed, mouth open to show those big teeth, and barking up a storm."

Tim laughed. "He's a good dog." Chester skidded to a halt in front of him and dropped the piece of wood on Tim's feet. He picked up the stick and threw it again. Chester took off like the Tazmanian Devil from the Bugs Bunny cartoons.

"We had another Dobie when I was growing up, a character named Ruffie. Every day me or my dad would take him for a walk. Ruffie made it his job to pick out one piece of driftwood. It had to be the biggest piece. Then he carried it back to the cottage." He chuckled. "People started calling him 'the log dog.' When he died, we didn't have to buy any firewood for a year and a half." He shook his head. "Crazy dog."

"We never had any pets. Well, not unless you

33

counted the gators." Truly, the gators were everywhere on the bayou where she grew up.

His eyes widened. "Gators, huh? That's too bad. Dogs are great." He clapped his hands as Chester careened back with the stick. Tim took it and threw it again. The dog whooped with joy and ran to get it. "His idea of heaven. Except he practically swoons when you scratch behind his ears."

Angelique could imagine Tim's fingers rubbing behind her ears, massaging her scalp, running his fingers through her hair. "I can imagine. And don't underestimate the love of a good gator."

He laughed and it felt somewhat intimate. Uh-oh. Another reason she should go into her house along with the fact that the liniment for her feet was calling her name. But she didn't want to.

The man she wished was playing with her hair had a lot to do with it.

Besides, the sun was about to set, the colors just beginning to bloom over the horizon.

So beautiful. Why had she never taken time to notice before?

She'd spent too much time looking into a mirror, worshiping her own likeness. Honing her own beauty to perfection.

Well, her beauty was no longer perfect. The scar on her cheek gave proof of that.

Still, when he looked at her, she saw something in his eyes that she never expected to see again.

Desire.

She'd have none of that; she couldn't, so she cleared her throat. "I should go on up. I've got an early day tomorrow."

He stared at her, his expression unreadable. "Okay." He whistled. "Chester!"

"You don't need to come back with me. I'm a big girl."

"I know I don't have to. I want to." He reached out, gently took her hand, and tugged her out of her chair then picked it up. "Let me get this for you."

He held her so lightly she could have easily pulled her hand away, but she didn't. Their connection felt right.

Intimate.

Both desire and fear skittered up her spine as they climbed her stairs together in silence. They reached her door and he put down the chair, took her other hand, and turned to face her. "Would you like to go to dinner with me tomorrow night?"

Yes. Yes she did. But…"I'd like that, but no big deal, okay? Someplace quiet? Off the beaten path?" Someplace where no one would recognize her.

He smiled. "I think I can manage that. How about I come get you around seven o'clock?"

"Sounds perfect."

"Until tomorrow then." He lifted her hands to his mouth and placed a soft kiss in each palm then curled her fingers over her palms. "Good night. Come on, Chester."

He left, his dog following him.

She sat on her stoop and looked out over the water until the stars began to sparkle.

Whatever she'd expected when she sought refuge here in Lobster Cove, a man like Tim was nowhere on the list.

Chapter Six

Tim decided that Mariner's Fish Fry was the perfect place for a low-key date. They could sit outside, stay off the beaten path.

It didn't hurt the blueberry pie was the finest kind.

He'd spent the rest of last night and most of this morning going over the pictures he'd taken of Angie. They were good. Really good. Maybe the best he'd ever done.

He'd managed to capture her graceful energy as she played in the surf. The gentle shower of light and shadow showcased both a sense of fragility and strength.

She was magnificent.

Last night had been a revelation. He hadn't felt so much peace in such a long, long time.

His phone went off. "Baldwin."

"Hey, Tim. It's Jeff."

"Hey, lover boy. How was the honeymoon?"

"Wicked good. Listen," Jeff said. "Do you still need me to crew on Thursday night?"

"You know I do." Tim frowned. "You're not going to bail on me, are you?"

"No, no, just confirming. Danny has a Little League game in the afternoon, but I can do both."

"Listen to you, Dad."

"Yeah, it's great! By the way, Beth wants to know

when you're coming over for dinner."

"I'll have to check my very crowded social calendar and let you know."

Jeff snorted. "Do that. What time do you need me on Thursday?"

"Race starts at seven thirty, so six? We can do a couple of spinnaker drills."

"Sounds good. See you then. Later."

"Yep." Tim clicked his phone off.

Jeff sounded good. Happy. And Tim was happy for him.

He picked up one of the photos he'd taken of Angie the other night when she sat on the beach at sunset.

Tim wished that he deserved to be happy, too, but he didn't. Not by anyone's yardstick.

****

Angelique found herself between a rock and a hard place. Every instinct she had was to gild the lily and use every bit of make-up magic she possessed to make sure she got everybody's attention.

Especially Tim's attention.

The sensible part of her argued that she used just enough make-up to disguise her scar, but not so much that she caused a stir.

Except she wouldn't mind stirring up Tim.

Unfortunately, her life was such that she had to dial it down. She sighed.

Lucien was hesitant at first about her getting a job, but he'd listened to her and in the end got on board with it.

He even laughed and told her it was about time she learned, hands on, about the back of the house.

Then he'd asked about the head chef, a woman named Alma whose ancestors hailed from Sweden—yes, the Sea Crest Inn had a Swedish chef—and told her to scope out the recipes.

He also told her to look out for Kermit, Gonzo, and Miss Piggy.

She shook her head. Whatever.

She pulled her hair back into a ponytail and attached it to the top of her head with more than a few bobby pins.

Sighing again, she plonked a straw hat over her hair and pulled on her sunglasses. She went out onto her front porch, sat in a poppy-colored butterfly chair, and waited for Tim.

And when had she ever waited for a man? Not until now.

She thought of Tim's exquisite gentleness last night. Maybe he was worth waiting for.

****

"Wow, you look gorgeous," Tim told Angie as he walked up to her house.

She blushed and touched the scar on her cheek. "That's kind of you to say."

"I mean it." He barely noticed the scar. It didn't make one bit of difference to him. She was still the most beautiful woman he'd ever seen. "Are you ready to go?"

She stood and nodded. "Where are we going?"

"Mariner's Fish Fry. Have you been there yet?"

"No. I really haven't been going out much."

"Well, you might want to get a jacket. It might get a little chilly later."

"Be right back," she said.

He watched her go into her cottage, enjoying the graceful sway of her hips as she moved. Cliché maybe, but sheer poetry in motion, like that old song said.

"Okay, I'm ready." She smiled as she closed her door and locked it.

Who could notice a scar when she gave them that dazzling smile?

He felt himself grinning like an idiot. "Great."

****

Angelique laughed to herself when Tim led her into Mariner's Fish Fry, thinking about what Lucien would say about this restaurant.

Would he even grant it the title of restaurant?

In the past? No. But lately, he'd become a little more tolerant.

Now he'd say the food would tell the story.

Before he met Hope? Not so much.

"Hey, Tim," a tall blonde said as they walked into the restaurant. "Here for dinner?"

"Hey, Katelyn. Yeah, we are. Got a quiet place on the back deck?"

Katelyn grinned. "Sure do." She looked Angelique in the face, her expression was friendly, but Angelique could tell that she'd noticed the scar.

"You look so familiar to me," she said as she tilted her head to the side. "Have we met before?"

Angelique's palms started to sweat. "No, I don't think so. I'm new here in town."

"Given your accent, I can tell. It's just that I have a good memory for faces and I could swear I've seen you before. Anyway," Katelyn sighed, "let me get you a table."

Tim rested his hand against the small of her back

as they followed Katelyn to the deck.

Rustic kitsch, she decided. They'd decorated the ceiling with multi-colored lobster buoys. Outside, weathered lobster pots were stacked against the wall. A lighthouse stood off to one side in the harbor. Picnic tables lined the patio and little red, white, and blue fairy lights glittered around the seating area.

Here was your first clue, and it was a big one, that you were now in Maine.

"This should be private enough." Katelyn set their menus on the table. "Can I get you something to drink?"

"Do you want something?" Tim helped Angelique onto the wooden bench.

"Some sparkling water, please."

Tim slid next to her then looked at Katelyn. "A sparkling water and a Thunder Hole Stout, please."

"Um, we've got club soda, is that all right?"

"Oh." Angelique blinked. "Sure. Thank you."

"I'll be right back with your drinks and to take your order."

"So, what do you think?"

"Think?"

He gestured to their surroundings. "About the ambiance here at Mariner's Fish Fry."

She wrinkled her nose. "It's pretty…fishy."

Tim chuckled. "That it is." He picked up a menu. "The lobster boil is good here, but everything is fresh so it's good. My family used to bring us here and order a full clambake. It was awesome."

"What's in a clambake?"

"What isn't? Lobsters, clams, mussels, potatoes, a sausage called *linguiça*, corn on the cob, seaweed." He rubbed his belly.

"That's a lot of food." She looked at her menu. The lobster boil sounded a lot like a crawfish boil, only with the seaweed.

Just the thought of crawfish made her miss her brother and her *Grand-mère*. It came out of the blue, unexpected and unwanted. She cleared her throat.

"You okay?" Tim looked puzzled.

"Of course. I just got something caught in my throat."

"I didn't even ask if you like seafood."

"I do." She studied the menu. Fried this, sautéed in butter that, slathered in the New England aberration called tartar sauce, no thank you. "Do you think they'd just broil me a piece of the catch of the day?"

"Probably. The kitchen staff is usually flexible. Ruark and Dawn, the owners, run a tight ship, but are always accommodating to their customers' wishes."

Angelique knew all about restaurant owners running a tight ship. "Talk about!"

"Say what?"

Oh dear. "I've worked in a few restaurants for some very tyrannical chef slash owners." True. Sooooo true!

It helped to think of Lucien as a tyrant. She didn't miss him as much if she clung to that thought.

Katelyn showed up with their drinks. "Are you ready to order?" She set the beer and water on the table.

"What's the catch of the day?"

"We got some nice yellow-tail flounder in. You want the fish and chips?"

Tim shook his head. "Is it possible to get a flounder filet broiled with," he looked at Angelique, "the

41

vegetable of the day?"

Angelique nodded at the vegetables.

Katelyn's mouth quirked up at one end as she tapped her pen on her dupe pad. "Sure."

"Great!" Tim beamed. "And I'll go for those fish and chips."

"Flounder or Haddock?"

"Flounder, please."

"Gotcha." She picked up the menus. "Flounder coming right up."

Looking at Angelique, she asked, "Do you want any like herbs and stuff on your fish? I've got to warn you, the only right answer is oregano."

"Oregano sounds lovely." She hated oregano, especially on its own as it was so bitter, but when in Rome—

"Awesome. Be right back in three shakes of a lobster's tail."

Tim moved a little bit away from her as Katelyn left. "I don't want to complain, but do you think you might take those sunglasses off sometime in this century? I'd like to see your pretty eyes when I talk to you."

Panic clawed at her throat. The waitress already thought she looked familiar. If she took off the glasses, that woman might put it all together.

And Tim would find out that she was Angelique Durand, notorious, disfigured supermodel. She didn't want to let him in on the secret yet, not until she knew him better.

He already knew about the scar, how could he not. It stood out like a bright red slash of ugliness.

No make-up could hide it.

She shook her head. "When it gets a little darker."

He shrugged. "Suit yourself. It seems like a shame to keep those gorgeous peepers of yours covered."

"Peepers?" She laughed.

"Yeah, like the song, you know, 'Jeepers, creepers, where'd you get those peepers? Jeepers, creepers, where'd you get those eyes?'" He'd belted it out.

Okay, that was a little embarrassing. "I've never heard of it before."

"You must have had a sheltered childhood."

"I did."

"Where did you grow up?" He poured his beer into the chilled glass Katelyn had brought him.

"Down south." She might as well tell him. It would look stupid and suspicious not to. "New Orleans."

"Really? Great city. I've been there a bunch of times. Kind of hard to be sheltered there, I'd think."

"Yet I was." When she'd been holed up on the bayou. She'd blown that popsicle stand in short order.

"This one time I was there I made sure I had dinner at Lucien Durand's flagship restaurant L'Enfer New Orleans. It was amazing, well worth the trip. Did you ever eat there?"

Oh, dear. "Yes. The food is very good."

"Good? The guy is a genius. I met him, even. He's pretty intense, but then most artists are."

Oh, if Tim only knew how intense Lucien Durand could get. Time to change the subject. "Where did you grow up?"

"Here during the summers and down in Addington, Massachusetts during the school year." He drummed his fingers on the table. "It was a good childhood."

Addington? *Addington!* Her brain swam so much

43

she got dizzy. What fresh hell was this? She could in no way let him know about her Addington connection.

It didn't bear thinking about.

She took a deep breath and changed the subject. "Is that why you're here now? Just for the summer?"

Tim's expression darkened. "Something like that. I'm taking some time off from work and doing some sailing. Have you ever sailed?"

No. She'd been in a couple of pirogues, poled through the bayou, but that had been hot, sticky, and buggy. Nothing that she'd ever want to do again. "No, I've never been sailing."

"You have to come out with me sometime. There's nothing like it."

"How so?" *Just keep him talking about himself so he won't ask too many questions.*

"It's just you and your boat and the elements, flying over the water, propelled by the wind. You just feel so alive and free." He looked out over the view of the harbor, out beyond the squat lighthouse, out to the breakwater. The slight breeze ruffled his hair and he squinted against the late rays of the sun.

A man surveying his kingdom.

"Do you have a big boat?"

"No. I have a Melges 24, which is pretty small. But it's the fastest thing out there, total state of the art. The hull is made from lightweight fiberglass and the mast, rudder, bowsprit, and keep fin are made from carbon fiber. They also designed it so you don't have to do any work on the foredeck, even flying the spinnaker."

"I have no idea what any of that means, but I'm sure it's wonderful." She smiled at his embarrassment over his enthusiasm.

"Sorry. I get a little crazy about sailing."

"Here you are, guys!" Katelyn showed up with their food. "Broiled sole with summer squash and fish and chips with coleslaw. Can I bring you anything else? Another beer, Tim? More water, uh—"

"I'm sorry, I didn't introduce you. Katelyn, this is Angie Doucette."

"Nice to meet you, Angie. Want another club soda?"

Ah, the sodium. Total bloat city. She sighed. "Yes, please."

"You got it. Be right back."

Angelique glanced at her broiled fish. They'd put butter on it, which of course defeated the purpose for getting broiled fish.

Damn. She really did miss Lucien.

Who lived in Addington, Massachusetts, exactly where the handsome man she was currently on a date with, came from. The world had become very small.

Too close for comfort.

Chapter Seven

"You want to take a walk out to the lighthouse? We have to work off all those calories you packed in," Tim teased Angie as he led her out of the restaurant.

He couldn't believe how little she ate. At least he'd gotten her to take her sunglasses off.

He also noticed every time he asked her something about herself, she turned the conversation back to him.

Sooner or later, he'd learn all her secrets, without giving up any of his own hidden demons.

He was tricksy like that.

Okay. And maybe he should stop watching the Lord of the Rings movies. Like soonishly.

"I don't know. I have to work tomorrow, bright and early."

"You didn't tell me where you work."

"I'm working at the Sea Crest Inn. I've got the breakfast shift tomorrow."

He grinned. "Really. I'll have to stop in. Alma bakes a mean Danish, for, you know, a Swedish chef. It's kind of like hur-dee-duhr-dee-deena-danish."

She snorted at his Muppets reference. She had a lot in common with Miss Piggy. "I know, right?" She slapped his arm. "Behave! Alma is very nice. I've heard they're very good."

"Haven't tried one yet? You've got to. I like the cheese ones the best, but everyone else likes the blueberry. You know how it is around here. All blueberry, all the time."

This time she exploded in a true belly laugh. "Only when it's not all lobster, all the time."

"Jeez, can I get an amen for that? I think the worst is the cartoon logo Lionel the Lobster for the October Harvest of the Sea Festival." He shivered. "I had bad dreams about Lionel for a long time after I first saw him."

Something creeped up from his feet to his head. He probably shouldn't have mentioned having bad dreams.

It felt too much like tempting fate.

"What's so bad about poor Lionel?"

He shook the mood off. "Well, since he's red, that means he's cooked, which means he's dead, with these black bugged out eyes and a smile only a zombie lobster mother would love."

"Zombie lobster? There is such a thing?"

"I don't know, but do you really want to find out?" He snapped his fingers. "Our boy Lionel probably has the B-52's 'Rock Lobster' as a theme song. It plays in the background as he feasts on his next victim's brains. Nanh-nanh-nanh-nanh-nanha-nanha-nanha-nanha," he belted out like he was Fred Schneider.

"That is so gross." She laughed so hard she could barely speak. "And you can't sing!"

"I'm cut to the quick! I'll have you know I sang in the chorus in high school. I was an exemplary student."

"You? In chorus? I don't believe it."

Tim pulled her down along the pier with him. "Actually, it was not one of my finer moments. Me and my buddy got stuck in choir because we needed a fine arts credit to graduate and chorus was the only place to go. We were not happy, so we made the teacher not happy, which caused her to flunk us and put us on the ineligible list." He shook his head at what a tool he'd been.

"What's an ineligible list and why is it important?"

Wow. She must have been really sheltered. "I was a senior and one of the captains of the football team. When you're ineligible, you can't do any extra-curricular activities, such as football. But never mind. I wised up and passed chorus in style. Finest kind for sure."

"I still can't imagine a group would let you sing with them, but never mind. I can't sing either."

"You're not a little songbird?"

"Can't warble a note." She stopped walking and looked at her watch. "I really should get home."

"Afraid of the zombie lobsters? I promise I'll be brave and save you from them." He didn't want the night to end. He just…didn't.

"No, just afraid of not being able to tell one Swedish Danish from another." She clasped her hands in front of her as primly as the most pious and fearful of nuns.

The sound of a bunch of motorbikes started out low in the background and grew as they came toward them. Angie's eyes filled with some extreme emotion. Fear? Panic? She leapt to the side, out of the light of a street lamp, into the closest shadow.

What the hell? "Angie? You okay?" He stepped toward her.

The roar of the bikes peaked and died away as they passed by the pier. He watched as she breathed slowly and carefully. "Can you take me home now?"

"Okay. I'll take you home."

He didn't want to. Son of a bitch, he didn't want to. But something had flipped a switch and terrified her, giving him an excuse to play the hero.

He could do that. It had been a long time since he'd been anybody's hero. He found he relished the chance. "Let's go."

****

Angelique knew how to handle men. She was born knowing how to wrap a man around her finger, starting with her father.

She didn't remember much of them, her parents, but moments with her father stayed bright and clear with her. Him taking her out on his pirogue, or then a boat, and taking her fishing. She'd caught the first fish.

He never said no when he had stuff in front of him that he knew she wouldn't eat. If she wanted to try it, he just smiled and let her. He loved hot peppers, what Cajun didn't? She'd never eaten one, but wanting to impress him, she chomped on a chili. Her mother had said no, but he smiled like the devil himself and told her to go ahead. So she did.

Then there was the time when he took her out to dinner. Just her, no one else, not her mother, not her brother. She ordered the exact same thing that he had, including the appetizer, oysters on the half shell.

Raw oysters on the half shell.

Even though he knew she'd hate them, he hadn't told her 'no.' He let her discover for herself.

Then she'd lost them both, mother and father, the loving guide who made her follow all the rules, then the one who gave her permission to make mistakes. She lost them both at once when they died in a car accident.

Grand-mère took over and then there was just work. Dirty, sweaty, smelly work. She knew she was loved, Angelique knew that better than she felt her own heartbeat, and she'd done what she had to do to help out.

But they'd never known the wildness in her, the part that would try to eat something no five year old would even think of eating, to please her father, yes, but also to fulfill the hunger in her to experience everything. She'd wanted more, at least for the chance to wear a fragrance more intriguing than eau de diesel. Angelique longed to be away from the stupid, backward, leering idiots of the bayou and out into the bright lights of the cities of the world, where everyone was sophisticated and no man had axle grease under his fingernails.

She'd be the queen of all of them, or so she had thought.

Pull yourself together, girl. She had one prime piece of beefcake walking right next to her, no axle grease anywhere to be seen or smelled.

Tim wore a dangerous scent, one no mechanic wore, ever. Clean. Slick. Dangerous.

While he lived in small-town Lobster Cove, he had too much of a man-of-the-world air about him. He'd seen a few things, done a few things, she thought, that ordinary men had not.

He never did tell her what he did for work.

The night rolled in, along with a heavy fog that brought in humidity and promised a late storm.

"Here we are," Tim said as the stood in front of the walkway to her cottage. "Can I entice you into asking me in for coffee?" He gave her a sexy grin.

"No, I'm afraid not. I really do have to call it a night."

"At least let me walk you to your door." He rested his hand lightly against her back as he guided her to the front porch.

"Thank you for dinner. I had a lovely time."

"Let's do it again sometime." He looped his arms loosely around her waist. Angelique shivered as she looked up at his face, knowing, waiting for the kiss she knew would come.

Desired to come.

He didn't disappoint. His mouth brushed across hers once, twice, three times before he deepened the kiss.

So light. So sweet. He didn't push her, just gave her a promise more than a kiss.

Too soon, he lifted his head and whispered, "Good night. Dream of me, okay?"

She needed to catch her breath. All she could manage was a small nod.

He walked off the porch and waited until she'd opened her door. She gave him one little wave before going inside.

She had an idea the man was going to drive her insane.

That did not happen to Angelique Durand. If there was any sanity to drive away, she did the driving. But then, she'd lost her edge on the steps of a Paris jail. Most likely, she'd never find it again.

Time to move on. It might prove interesting to chase as well as be chased. She smiled at the thought.

Chapter Eight

Fuck him! The fetid air choked Tim as he fought against the tight, rough restraints around his hands and feet. Heavy boots kicked him over and over, and he screamed against the duct tape over his mouth but no sound would come. Wet from his own sweat, blood, and most likely urine, he hunkered into as small a ball as he could.

He heard loud cracks and roars from the war approaching from all sides. The blasts came incrementally closer until they were practically on top of him

One last explosion came so close he could feel the heat and the sharp, hot pieces of shrapnel spread by the bomb. The deadly spray relentlessly pelted him until the skin on his back turned raw and bloody.

With a scream made of pure, unadulterated terror, Tim sat bolt upright in his bed. His chest rose and fell as he dragged air in and out of his lungs, not the stink of Iraq but the fresh salt air of Maine.

He fell back onto his bed, his eyes wide open as he remembered where he was. His body drenched in sweat, his face streaked with tears, he worked to get his breathing back under control.

The earlier predicted electrical storm raged above Frenchman's Bay with lightning stabbing straight down from the roiling sky, thunder booming loud enough to rattle the windows and doors.

He got up and staggered to his kitchen for something to drink. Not water.

Never water. It reminded him too much of the times he'd been water boarded. He also knew better than to take a shower, no matter how disgusting he felt.

He opened his fridge and pulled out a beer, pressing the cold bottle against one cheek then the other.

Moving into his living room, he turned on the lights and flopped down on the couch. No way could he go back to that bed tonight. He grabbed the remote and clicked on the TV, channel surfing to find something innocuous. Something boring.

What had he been thinking of, trying to start a relationship with Angie? No way was he fit to be around any woman.

****

Lord, Angelique hated her life. Hated with a capital H. The breakfast shift had been a madhouse. The brat at table five had managed to mash half of his muffin into the tablecloth and the chair cushion. Then he'd crawled under the table and mashed the rest of it into the carpet. Now she was on her hands and knees, under the table, working her butt off to scrape the crumbs and other debris out of the rug.

So gross.

To top it all off, her fake glasses had filmy spots on the lenses and kept slipping down her nose. She didn't dare take them off or else she'd ruin her disguise.

The hostess stuck her head under the table. You've got a new party, a four-top. Table 8."

Angelique sighed. "I'll be right there."

"I already coffee'd them, so they're good for the next few minutes, so you can go wash your hands."

She resigned herself to her fate. "Thanks."

Slowly backing out from under the table on her hands and knees, a sense of defeat came and rested on her back and shoulders.

Even with better shoes, her feet still ached. Throbbed. And no matter what she did, she still got red spots and itched because of the uniform. Wasn't that attractive?

A big, fat ol' no to that.

The family at the four-top looked nice. The parents were making sure their children, a boy and his little sister, actually behaved.

She rolled her shoulders and prepared to woman up. She'd wallow while she washed her hands then be Angie the Wonder Waitress once she turned off the tap.

She marched over to the table as fast as her sensibly but ugly shod feet would carry her.

The man at the table had pinned all his attention to a very sweet-looking blonde girl, who looked to be pretty spoiled. Angelique recognized all the signs, especially the boo-boo lipped pout. The boy, older, sat there engrossed in a comic book.

Angelique pasted a smile on her face. "Hello! I'm Angie, and I'm your server this morning. Have you decided what you want?"

Everybody but the little girl smiled at her. Okay, the boy blinked once, and even though he was a child, he hid his reaction to her scar well. But the little girl…she stared at Angelique's face.

The man looked from the little girl to his wife then to Angelique. "We're here for Alma's Danishes, of course."

"I don't want a Danish."

"Cookie, just try one before you decide you don't like it."

The kid looked like a Cookie, for sure, a girl who made sure everyone paid attention to her and only her.

A diva waiting on a diva? Angelique could most definitely give this kid a run for the money.

After all, Angelique had written the book on little sister diva-hood.

She flushed hot and, as she suspected, lobster red. She was catty, but she'd never picked on a little kid; she should be ashamed of herself.

Angelique *was* ashamed of herself. And what did it say about her appearance that she frightened little children? She wanted to cry.

"Do you want to order now or do you need some time?"

"We'll wait a little. We're meeting someone here," the man said.

"Well, why don't I bring y'all some drinks while you're waiting and deciding?"

"That sounds lovely, thank you." The woman smiled gratefully.

"Hey, sorry I'm late! I had to take care of some stuff for the new book."

Angelique's head ripped around. Tim Baldwin had just come racing up to the table.

"Hey, Angie. Hi." Tim looked taken aback even though he smiled at her as he ran his hand through his hair.

"You know each other." The man waiting for Tim grinned.

"We're neighbors. Chester introduced us. Angie, this is Jeff Myers, my best friend in the whole world, his wife Beth, his daughter Cookie, and his smelly, ugly son, Danny."

Danny guffawed. "You smell worse, Uncle Tim."

"It's nice to meet you all." Angelique felt herself flush. "Tim, do you want some coffee?"

"You bet."

"How about you sit down, I'll get you that coffee and come back to take your order?"

"Sounds great." Tim had turned his smile up to heart stopping.

"Be right back."

She high-tailed it to the coffee station, so unsure of what her next step should be.

Oh, don't be stupid. Going to the table, taking their order, and then hauling out their damn food was her next step.

She was a waitress. She needed to act like a waitress.

****

"You been holding out on me, buddy?" Jeff shot Tim an amused glance. "How long has this been going on?"

"Has what been going on?" Tim would not give Jeff any fodder to torment him with.

"Jeff, behave." Beth sat back in her chair. "She's very pretty."

"No, she's not," Cookie chimed in. "She's got a big scar on her face."

"Cookie." Jeff's tone was stern. "That's the last thing you're going to say about that."

"I think it's cool." Danny automatically

contradicted anything Cookie said.

"So anything going on there?" Jeff took a sip of his coffee.

"She's my neighbor."

"Really. Go on."

"That's it." Or at least that was all Tim was admitting to, especially after having the nightmare last night.

"She's very pretty and seems very nice." Beth smiled.

Beth had been the good fairy in a previous life, Tim was sure of it.

Time to change the subject. "How was the honeymoon?"

Beth sighed. "A dream come true. I never thought I'd ever see Paris and it was so much more than I had ever imagined."

Jeff took Beth's hand and brushed a kiss over her knuckles. "We had a good time."

Tim just bet they had. If the two didn't stop looking at each other with so many stars in their eyes, they'd blind everybody.

"I got to spend time with Granny Nancy," Danny said. Granny Nancy was Jeff's mother and still lived in Addington. "I got to meet Brock and Buck Nelson. They were so cool."

Brock and Buck Nelson were professional football gods. They were also close friends of Jeff's, who was the Lobster Cove High School football coach. They'd be doing a football clinic here in Lobster Cove in August as a personal favor to him.

Go Lobster Cove Sharks.

"Finest kind," said Tim.

"I met Coach Deke, too!" Danny nearly fell off his chair over meeting Deke Nelson, a pro-football coaching god.

Jeff put a hand on his son's shoulder. "Let's make Uncle Tim talk about Angie the new waitress. Tell him to leave no detail out."

Danny nodded at Tim. "Leave no detail out."

"Shush." Beth turned a stern eye to Danny. "Don't make Uncle Tim feel uncomfortable."

"But she's hot!"

Beth's eyes narrowed. "Daniel William Myers, when did you start calling women hot?"

"Well, she is!"

"No she's not. She's got a scar. She put make-up on to hide it, but she's still got an ugly scar."

"Cookie, you stop that talk now." Jeff's tone defined icy and stern.

"And you are way too young to be calling women hot," Beth told Danny.

Danny shrugged and dived behind his Refractor comic book. Cookie pouted like the Olympic Gold Medalist in pout that she was.

Just like her mother, Jeff's ex-wife.

Tim had done his best to talk Jeff out of marrying Katie, but whatever Katie wanted, Katie got. What she had wanted was Jeff.

She threw him aside as fast as she could when he didn't live up to her expectations.

Their little girl paid the price. She really was a cute kid, but it took a while before she shook off the bratitude caused by Katie and returned to the sweet little girl she actually was.

Today was obviously a bratitude day.

Never mind. Angie was headed his way with his coffee.

It seemed that the sight of Angie fixed everything.

He paid attention to her face as she came closer. She did wear a lot of foundation, and she had cleverly applied her blush, but you still saw the scar. The glasses put all your attention onto her eyes. You almost didn't see it.

Almost.

He'd not worked with models or other people who had skill with make-up. Maybe she'd worked with someone who knew how to paint her face to minimize the mark of her courage.

He'd never sold a single picture to a fashion magazine, hadn't wanted to. He only caught the magic when he tried to catch the uncatchable.

The things only a magician could see through his camera lens.

The gruesome. The hopeless.

Unfortunately, the terrorists had broken his secret photographer magic decoder ring when he'd been kidnapped.

"Here's your coffee," Angie said as she put a nutty, fragrant, steaming, white stoneware mug in front of Tim. "Do you all know what you want?"

Tim watched her as she took everybody's order. He decided to go just for a couple of Danishes.

"Thanks, y'all. I'll be right back with your food." Angie took the menus.

Tim watched her walk away. When he turned his attention back to the table, both Jeff and Beth were staring at him with big grins on their faces. "What?"

"Nothing. Nothing at all," Jeff said.

Tim knew better. He smelled a matchmaker in the room. Two of them in fact.

He wished he had more to offer Angie.

But he didn't. He was broken in more ways than one.

Chapter Nine

Angelique's hands shook as she put together the order for Tim's table. Why did he have to come in and see her in the hideous green shirt and butt ugly shoes?

She should have realized that he was going to have food here at some point.

Now all she had to do was get said food out to them without spilling the drinks and dropping the tray. Grimacing, she hefted the heavy tray onto her left shoulder and hip-checked open the door that led to the dining room.

A couple of big parties had come in while she'd been in the kitchen and one of them sat at a couple of tables they'd pushed together in her station. Just ducky.

She started to count how many were there and took her attention off where she was going. She misstepped and the tray began to fall. Panicking, she tried to steady it, but it flew up into the air, defied gravity and flew for a bit until it crashed into the wall right behind Tim's table.

The plates full of food bounced off the wall and clattered over Tim and his friends, finally crashing in a huge, ungodly mess.

Cookie screamed immediately, jumped into her father's lap, and wrapped her arms around his neck, clinging to him like a demented howler monkey. She thought she heard the boy say totes rad, but she couldn't be sure.

They all stood, just seconds before Birdie McCorkle flew into the dining room all a twitter.

Great. Angelique could just kiss this job good-bye. The upside? She could ditch the fugly green shirt and the even fuglier shoes.

One always had to look on the bright side, right?

A couple of bussers dove right in and started to clean up. Angelique closed her eyes, said a quick prayer, and ran into the breach.

"I'm so sorry!" She started to gather up pieces of broken crockery.

"It was an accident," Beth said as she used a napkin to wipe off Danny's shirt.

"Of course it was." Jeff croaked out, because Cookie still had a death grip around his neck.

At least she'd stopped screaming.

Angelique noticed Tim just standing there like a statue, like he couldn't move. His hands fisted tight and his face paled. His lips nearly disappeared, stretching into a line above his chin.

He stared straight ahead, his pupils fixed and dilated.

"Let me get you another table, Coach," Ms. McCorkle said, "and of course your breakfast is on the house." She turned to Angelique. "Go on back to the kitchen and tell Alma to re-do their order a.s.a.p."

Angelique nodded and ran to the kitchen. "Alma—"

"I heard. I'm on it already. Why don't you go to the sink and try to clean up a bit?"

Angelique looked down at herself. *Zut alors!* "Okay. Thanks."

"Don't worry about it. Things like this happen all the time. Nobody's hurt, so it's all good."

By the time she'd gotten herself sort of together, Alma had the food ready for Angelique to take out.

"Watch your step this time," Alma warned.

"You know it." She picked up the tray and went back into the dining room. Tim's friends were seated at a different table but Tim was nowhere to be seen.

"Here you are. I promise not to throw this on you again." She set the tray down on a nearby tray stand. "Where did Tim go?" She placed a plate with chocolate chip pancakes in front of Cookie.

Beth and Jeff exchanged a glance. "He said he had somewhere to go and left."

"I see." She put a cheese omelet down in Beth's spot. "He looked a little shaken up."

"I'm sure he's fine." Jeff frowned.

She bit her lip. "I'm sorry I dumped y'all's breakfast on you. Can I get you anything else?"

Beth shook her head and smiled. "It's all good. I think we're set for now."

"Well, *bon appétit*."

"Angie," Birdie McCorkle quietly called and motioned for her to come over.

Angelique sighed. The moment of truth. Her butt was so totally fired.

Her hands started to shake. "Birdie, I'm so sorry. I'll get my stuff out of my locker and—"

"And why would you be doing that?" She shook her head.

"Obviously because you have to let me go because of what happened."

"That was an accident. I called you over to find out

if you're okay."

"I'm not fired?"

"Not today, lass. You're not hurt or anything?"

"N-no."

"Right-o. Here's a clean shirt for you to change into and then go back on the floor."

Angelique blinked as she took the tee. "Thank you."

"Get on with it." She nodded then turned and left Angelique alone.

She'd dodged a bullet, thank God.

But what was up with Tim? She wanted to pay him a visit when she got home, but she got the feeling he didn't want to talk about what had just happened.

She, more than anyone, should respect that.

****

"You sure you want to take the boat out today in this wind?"

Tim didn't look at the guy watching him launch *Fantasy*. "Yep."

"You at least have someone sailing with you?"

"Nope." If this jerk kept talking, Tim was going to have to punch him.

"Got a death wish?"

Yes. He could make it a murder-slash-suicide deal. "I know what I'm doing."

"Hope so."

Tim gritted his teeth and went about the business of rigging the boat.

Two episodes in twenty-four hours. A nightmare and a panic attack.

The need to fight the water and wind rode him hard. Boat ready to go, he turned her loose and steered out to Frenchman's Bay.

The wind bit into the jib right away, so Tim changed course and let the sail out a little. The waves slapped viciously at the hull, sending cold spray up on either side of the boat.

It was nearly summer, but the water never got truly warm, even in August. He supposed he should be wearing a wet suit in case he capsized, but the hell with that.

The hell with all of it.

He would conquer the water. Conquer it and defeat it so it would never be able to terrify him ever again.

He could have walked away from the nightmare. He knew how to manage that. Getting doused with liquid when Angie lost control of the tray, so soon after the horrendous night he'd spent, had triggered a panic attack the likes of which he'd never experienced.

And in front of Angie no less.

What a pansy ass bitch he was. He should have been all over helping fix the situation. Instead, he'd stood there like a damn fool.

What happened to him? He used to be so cool; nothing rattled him, not bombs, not bullets, not nothing.

Now he lost his shit over broken pottery?

Damn terrorists. They'd taken away what made him a man.

He reached out of the harbor, past the breakwater, and into the bay. Immediately, the air got heavier and changed direction, so he had to make adjustments to the sails and course.

Tim could have changed direction so he could still reach across the bay, but he wanted to work. Instead, he turned so he could beat upwind.

He situated himself on the high side of the boat and leaned out as far as he could to keep the boat flat against the sea, using the tiller extension. That way very little air spilled over the top of the sails and he got more stability from the keel and didn't lose the ability to steer the boat because more of the tiller stayed in the water.

Both the tiller and the keel didn't work as well when the boat heeled so far over; hence, Tim hiked out as far as he could on the high side.

The salty waves chopped high, spraying him in the face. His heart started to beat a little bit faster but not so fast that he froze or freaked out.

He welcomed the challenge. He craved the victory over his demons.

Boo Yah.

What was he going to say to Angie?

Both Jeff and Beth knew about his PTSD and were so supportive. He doubted they'd tell Angie about his pitiful story and condition.

Jeff and Beth were true stand-up people. They'd let Tim tell Angie in his own time.

Which he wouldn't do soon, or ever, for that matter.

The wind kicked up and he pulled in the jib to counteract it then he tacked to change course. The chop increased and water sprayed him in the face. Cold, nearly frigid, water started to ship over the lee rail and pooled in the boat's cockpit and sloshed over his feet.

Determined to conquer his fears, he gritted his teeth and faced the elements.

The damned terrorists were not going to win, not this time.

Chapter Ten

Angelique stared at Tim's front door. Her nerves jingled and jangled like a set of handbells played by rabid chimpanzees.

After her breakfast and lunch shifts, she went home, took a shower, and gave herself a pep talk.

Usually clueless, or rather, not keyed into anyone else's emotions than her own, it startled her to be so concerned about Tim.

Something just didn't add up.

And what did she know?

Nothing. She had to think about someone else.

Which was something she never did.

Argh. She had to get over herself. *Just knock on the door and see if he is okay.*

It wasn't rocket science.

She pounded on the door.

A barrage of low pitched, scary woofs streamed from behind the door.

Chester. Great.

"What are you doing here?"

Angelique turned at the sound of Tim's voice coming from behind her.

To quote a southern phrase, he looked like he'd been ridden hard and put away wet, which she usually snorted over because of the sexual innuendo, but not right now. The man looked as if the hounds of hell had

Doreen Alsen

ridden right up his butt and camped out there.

She dug deep and pulled up her inner diva, who was closer under her skin than Angelique was comfortable with. "I want to apologize to you about dumping a tray full of food on you this morning. I of course apologized to Jeff and Beth and their children, but you were gone before I could get a chance."

He swallowed, took a moment to stare at his shoes, then brought his head up to meet her gaze. "It's okay. No big." He scuffed his Topsider clad foot over a lump of crushed quahog shells on his front walk. "Are you okay? Did you get into trouble?"

"No. They were good to me. Kind."

"Good. It was an accident after all."

"You looked a little weird there. I hope I didn't hurt you."

He sighed and studied the tops of his shoes again. After an overlong moment he said, his voice flat, "You didn't hurt me."

"Well, good." Angelique Durand, the queen of holding men in the palm of her hand, didn't know what to say to this man. How the mighty have fallen. "I'll go now, then. I'm glad you're okay."

"Oh yeah, I'm just finest kind." He brought his head up and caught her gaze with his. "Thanks. I've got to go let Chester out, so I'll see you around."

Yes, Chester was barking like it was his job, which she supposed, it was. Fish gotta swim, dogs gotta bark.

"Yeah. I'll see you around."

She left, clutching the tatters of her pride around her.

****

Tim watched Angie scurry away. He'd pretended

68

to be happy.

He really just wanted to wrap his arms around her, take her up to his bed, and lose all his miserable problems in her body.

And wasn't that just the best reason to take a woman to bed?

No. If she were just some other piece of tail, he'd have no problem with using her and discarding her, getting rid of all the sexual frustration that had been building in him since before he'd been kidnapped.

This woman deserved more. If he couldn't give her more, he shouldn't touch her.

But, oh, Christ on a crutch, his hands itched to run up and down, all over her body.

He let himself into his house and Chester nearly knocked him over in Dobie ecstasy. "'Kay, buddy. Need to go out?"

The dog started running in circles around him. "Yeah, yeah, let's go."

He let Chester out the door to the beach, grabbed his leash, and, out of habit, his camera.

He felt, rather than saw, the exact moment Angie came out of her cottage and headed down the beach. She walked away from him, her slim body surrounded by the soft light of late afternoon.

She might as well be the angel she was named after.

He picked up his camera and pointed it at her, placing her in the middle of the frame. Some kids were flying kites, which dipped and swooped in the brisk wind. He managed to get them in the image and snapped the picture.

She'd been worried about him. So much for his

hope that she hadn't seen him freeze.

Damn.

On the other hand, the thought of her concern thawed something deep inside him, something that had frozen up in the hot desert of Iraq.

All the more reason for him to stay away from her.

As she faded from view, Tim put the camera down. "Chester! Want to go for a walk?"

Chester ran down the stairs and headed for the beach. Tim had to hurry to catch him, so he could point the dog in the opposite direction Angie had taken. "Let's go this way, buddy."

Chester turned on a dime and raced away like he was Secretariat.

Tim understood the need for speed, only when he indulged, he was racing away from his demons. His dog wouldn't know a demon if it jumped up and bit him on the nose.

But it looked to Tim like he'd gained a new demon to fight. Her name was Angie and his nearly overwhelming desire for her.

Looked like there would be a lot of cold showers in his future.

****

Angelique pushed a cart laden with towels, sheets, and cleaning supplies down a hallway in the Sea Crest Inn. Cleaning up other people's messes totally sucked.

The pigs in the last room she'd made habitable for the next guests left dirty diapers on the floor. Really?

Really.

She almost threw up, as the diapers smelled like they'd been there since Y2K. What did they feed that kid? Dead, putrid skunks?

O. M. Effing. G.

So totally pukeworthy.

She'd spent a few terrible moments in front of the toilet gagging. She'd, against all odds, gotten over SmellyDiaperGate.

The next room was even worse, as the happy couple staying there had managed to discard their used condoms on the floor instead of the wastebasket or toilet.

What was wrong with these people?

She did have to admit that in her previous superstar life she hadn't given one single thought about the person coming around to clean up after her. Another new regret. *Yay!*

This job, however, went a long way in preserving her anonymity. Much more so than working in the dining room, so she'd pull up her big girl panties and cope.

She finished making up the rooms, stowed her cart and supplies, and took the dirty linens and towels down to the laundry room. The bag holding the soiled wash felt like it was weighted down with boulders. By the time she muscled it to the basement, her lower back and biceps were screaming at her.

And, oh look. She broke another nail. *Peachy.*

After clocking out, she slipped out the kitchen entrance and made her way around the grounds. She happened to pass by Keen Quinn's workshop. The son of the owners of Sea Crest Inn, he handcrafted all the Adirondack style furniture featured by the Inn.

From the sound of it, she figured his wife, Bobbie Darling, kept him company.

"I tell you, Keen, that man is infuriating. I have his

71

book signing all set for the end of June and he's not helping at all with the publicity." Bobbie owned the bookstore next to the Inn, Cliff Notes.

"He's been through a lot. Maybe you could give him some leeway?"

"I suppose you're right. I'm just really excited about the event and want to get the word out."

Angelique kept on walking past and remembered Tim telling Jeff that he was late because of stuff to do with his book.

She wondered what kind of books he wrote. She'd have to ask him.

She wanted to see him again. She'd enjoyed her date with him, up to the point when she'd heard the motorbikes. She felt her face heat at the memory of hiding when they passed by.

She took the chance that someone would recognize her every time she took a customer's order at the Inn. It felt rather presumptuous to ask him to come over for dinner. She shook her head.

There was also the fact that he hadn't seemed too happy to see her the other day when she knocked on his door, checking up on him. So an intimate dinner was out of the picture.

She herself wasn't ready for that yet. She thought about him joining his friends for breakfast. What about a casual brunch on the beach? On her patio?

Low key. No pressure. No innuendo, which was more important to her. She'd been gossiped about enough.

A brilliant plan took shape in her mind.

****

"You want what?"

Angelique sighed and rolled her eyes. "Do you have a hearing problem, Lucien? I need some of *Grand-mère's* recipes."

"Why?" Lucien sounded suspicious. What a surprise. He always sounded suspicious when he talked to her.

Granted she'd given him lots of reason not to trust her.

"I'd like to learn how to cook them."

"You've never been interested in learning to cook them before."

"I never had to learn before because you would make them. I miss that kind of food. Maine cuisine is nice and all, but there are only so many lobster rolls you can eat. I really crave some good ol' Cajun dishes."

"Which ones do you want?" Lucien still didn't sound convinced.

"Gumbo, so if you could send me some of your special *filè* powder, that would save me from trying to find it here or settle for someone else's version, her shrimp and ham gumbo, and if you wouldn't mind, that oyster preparation you invented for Hope." She knew Lucien wouldn't be able to resist that one.

"You have to swear on a stack of Bibles that you will never share that recipe."

"Cross my heart and hope to die." She thought about asking for Hope's apple pie recipe, but most likely, it was too soon to be asking Hope for favors. "And beignets."

"Beignets? You want to eat something deep fried?"

She remembered mornings spent at the Café du Monde drinking chicory coffee and nibbling on a warm beignet topped with powdered sugar. Homesickness washed over her. She couldn't go back to New Orleans. Everyone knew her there and all her old crowd would laugh at her. "Yes. I very much want to learn to make beignets."

Silence from the other end of the line. "Lucien? Are you still there?"

"*Oui.* I'll scan and e-mail the recipes to you today and send the *filè* to you. Do you need it soon? Should I overnight it?"

Her heart once again swelled with love and with extreme gratitude that this man was her brother. "You don't have to overnight it. I'm not making these dishes all at once."

"You can get good oysters there, *n'est-ce pas*?"

"Lucien. Lobster Cove is a fishing town. The whole coast around here is all about the fish. I think I can find some good oysters."

"Make sure they're in season and local."

"In season? When did you start to care about things being in season and local?"

"Since my amazing wife taught me a thing or two. If you need any advice, just give me a call and I'll talk you through it."

"That's so sweet, but I've got to figure this out on my own. I'm a Durand, after all. The Force runs deep in our family."

For too long Angelique had represented the dark side of the Force. Darth Durand. Time to find Angelique Skywalker.

"Okay then. Let me know how things turn out. Angelique?"

"Yes?"

"I'll strangle you with my bare hands and drop

your dead body in the bayou for the gators if you reveal my Oysters Hope recipe."

She smiled as tears welled in her eyes. "*Merci*, Lucien."

"Take care of yourself and let me know if you need any help." He clicked off.

Angelique wouldn't be making that call. Determined to make this happen, all she had to do is keep her eye on the prize.

She smiled. She had the feeling that Tim Baldwin was worth the effort.

Chapter Eleven

"Alma, I have a favor to ask." Angelique approached the head chef at the Sea Crest Inn.

"Shoot!" Alma stopped stirring the pot she had bubbling on the stove.

"I'm trying to make some old family recipes, you know, Cajun things, and one of the things I want to try is my *Grand-mère's* recipe for beignets, but I don't have a deep fryer. Can I try them out here when the dining room is closed and the kitchen isn't busy?"

"Beignets! Absolutely, as long as you give me the recipe and let me help out. Are they any good?"

Angelique grinned. "Better than the ones you can get at Café du Monde. My *Grand-mère*, she could cook." She silently begged Lucien's forgiveness about giving this one recipe to Alma.

"Yum! I've only been there once, but I fell in love with New Orleans. I still dream about the meal I had at L'Enfer, the restaurant owned by that famous chef guy, whose name escapes me right now."

Angelique stifled a grin at how Lucien would react to being called 'that famous chef guy.' "Lucien Durand."

"That's him! What other of your grandmother's recipes do you have?"

"Her jambalaya and her gumbo." She purposely left off Lucien's secret oyster recipe.

"I'd love to try those, too, if you wouldn't mind." Alma clapped her hands together. "I could put a version on the menu, like switching scallops for shrimp in the jambalaya, and lobster for shrimp in the gumbo."

"Sounds like fun." Angelique kept it to herself that there were already too many lobster preparations in this town, but what could one do?

"If the beignets come out good, I'd love to put them on the breakfast menu along with the Danishes and other pastries."

"I don't have a problem with that." It occurred to her that Lucien might. Well, what he didn't know wouldn't hurt her. "Would tomorrow afternoon work?"

"Around three thirty. The lunch rush is over and we don't need to prep dinner yet. Is there anything special you need?"

"There's a special flour mix, with a couple of different flours in it. And cottonseed oil. We have to have cottonseed oil."

"I'm not sure we can get that around here, but let me check."

"Other than that, it's yeast and powdered sugar."

"That I've got. I'll get stuff together and we can dig in tomorrow afternoon!" The pot on the stove started to bubble over. "Oops!" Alma went back to stirring the liquid in the pan.

"I won't keep you from your work," Angelique told her. "Thank you!"

"No problem."

So, she'd put the first part of her plan in place. First, make the beignets. After that, she would invite him over for coffee and beignets *al fresco* in the morning when he came out to walk Chester.

Then, if a little breakfast on the patio worked, if he didn't run away screaming when he learned who she was, she'd invite him in for dinner, *Grand-mère's* gumbo, preceded by Lucien's Oysters Hope. Champagne and something outrageous and chocolate to finish it off.

No going to bed yet. She wanted to spin this out and enjoy courting him.

She smiled as she walked the long trek home from the restaurant to her cottage. Warmth slipped out of her heart and surrounded it.

Something very close to hope enfolded her in its loving and nurturing arms.

****

It turned out that making beignets was very hot and greasy work. They'd overworked the dough the first time and made doughnuts the shape and consistency of rocks.

And wasn't that sexy?

The second batch was better, but only marginally. Alma hadn't been able to find cottonseed oil and the substitution of vegetable oil meant some changes to the recipe.

"I'm putting in an order to this place in Boston where I can get anything I want and we're getting cottonseed oil. I told Betts and Birdie McCorkle that we were putting beignets on the menu and they about swooned. And of course, Keen nearly had a kitten. Cops, even the ones on leave, do love them some doughnuts. Not that we can call these babies doughnuts." Alma cut the new batch of dough they'd made into squares. "Check the temp of the deep fryers, make sure they're at exactly 370 degrees."

Angelique did as she was told.

As she imagined her plan, she saw Chester lumbering up her steps, Tim following him, her smiling like a Renaissance painting of a Madonna, which she'd learned about that one almost completed semester at Barrett University in Addington, and asking if he wanted a taste of New Orleans. She'd set the table on her patio with a pretty cloth and some colorful fruit in a cut glass bowl.

She sighed as she checked the thermometer of the fry-o-lator. There it was, 370 degrees. "It's ready."

Alma gently lowered the squares of pastry dough into the oil. "I think these will turn out right."

Angelique held her breath. "I hope so."

Alma patted her on the back. "If it doesn't, we'll just try again."

Angelique wasn't sure if her lower back and feet would hold out. She did some twists and bends. She'd say manual labor killed a person, but she remembered the days of wearing scanty underwear while standing in nearly impossible poses on four-inch stilettos.

Why was this worse?

It must be the sensible rubber soled shoes. Who knew shoes could be this ugly? She supposed she must have known as she'd worked in the front of the house in restaurants for years, but she'd thought those shoes had been in her nightmares.

Her leg and lower back muscles were used to heels. High heels. Sky-high heels. Her calves were cramping up, just like they did when she went to bed after she'd taken her shoes off.

Sometimes it got so bad, she'd wear her heels to bed so her legs didn't cramp and she could sleep.

This flat shoe thing was just a new, unpleasant phase of her life. Yet another big girl panty moment.

Soon she'd get a better job and be able to wear beautiful, feet-killing shoes.

She giggled because she couldn't wait.

Chapter Twelve

Angelique set a small table on her patio. She covered it with a cheerful blue cloth covered with daisies and placed a small vase of wildflowers in the center of it. She found some mismatched, but charming, antique china plates, cups, and saucers and put them on the table. She had a pitcher of hand-squeezed orange juice on ice and warm beignets in her oven. She peeked through the hedge separating the terraces, waiting for a glimpse of Tim and his dog.

She even bought some gourmet dog food for Chester.

She also decided to do something she'd never, ever done before, to meet a man without wearing make-up. Well, okay, she did throw some mascara on, she couldn't quit cold turkey, but she didn't try to hide the scar. Grimacing, she pushed the black-rimmed hipster glasses up her nose.

She rubbed her hand over her stomach. She was totally terrified.

Wearing her favorite sundress, pale pink with raspberry-colored peonies, she felt pretty confident she could get him to join her for breakfast. The guy had to eat, right?

She heard his porch door slide open and Chester galumph out. She put her hand over her stomach, trying to tame the butterflies knocking around in there. After kicking off her sandals, she bopped down her stairs as casually as she could to intercept him.

"Hi." Smiling, she clasped her hands in front of her.

"Hey." Tim stopped as Chester ran along the beach. He hadn't shaved yet and his T-shirt fit his impressive physique like a second skin.

"I wanted to thank you for dinner the other night, and I thought maybe, if you haven't had breakfast yet, you might want to join me."

"Breakfast?"

"Yes, that meal you eat at the beginning of the day. I got a craving for some New Orleans food and made my *Grand-mère's* recipe for beignets. I made way too many. You'd be helping me out as I can't possibly eat them all."

"Beignets, eh?"

"Better than the ones from the Café du Monde."

"Well, I'll just have to test them out, won't I? Let me call the dog."

"I've got breakfast for him, too." She felt her face flush.

"He's a lucky dog." He whistled and Chester stopped in his tracks and barreled back.

They headed up to her patio and Angelique pointed to the table. "Take a seat. I'll be right back with the beignets and coffee. There's some orange juice there if you want some."

She made short work of grabbing the food and returned to her little party.

Sitting on her delicate chair, Tim looked like Gulliver at a Lilliputian tea party. She put the covered plate with the doughnuts on the table. "Do you want some coffee?"

"Please."

She poured then sat. "You take it black, right?"

Tim smiled. "You remember."

She grimaced. "It was a memorable morning. Oh, I almost forgot!"

Picking up the dish of food for Chester, she put it on the stone floor. "Here you go, boy."

Chester snarfled then attacked the dish muzzle first.

"He likes his food." She scratched behind his ears.

Tim laughed. "That he does."

She uncovered the plate of deep fried delights. "Take one. Let me know what you think."

He did and took a bite. It crunched like it was supposed to and left a trail of powdered sugar on his lower lip. After he chewed and swallowed, he licked the sugar off his mouth.

Oh. My. She could totally recall all the other ways he'd used his tongue the other night.

She had to clear her throat. "So?" Her voice squeaked a little.

"Excellent. Just as advertised." He popped the rest of the beignet in his mouth.

She took one, put it on her plate, and tore a small piece off. "Listen, I had an ulterior motive putting this all together."

"Really?" His eyes squinted a little. "Want to tell me about it?"

"No." She gave him the smile that she knew left men weak in the knees. "You have to guess."

****

Guess? What the hell? He had a myriad of options

playing out in his mind.

All of them sexual. None of them he thought she'd welcome.

Or would she? He used to be able to read women and know what they wanted before they knew themselves.

Now? He had trouble reading a grocery list, never mind the fairer sex.

His mouth went dry and he licked his lips. The look she was giving him certainly did raise his temperature and blood pressure more than a little bit. "You're going to have to help me out here."

She cocked her head to one side. "Well." She tore a corner off her beignet and put it in her mouth. "First, I wanted to make it up to you." She shrugged. "For throwing your breakfast all over you."

No. Just no. He wasn't going to talk to her about it. "Apology accepted."

She smiled. "I owed you a pastry or two. And we're neighbors. I'd like us to be friendly."

Friendly? Huh. Just how friendly was she willing to be? "I'd like that, too."

"Good!" She licked the sugar off the bit of pastry she still held before putting it into her mouth. "Mmmm. Just like *Grand-mère* used to make."

"Would that be your grandmother who kept the gators?"

"You remember!"

"That's not an easy tidbit of information to forget. She did give you a great beignet recipe, though. One worth putting up with the gators." He toasted her with his coffee cup.

She snorted. The sound didn't exactly define the

word feminine. Still, he loved it. She'd charmed him.

Her quick, winsome smile, her saucy, dark eyes, her grace, and beauty made her a dangerous, sensual presence.

Who could resist her? Not Tim, that was for damn sure.

"But what were they doing there?" he asked her.

"Having breakfast, shoog!" She laughed.

That laugh hinted at a lot more than breakfast. He liked that about her.

He thought of asking her again about her disappearing act the night they went to Mariner's. However, if he asked her that, she might insist about the, uh, event at the Sea Crest Inn.

He kept his mouth shut.

"You look upset, shoog. Don't you like breakfast?"

"I like breakfast fine. These," he picked up another beignet, "are pure sin." He took a big bite and smiled as he chewed. "Finest kind."

"I'm glad. I'm not usually a breakfast person, but for you I made an exception. But I'm warning you, I have ulterior motives."

"Do you now?"

"I want to get to know you better, especially after that kiss the other night." Her face turned pink and it was adorable.

A low-level hum of arousal surrounded him. "That was a pretty great kiss. We should try it again sometime."

"I'm hoping we will, but I want to know a few more things about you."

"Like what?" He stopped himself from sighing. He should have figured out something like this was going to happen.

"Like what do you do all day."

"What I do?"

"Yes. Like what's your job and why are you here in Lobster Cove. That kind of thing. I mean I know you spent summers here when you were growing up and you're taking time off work. I guess I want to know what kind of work you do. Your friends mentioned a book. Are you a writer?" She shrugged. "You can tell me if I'm being too nosy."

"Hmmmmm." Okay. To stall or to lie, that was the question. "I guess you could say I'm a kind of writer." The kind of writer who told stories via photographs, not that he'd tell her that. "What do you do when you're not in Lobster Cove?"

She looked down at her hands. "I'm between jobs at the moment," she said.

"What did you do?" That-a-boy! Turn the conversation around to her.

"I was in sales. I'm here looking for the next direction for my life to take."

"What do you want to do?"

"I have no idea. Right now I'm going with the flow, thanks to my brother letting me borrow his beach house."

"I was surprised when I heard it'd been sold. Charlie and Violet had lived there since before I was born."

"Your family was close to them?"

"They were sort of honorary grandparents." Tim smiled at the memories flooding him. "Charlie always had peppermint candies in his pocket and Violet was always baking something, cookies, muffins, that kind of thing."

"What about your own grandparents?"

"Down in Massachusetts. My mom's parents are in assisted living and my dad's father moved down to the Cape when he retired."

"Where on the Cape? I've never been but I'm told it's beautiful."

He rubbed his chin with the back of his hand. "Wellfleet, on the Outer Cape. It is a beautiful place, especially in the off-season. In season it's packed with people, just like here."

"I don't mind the crowds. I've mostly lived in cities, so this is different for me."

"Yeah, not a gator to be seen."

"Just zombie lobsters." She shifted in her seat. "Do you want more coffee? Orange juice?"

He cast a glance over to Chester who lay there, the picture of patience as he waited for his walk, and decided Chester could wait a little bit longer.

He stood and came over to Angie's side of the table. He took her hand and pulled her standing, into his arms. "This is what I want right now."

Then he kissed her. Her mouth moved under his as she responded to his persuasive lips and tongue as she melted against him.

He ran his hands up and down her slender back, cupped her sweet behind, and pulled her in even closer while his tongue plundered the sweetness of her lips and tongue. He felt himself harden as he rocked her against his pelvis.

As if from far away, he heard a woof. Next thing he knew a very impatient Doberman wedged himself in between Tim and Angie, effectively ending their steamy clinch.

"Okay, Chester," he said as he rested his forehead against Angie's. "You want your walk."

The dog woofed again.

"Maybe you better go take him."

Chester wagged his stump.

She laughed. "I think that's a yes."

"Will you be here when I get back?" Tim wasn't ready to end the morning.

She glanced at her watch and shook her head. "I'm sorry. I have just enough time to clean up and get to work."

"Do you want help cleaning up?" *Please need help.*

"No, I've got it. Go on. Enjoy your walk." She raised herself up on tiptoes and pressed a gentle kiss to his cheek.

"You're sure."

"Yes, I'm sure. I'll talk to you later."

Chester took that moment to whine like he did when he had some business to conduct.

"Talk to you later," Tim said. "Let's go, buddy."

Chester bolted off her patio. Tim had no choice but to follow.

Chapter Thirteen

Angelique sighed as she tidied up the Sea Crest Inn's main lobby. Why did people never put the magazines back where they found them?

Some of them were very old, but a few of them weren't. She picked up a shiny, glossy fashion rag from a few months ago and froze at the sight of her face, her unscarred face, smiling at her on the cover.

It was from her last photo shoot. She'd assumed after all the notoriety, the magazine would not to use her face on its cover.

Yet, there she smiled, larger than life in all her former glossy glory.

She hugged the magazine to her chest, all set to run out and burn it, but then she realized she could run but she couldn't hide.

"The beignets are a huge success."

She clutched the magazine to her chest. "I'm so glad!

"Betts really wants to thank you for sharing the recipe with Alma. The reviews this morning have been very positive. They're a hit!"

"That's so awesome." Her fake glasses slipped down her nose. When she went to push them up, she dropped the magazine.

Before she could reach down and pick it back up, Birdie beat her to it. Angelique's heart leapt up into her throat.

True she was dressed down and the picture had been photo-shopped, but still…what if Birdie put two and two together?

She'd been sent to jail for stealing. How would Betts Quinn feel about having a thief working for them?

Not good, she bet.

"Here you go!" Birdie handed her the magazine without looking at the cover. "I'll let you get back to your work. You're doing a great job, Angie me-lass. I'm glad we took a chance on you."

"I'm grateful to have the job."

"It seems to be working out all around. By the way, I want to let you know that there are going to be some photographers and reporters on the premises next week."

What? No! The hairs on the back of her neck stood up. "Why?"

Birdie lifted her eyebrows. "Why? The Sea Crest Inn is being featured in The Boston Globe as one of the top ten destination inns in New England. It's quite an honor for us."

Her hands fisted in the magazines. "Oh."

Birdie squinted at her. "We'll be after arranging a photo shoot of all the staff sometime next week, but we'll let you know the day before. Are you all right, lass? You look a little peaked."

"Yeah, sure. Never better." What a good liar she was.

"I'll let you get back to work, then."

Angelique watched Birdie walk away, so shaken her teeth started chattering. *Le bon Dieu!* A week of photographers and cameras watching her every move.

Angelique Durand, welcome to hell.

****

"So, when are you coming to dinner?"

Tim sighed. His best friend's wife wanted to domesticate him. "When do you want me?"

Beth laughed. "Any night works." She narrowed her eyes. "Why don't you bring a date and let me know when you want to come?"

"A date." God, he hated this. Beth had written the extra-credit work he had to do to be eligible to play football, like a million years ago. He owed her big time, so he couldn't say no to anything she asked.

"Yes." She beamed at him like a lighthouse. "Your neighbor, the one who works at the Sea Crest."

Sweet Jesus, save him. "Aren't you afraid she's going to spill your food all over you and break your best china?"

"She won't be doing the serving, so the china is safe." Rolling her eyes, Beth crossed her arms across her chest. "She's nice and you're lonely."

"I'm not lonely."

"You are too lonely. And a hermit. It's not healthy, Tim. Besides, she's new in town and doesn't have a friend except for you. Bring her over to dinner." Beth laid her hand on his arm. "It's not as if you're asking her to marry you."

Jesus. Just the thought of marrying someone when he had this shit storm going on in his head, day and night—"I can take care of my own love life."

"I'm sure you can. I'm not talking about a love life. I'm talking about bringing a nice woman, whom you like, whom we like, to dinner at our house. Nothing fancy. I'm thinking burgers on the grill, that kind of thing."

"I don't know."

Beth cleared her throat. "Tim. Ask Angie and bring her to our house for a meal. Just simple hamburgers, some salt and pepper corn, some potato salad." She shrugged. "I'll throw in blueberry tarts from Julie's Coffee and Sweet Shop for dessert." Beth raised and lowered her eyebrows. "You know you want them."

Tim shook his head. She wasn't going to give up until he gave in. "Okay, okay. You've worn me down."

Beth bounced on the balls of her feet and her hands clapped twice. "And you'll bring Angie?"

"If she'll come." He had no idea if Angie wanted to get to know his friends over a simple cookout.

A wish, sudden and unwelcome, descended on him. He really hoped she'd say yes. A normal night, doing normal things, with normal people.

He was amazed at how much he wanted it, how much he craved it. He'd be much better off alone. Nothing about his life was even in the same zip code as normal.

Angie would be much better off without him.

"She will." Beth nodded. "I've got a real good feeling about you two."

"It's a cookout, Beth. Don't make it more than that."

"It's a step forward, a big step forward that you need to take." Beth gave him a gentle smile. "Relax and enjoy it."

"You know, I wasn't kind to you back in school. I didn't know who you were. All I knew was that you were willing to write the extra credit papers Jeff and I needed to give the chorus teacher, so she'd pass us and make us eligible to play football again."

"You called me the music geek."

Tim winced. "You knew? I'm sorry. It wasn't one of my finer moments."

"No, it wasn't, but you were young and stupid and blind to all my superior qualities." She chuckled. "Fortunately for you I'm a forgiving woman. Forgiveness is a beautiful thing."

"I don't deserve it."

She touched his arm. "You deserve it more than most people. Now go and ask that beautiful woman to come over to our house for a simple, no-strings-attached cookout."

He sighed.

"I mean it. Shoo. And don't take no for an answer."

"Jeff's a lucky guy, you know that?"

"I remind him of it every day. Go away."

"You didn't used to be this pushy."

"I didn't used to be a lot of things. People do survive all sorts of stuff and go on to live happy lives."

Tim longed for that with all his heart, but didn't hold out much hope.

But he'd ask Angie to go to a cookout at his best friend's house. And he thought she just might agree.

Chapter Fourteen

"A cookout at your friend's house?"

"Yeah. It's no big. Burgers and such."

Angelique had never been to a friendly neighborhood cookout in her life. "They invited me?"

"I do think that if I don't bring you, Beth will march over here and rectify my mistake."

"She sounds like a tyrant." What if Tim's friend followed fashion? Angelique was already panicked about reporters running all over the Sea Crest Inn. How could she find out before she accepted the invitation?

Tim's eyes softened. "She's the best person in the world."

Angelique thought of her sister-in-law Hope. Also on the top ten list for best person in the world.

A list that Angelique which would never, ever be on.

"So will you come with me?"

"I don't know. What if I have nothing in common with them?"

"They're not that hard to get along with. Jeff is the high school football coach and Beth is a piano teacher and the organist at the Catholic church."

Huh. She didn't think a church organist would be that into fashion. Maybe she should take a chance.

Any excuses she could come up with felt so lame, even to her. Besides, she wanted to spend time with

Tim. That's what breakfast the other day had been about. "When does she want us to come?"

"She didn't let me know, because she wants to make sure you're not working so you can come."

Oh, really. "Any evening is good. I work mornings and afternoons." Unless she called in sick while the press was crawling all over the Sea Crest Inn.

He cleared his throat. "I'll let Beth know and get back to you."

"Sounds great." And about that Beth. "You're very fond of her."

He looked puzzled.

"Beth, I mean."

"I am." He stared at the floor. "She's made my best friend the happiest man in the world. They had a long, hard road to get to where they are now."

Lucien and Hope also had trouble getting to the happiness they shared now. Her cheeks heated up at the thought of how she nearly ruined it for them.

But she hadn't really ruined it. Nothing could have ruined Hope and Lucien coming together. They were meant to be.

She'd just wanted to get her way and be a supermodel. She'd been selfish, petty, and just all around nasty.

And now she was so tired of being that. Of being tormented by all her past mistakes.

She'd take the risk. Time to go to a cookout and hang out with Tim's friends. It might be awkward, it might be off the charts uncomfortable, they may recognize her, whatever.

She was all in.

****

What do you bring to a cookout? Angelique didn't have the first clue.

She probably should have done some research online. As much as she knew about un-catered meals, she knew that she should offer to make something.

"I should bring something."

Tim shook his head. "No. Beth's got it all under control. She's amazing that way."

Angelique felt something in her stomach tickle uncomfortably. "Were you in love with her?"

A strange emotion crossed his face. Why could she never figure him out?

"Never. I was too full of myself back then. Totally clueless. Besides, she was always Jeff's."

"They look very happy."

"They are. They deserve it." He rubbed his hand over his chin. "What would you want to bring them?"

"Maybe wine? Flowers?"

"Flowers." He nodded. "Beth likes them."

"Okay. I'll stop by Flowers in Bloom and pick something up. Do you know what she likes?"

He hitched up one shoulder. "I think Inge at the flower shop might know."

"Sounds good."

He leaned in and kissed her, a soft, sweet brush of his lips. "I'll come fetch you around four. They eat early because of Danny and Cookie." He snapped his fingers. "Actually, a little something for the two kids might be a good idea."

Le bon Dieu, what did she know about gifts for children? "Like what?"

Tim's brow furrowed. "I don't know. Books, maybe?"

"What kind of books?"

He shrugged. "Kid's books."

"That clears things up."

"Never mind. Flowers for Beth are enough. I'll be by to pick you up later." He leaned in and kissed her again.

"No problem. I'll see you then." It looked like there was a trip to Cliff Notes bookstore on her way home from work.

Tim smiled. "Count on it." He bounded up the stairs to his house.

She touched her lips as she watched him go. He was so unpredictable and mysterious.

She liked that in a man. She was looking forward to uncovering his secrets.

****

"She's nice," Jeff said as he handed Tim a beer. "Pretty."

Tim looked over to where Beth and Angelique were chatting at the picnic table in Jeff's backyard. They'd bought the house right before they got married and were in the process of putting their personal touches on it. Beth was trying her hand at gardening, and she'd been ambitious so the flowerbeds were a riot of brightly colored flowers of every size and shape.

Jeff and Danny were in the process of building a tree house in the big maple tree in a corner of the fenced-in backyard.

At that moment, Danny played tug of war with Chester, Jeff presided over the grill, flipping the burgers, and Angelique and Beth still talked at the picnic table.

Angie looked particularly lovely, in a bright red

dress and some high-heeled strappy sandals that did amazing things for her legs. His hands itched to touch her, to take off that sexy red dress and explore every inch of her body.

"Hey, Beth?" Jeff called.

"Yeah?"

"Burgers are about ready! Bring out the other stuff."

Beth stood and gave him a jaunty salute and tapped Cookie on the shoulder. Angie stood as well and followed them into the house.

"What's her story?" Jeff slid some split hamburger buns on the upper rack of the gas grill.

"Hmmm?"

"What's Angie's story?" He waved the spatula in a circle. "Where's she from, that kind of thing."

"Oh." Tim hesitated, as he didn't know what to say. "From the south, obviously. New Orleans, specifically."

"How'd she end up here in Lobster Cove? It's a long way from the Big Easy."

Tim rubbed the back of his neck. "I think it's that she needed a break, a change of scene. She says she's in between jobs."

Jeff chuckled. "Well, you can't get further from New Orleans than Lobster Cove."

"That's for sure." Tim took a pull on his beer.

The women returned with heaping bowls of food, potato salad, a monster-sized green salad, and steaming ears of corn. "Danny!" Beth said while she put a bowl on the table, "Go wash up!"

"'Kay." The kid raced into the house. Chester looked clearly bereft, but then he brought his rope toy to Tim.

"Sorry buddy. I'm not touching that."

Jeff nudged him. "C'mon."

Tim followed him to the table and took a seat next to Angie. She gave him a gentle smile. He smiled back. He couldn't help it.

She had a lovely smile. He found it quite compelling.

His heart beat a little faster. He had to remember that he was no good for her.

No matter how much he didn't want to.

****

"Your friends are nice. I like them." And didn't that surprise Angelique.

She hadn't thought she'd have anything in common with a homebody church organist and piano teacher, but she had. And she really liked Beth's son Danny and Tim's daughter Cookie.

Who knew she liked kids? She certainly hadn't.

"The boy is a handful. I got worn out just watching him," she told him.

"He seems to have gotten more than his share of energy. But I remember being like that as a kid. Why walk when you can run?"

She laughed. "Anyway, I had a very good time."

"I'm glad."

She waited for him to say more, but he didn't.

So they walked in companionable silence. Angelique liked it, not having to fill the air with conversation. Usually, she felt antsy when the talking stopped.

He looked at her. "Would you like to go sailing?"

"Go sailing?"

"Yeah. With me on my boat."

Ouch. Sounded athletic, which she avoided at all costs, except for the damn yoga. "Is it dangerous?"

He laughed. "Of course it's not dangerous. I wouldn't ask you to come with me if it was. I'm a really good sailor."

"Oh. How big is your boat again?" Maybe he had a big luxurious yacht and they could snack on caviar, chocolate-covered strawberries, and champagne.

"It's a twenty-four-foot Melges."

"Is that big?"

"It's big enough. It gets the job done."

She felt her face flush and get all tingly. "I don't know anything about boats. I'm sorry."

He sniffed. "I'm the one who should be sorry. I shouldn't tease you. Look. I'm talking about a short sail to Bar Island, have a picnic, then head home."

Her interest perked up. A picnic. She liked picnics as much as the next person.

Especially if they included chocolate-covered strawberries and champagne. "A picnic sounds fun."

"It'll be great. When's your next free afternoon?"

Angelique mentally went through her work schedule. "Wednesday, but let me double check."

"You got it. It'll be fun. Let me know and if I'm not home, just leave me a note in my mailbox."

"Okay."

He walked her to her front door. "Good night, Angie."

"Thank you," she could barely do more than whisper.

He kissed her and sensation zapped through her body.

He stopped the kiss and stepped away. "Let me know about Wednesday."

"Okay. Good night."

"Good night." He backed down her front walk until he hit the sidewalk.

She sighed as she watched him fade into the night. If she wasn't careful, she'd be halfway in love with him before it was too late.

What had happened to love 'em and leave 'em Angelique Durand? She didn't recognize herself, but she started to like what she saw.

A gourmet picnic! A romantic boat ride to a beautiful island! How could this get any more perfect?

Chapter Fifteen

"Thanks, Sally." Tim handed Sally Pelletier his credit card. "I appreciate it."

"Let us know how it goes." Sally rested her chin on her hands, which were steepled in front of her. "Don't leave out a detail."

Tim stopped and hung his head. "Sally." He lifted his head up to look her in the eyes. "You know I don't kiss and tell."

"I do and it's so frustrating! I have to imagine it all."

Christ on a crutch. The thought of Sally having romantic fantasies about him just didn't bear thinking about. "Go grab a Scarlette LaFlamme book."

"I've read them all three times. The woman can't write fast enough for me. Go," she said. "Faint heart never won fair lady."

"Bye Sally." Tim hotfooted it out of Maggie's Diner and breathed a sigh of relief. Sally could be a trial.

He'd already gotten the six-pack of Thunder Hole on ice.

It would go perfectly with the muffulettas he'd begged Maggie to make.

He headed to Julie's Coffee and Sweet Shop for some of their lobster-shaped sugar cookies. He'd considered the blueberry tarts but he thought Angie would see and love the whimsy in the lobster-shaped cookies. They were finest kind.

Not to mention they had an inside joke about lobsters. He hoped they had lobster cookies decorated with red sprinkles.

Zombie cookies.

A nice sail, a simple informal picnic, it was going to be great!

Tim practically bounced home. They were going to have a great day out on the water, a lovely time hiking the trails on the island, and then have an awesome lunch, featuring Maggie's version of a muffuletta.

Taking a deep breath of the bracing sea tinged breeze, he marveled at the difference between the air in Lobster Cove and the air in Iraq.

He shoved all the vicious memories of Iraq as far away as he could. He was taking a beautiful, interesting woman on a boat ride.

He wouldn't let anything ruin the day.

****

Angelique had chosen her fashion with care for going sailing. She thought she looked pretty cute in white capris, a navy blue and white wide striped boatneck sweater. She'd found the most adorable white canvas slip on espadrille wedges, on sale, no less. She really didn't need another pair of shoes, but these babies were too cute to pass up. Besides that, she bought them with her own money. New shoes for a new life.

She'd pulled her hair into a high ponytail and pulled it through a navy blue ball-cap decorated with a red-beaded lobster.

She'd poked her one-carat emerald cut sapphire

studs into her ears and looped *Grand-mère's* gold locket around her neck. After she spritzed some Coco Mademoiselle on her wrists, cleavage, and behind her ears, she was all ready for an afternoon sipping champagne on Tim's yacht.

She hummed "Anchors Aweigh" while she waited for Tim to pick her up. She resisted the urge to peek through the hedge separating their patios to catch a glimpse of him.

When had she ever waited for a man? Usually she let—no—she made the man wait. Just another new adjustment to her new life.

Or maybe it was simply Tim. So different from the men she usually dated.

Were they even dating? She supposed so, as they'd gone to dinner, they'd gone to a cookout at his best friend's house, and now this afternoon.

They'd shared a couple of steamy kisses.

That constituted, to her way of thinking, dating.

"Angie."

She saw Tim standing in front of her stairs. He wore a green polo shirt, Ralph Lauren logo, she noticed, well-worn jeans, and boat shoes without socks. His hair was already windblown and he smiled at her. Her heart skipped a beat or two.

Yum.

"Are you ready to go?"

She stood. "Aye, aye, Skipper." She grabbed her over-sized Vuitton tote bag, pulled her sunglasses out of it, and put them on.

He laughed. "Then let's go. We're wasting daylight."

She grinned. "Well, we can't have that, can we?"

"Daylight's a terrible thing to waste." He held out his hand to help her down the stairs. As usual, it was warm, dry, and calloused.

Thrilling. And she wanted to feel his hands on other parts of her body instead of her hand.

How could she make that happen sooner rather than later?

Chapter Sixteen

Tim steered his Mercedes G550 north out of Lobster Cove and headed for the Spinnaker Yacht Club. He'd already launched and loaded the boat so they could take off right away. His stomach jumped with the desire to get going.

To get out there, skating with the wind across the water.

Of course, that might also have something to do with Angie sitting in his passenger seat.

Man, she looked good, although he had serious doubts about her shoes being practical for sailing. He intended to take it easy and keep *Fantasy* as flat as possible, but she'd still need to be light on her feet and able to move from the low to the high side every time they tacked.

He liked the sparkly lobster on her hat. Actually, he liked the whole package. The hat just brought more of the cute.

He'd stowed his camera in a waterproof bag under the hull, in case he could talk her into letting him take some pictures of her on the island.

He wouldn't push the issue, especially as he hadn't told her yet that he was a photographer. That day wasn't today.

In no time, he turned into the Yacht Club's crushed clamshell parking lot and grabbed a space. He put the car in reverse, turned off the engine, and pulled up the hand brake. "We're here. You ready?"

She smiled at him, her eyes bright. "I am if you are."

"Let's go." He got out of the car and noticed she made no effort to do so. Of course. His mother had trained him better. After rounding around the back of the Mercedes, he opened her door and offered his hand to help her out. "My lady Sparky."

Laughing, she put her small hand in his and let him help her out. "Thank you, kind lord Skipper."

"Just trying to prove that chivalry is not dead."

"And doing a good job of it."

"Does calling me Skipper make Chester the new Gilligan?"

She giggled. "I don't think so."

He offered her his arm and she threaded her arm through his. Her bright eyes dazzled him to the point that he momentarily lost his power of speech, so much so that he had to clear his throat. He nodded toward the dock where he'd moored the boat and cleared his throat again. "C'mon."

"I'm looking forward to going sailing with you."

Tim picked up her hand and kissed it. "Me too."

****

They'd passed a whole bunch of really big yachts on the way to get to Tim's boat. As they walked along the dock, the boats got increasingly smaller.

She had the feeling that she was leaving Kansas with Dorothy and Toto.

The Welcome to Oz sign came up fast on the horizon.

She should have picked out the red espadrilles

instead of the white, because, you know, ruby slippers and all that.

Tim led her past all the increasingly smaller boats until they got to the end of the dock. Tied to it was what, to Angelique's way of thinking was the smallest boat in the world.

"Here we are," Tim said. "I'll board her first, then help you."

"I thought you had a yacht."

He grinned. "I do. This is she."

The boat pitched and rocked as he stepped down onto it. He raised his hand out to her. "Take my hand. I'll steady you as you step across the lifeline."

She froze, just couldn't make herself move.

"It's okay. You'll be fine." He cleared his throat. "I'm not going to let anything bad to happen to you."

Taking a deep breath, she took his hand and inched to the edge of the dock.

"That's it. Now put one foot over the lifeline and then the other."

"Okay." She lifted her leg and got halfway over the rail when the boat pulled slightly away from the dock. So there she was, one foot on the boat, the other on the dock, with the distance between the two getting bigger. "Tim?" She squeaked.

"Don't panic. I got you." He pulled on a rope and got the boat back in closer. "Now bring your other foot over."

She whimpered a little but got her other leg onto the boat. She heaved a sigh of relief. "I thought you'd have a gangplank or something."

He barked out a laugh. "A gangplank would probably be bigger than the Melges. Sit here while I tie us loose and cast off."

"Okay." She sat on the bench and watched him as he worked to get them moving. It seemed very complicated.

And the boat floated closer to the water than she'd expected. Just what had she gotten herself into?

****

Tim had been right about Angie's shoes. They were not practical boat shoes. He headed for the breakwater then he would change course to get them to Bar Island.

He supposed while they were still in relatively calm water he should teach her a thing or two about sailing the boat in case he needed her to jump in and help.

"Here are some things it might be helpful for you to know."

She turned those gorgeous dark eyes to him, so he launched into an explanation about the two sails, the main and the jib, how there were no ropes on a boat but lines, to trim the sails, and halyards, to raise and lower them. He showed her the winch and how it worked.

She listened solemnly, like a novice nun at mass with the Pope.

"It's easy, you'll see. Fun!" He grinned and pointed the bow high into the wind. The breeze grabbed the sails and they started to cut through the water on a beat, heeling slightly.

The sun glittered the waves, the air smelled crisp and cool, and the sky was blue and cloudless.

What a great day!

Chapter Seventeen

Well, this wasn't quite what she signed up for, Angelique thought. Not at all.

She watched Tim tie up in a slip at a rickety dock. Okay, it looked rickety to her. He assured her it was absolutely sturdy and safe.

She didn't trust him. Not when it came to this sailing stuff.

"We having fun yet?" Tim's oh-so-cheerful voice came from behind her.

She turned to face him. "*Mais* yeah, *cher*."

"We're about to have more fun. I'll get off the boat first then help you out." He leaped onto the dock with all the grace of Mikhail Baryshnikov and extended his hand. "C'mon."

She sighed. Stood. Took his hand.

Fortunately, it was easier to get off the boat than it was to get on.

"I've got to unload some things for our picnic. Why don't you go on up and I'll be right there?" He motioned to dry land with his head.

"Okay." Ready to do just that, she moved down the dock. Except that her feet didn't quite work. She couldn't quite catch her balance. "Whoa!"

Tim grabbed her from behind by the arms. "You need to get your sea legs."

"Is that what this is?" The dock felt a little bit

steadier.

"Yep." He escorted her down the dock, staying close enough behind her, all warm and protective.

Now that she liked.

"You good now?" He turned her around so they were face to face and kissed the tip of her nose.

She nodded. "*Oui*."

"Good. Just wait right here and I'll be right back."

She looked around at the landscape. Quite barren, some trees, a lot of sand, no sign that anything human lived on Bar Island.

Maine's version of the bayou, only very windy and no gators. What if it had something worse than a gator, like a bear or a moose?

She swung her head around, first in one direction, then the other, trying to find any clue that might indicate any bear or moose lurking.

"What are you looking for?"

Now, how could she tell him that she was on the hunt for mean animals with big teeth or a coatrack as headgear? "Oh, nothing. Just checking out the scenery."

"It's great, isn't it?" He carried a big red cooler that had a red tartan blanket on it.

"Let's go. I know the perfect spot."

She trudged along beside him, her shoes sinking in the sand, which made keeping up with him very difficult. She started to break out into a sweat and wasn't that attractive? *Uh, negative.*

Big negative.

"Here we are. Let's pick a shady spot." Tim grinned.

Thank you, Jesus. Angelique wanted to drop to her knees in gratitude.

Doreen Alsen

He guided her to a pretty little place, well shaded by some evergreen trees and scrub pines. The trees sheltered them from some of the wind.

He laid the blanket on the ground. "You hungry?"

His sexy smile sent shivers up and down her spine. "I could eat."

"Good!"

She let him help her down to sit on the blanket then sat next to her and gave her a small kiss.

The kisses made the misery almost worthwhile.

Almost.

For sure, the chocolate-covered strawberries would go a long way to bridge the gap left by the kisses.

****

Tim opened the cooler and reached in for a couple of beers. What a great day.

Blue sky? Check.

Puffy clouds? Check.

Sunshine? Check.

Steady wind? Check.

He opened the beers and handed one to Angie. "I bet you're thirsty."

She stared at it for just a couple of seconds before she took it from him. "Thank you."

"I hope you're hungry." He reached into the cooler and took out the sandwiches he'd gotten from Maggie's Diner. "I didn't know what you liked then I had this great idea. I coaxed Maggie into trying her hand at making a muffuletta. I hope it's close to what you're used to." He put it down in front of her.

"I haven't had a muffuletta in a long time."

He nodded. "I've got some chips," he said as he rummaged around in the canvas bag in which he'd stored the dry stuff. "Here. I've got a couple of flavors."

"Humpty-Dumpty potato chips?"

He grinned. "Finest kind. I've got salt and vinegar and another bag of sour cream and clam dip."

She wrinkled her nose. "Clam flavored chips?" *Please no.*

He nodded. "My favorite."

Going back to the cooler, he pulled out a couple of Baggies filled with raw vegetables and a vat of onion dip. He pulled out a plate to put them on, along with a huge pile of napkins.

If a muffuletta was anything like a Maine Italian sub, like Maggie had told him, there was a mess about to be made.

He unwrapped his half of the sandwich with gusto. He loved Italian subs and couldn't wait to dig in.

He glanced at Angie who seemed to be waiting for something.

Duh! Of course. She was waiting for a toast.

He held up his beer bottle. "Let's toast to a great day of sailing and to you the beautiful milady Sparky, for coming along with me!"

She brought her beer up slowly and they clinked bottles.

Tim took a big swallow. He noticed Angie didn't. After her delicate little drink, she lifted her beer. "To milord Skipper for inviting me."

"Thank you, lady Sparky." They bumped bottles again, but still Angelique didn't drink very much.

Damn she was so lovely. There weren't enough adjectives to describe how beautiful she was.

"So, check out your sandwich. Maggie's going to

be on pins and needles, waiting to hear how you liked it."

She unwrapped her wedge of muffuletta part way and with great care. The sandwich was big, filled with marinated olive salad, and layers of mortadella, salami, ham, and provolone cheese. She couldn't get her mouth open enough to get a full bite, so she nibbled first the top half of it, and then the bottom. Olive oil dripped down her chin.

"It's good, yes?" Tim opened wide and took a monster bite and blissfully chewed on it.

Angie put her sandwich down and grabbed a napkin to wipe the olive oil off her face. "It tastes very authentic."

"Great! Do you need another beer?"

"No, thank you. I'm good." She nibbled another bite off the muffuletta.

Yep, Tim thought as he chewed off another chunk of sandwich. Fair winds, good food, and a beautiful woman at his side.

Finest kind.

Chapter Eighteen

Wearing a bright yellow weather coat over an electric orange life preserver, Angelique gripped the lifelines on the high side of the boat for all she was worth.

The weather had turned on a dime and Tim declared it time go home.

So here she was, holding on for dear life, on a very small boat that heeled almost ninety degrees from the water. Tim told her everything was okay and that *Fantasy* couldn't capsize, which meant they'd go into the water and have to right the boat, or turn turtle, which meant the boat would go arse over teakettle, as in bottoms up.

Somehow, that wasn't reassuring right now.

She dared a glance at Tim, whose muscles bunched and flexed as he fought with the wind. As he'd given her the only rain jacket, his clothes stuck to him, delineating every muscle he had.

He had a lot of them.

Usually she'd enjoy being with a strong, muscled, all-wet man. This was not one of those times.

Right now she was praying to every god listening that she wouldn't die here in the cold waters of Frenchman's Bay, Maine.

"Hold on! We're gonna get a gust!" Tim yelled over the roar of the wind.

What!

The wind hit and the boat nearly went over onto its side, with the spreaders touching the water. She screamed her lungs out. Barely able to breathe, she scrabbled up as far as she could and held on to anything she could grab.

Tim swore a lot as he reached over to release the jib sheet. For a brief, dizzy moment, she knew, absolutely knew, they were going to die.

Then not. After he let out that damn sail, the boat got a little bit flatter.

Thank you, all you gods and goddesses. Now, they had to get home. In one piece.

And sane.

Don't forget sane. She didn't think Betts Quinn would like to have a babbling idiot working at the Sea Crest Inn.

"It's settling down a bit. Bad news, we had a rough ride. Good news, we'll get into port faster."

"Oh, thank God." She'd never wanted to be on solid ground so much before.

"It's been a little hairy out there, but you did great," Tim yelled as a wave smashed against the transom, sending more cold salt water into the cockpit.

Her pretty new espadrilles were a lost cause, totally saturated.

Ugh!

Even if they ever dried out, the salt would have ruined them. She might even have to cut them off her feet. If that had to be, she was going to weep.

She glanced at Tim. He looked all manly and sexy as he fought the elements for their survival. She sighed.

It didn't matter how gorgeous he was. She would

never ever set foot on a sailboat ever again.

****

"I'm sorry about the trip back. Try as I might, I don't have control of the weather." Tim helped Angie down her path and up the stairs to her front door.

"Don't worry about it. It made for some terrifying circumstances."

"That bad, huh?" He grimaced. "You were pretty brave. I'm impressed."

"You do what you have to do." And it was really not as horrible as spending twenty-four hours in a Paris jail.

He put his hands on her waist, pulled her against him, and kissed her.

She twined her arms around his neck, moved in even closer, and kissed him back.

He thought he could do that all night, drown in the taste, the warmth, the light flowery scent of her. Then he felt her shiver in his arms.

Trembling meant she wanted more, shivering meant she was cold. He broke the kiss. "Hey, you're shivering. Are you cold?"

She turned those deep dark eyes of hers up. "A little."

"Well, you need to go in and warm up. I had a great time with you today, really…I don't know…none of the words I have can describe it. I hope you did, too." He kissed her forehead.

She sighed. "It was…different."

Uh-oh. "Different good or different bad?"

She took a step back, out of his arms. "Just different. I really didn't know what to expect."

Uh-oh squared. "I should let you go in." He kissed

117

her hand. "Dream of me."

She sent him a sassy smile. "Maybe. If you're lucky."

"You'll have to let me know. Good night."

"*Adieu.*" She stuck her key in the lock, opened her front door, then closed it softly behind her.

He stood on her porch a little longer, staring at the door. His heart pounded a little harder as he tried to figure out his next move. Maybe he should leave it up to her.

Yeah. That was an idea whose time had come.

Chapter Nineteen

"Angie! There you are!" Birdie McCorkle captured Angelique in the back of the walk-in refrigerator. "It's almost time for the picture."

Angelique closed her eyes and prayed for strength. The reporter from The Boston Globe and his photographers were crawling all over the Sea Crest Inn, like fleas on a dog. She'd been shaking all day, along with ducking into corners and hiding. Of course, the shaking could from the fact that she'd been hiding out in a refrigerator for the past twenty minutes.

She patted her hair. She'd specifically let it frizz out that morning. "Do I have to? I'm having the worst bad hair day in the history of womankind."

She looked down at her green logo polo tee and pulled it away from her mid-section. "My shirt is really dirty. I spilled a whole order of Finnan Haddie down my front." She'd dumped the milk and haddock dish down her front on purpose.

"No problem, lass! No one's going to be after looking at your hair and we've got enough T-shirts to choke an elephant." She patted Angelique's shoulder. "I'll be right back."

That was Angelique's cue to exit, stage left.

She cracked open the door of the walk-in and poked her head out and looked in both directions before she left the fridge.

As far as she could tell, the coast was clear.

She pulled a baseball cap out of her apron pocket and slammed it on the top of her head, put her face down and took leave of her self-imposed, very chilly prison.

She shook for more than one reason.

Angelique touched her eyelashes, all stiff with the three coats of mascara she'd applied. They nearly cracked in half from having been in the cold.

What had become of her? Her life dependent upon frozen mascara.

Someone was the new Queen of Ridiculousness. Oh, look.

It was she. Angelique Durand. The person she no longer wanted to be.

Oh. Her glasses. She shoved them back on her face and stepped into the dining room.

"Angie?"

Angelique started, feeling like she jumped a mile into the air at the sound of Tim's voice. She turned around. "Hi, Tim."

He looked glorious, dressed in old jeans, a blue polo shirt, and his usual Topsider boat shoes without socks. "I almost didn't recognize you."

She resisted the urge to slap her hand against her chest and pasted a winning smile on her face. "Tim. What are you doing here?"

"Maybe I came here to say 'hi' to you?"

Be still my heart. "Did you?"

He chuckled. "Of course I did. And maybe to steal a kiss." He leaned over and gave her a quick peck on her lips. "So much sweeter than your beignets."

She slapped at his shoulder. "Oh you sweet talker."

"And don't you forget it." He touched her totally frizzed hair. "This is a new look for you."

Yes it was. "Do you like it?"

"It's very pretty. You're always very pretty." He slipped a finger down the slope of her nose. He looked over her shoulder then stiffened. "Who are those people?"

Angelique knew who he was talking about but didn't dare look. She actually stepped a bit more into him so the reporter couldn't see her. "Apparently the Sea Crest Inn is being featured by The Boston Globe and they've sent a reporter and a few photographers to cover us."

She wanted to throw up. She glanced up at his face. He was looking a little green around the gills himself.

"Well, I've got to go to Cliff Notes. I'll see you tonight maybe?"

"Maybe."

He pulled the bill of her ball cap down over her forehead. "Chester and I will be on the beach. See you later." He gave her a quick kiss on her mouth and left lickety-split.

She watched him leave then looked up to see the reporter and photographer staring at her. Instantly nauseated, she retreated to the first bathroom she could find.

****

"Was that who I think it was?" The reporter pulled out his recording device out of his shirt pocket.

"Which one? The guy or the girl?"

"I'm pretty sure the guy is T. L. Baldwin. Looks like we found his hiding place. I'd kill my own grandmother to get an interview with him."

"Could be. The girl looks familiar, too, but I can't place her." The photographer shifted his camera strap to his shoulder.

"Let's finish up here then grab a drink at Murphy's Bar and chat up the locals. It'd be quite a coup to get a hold of Baldwin."

"You got it."

****

"Oh, you're here!" Bobbie Darling came around the counter in her bookstore, Cliff Notes, with a big smile.

Tim smiled back. "I told you I would be."

"Well, let me show you where we'll have the book signing. Can I get you some coffee?"

"No thanks." He followed Bobbie to an area of the store decorated with some chairs and a couple of couches. People sat there reading or tapping on their laptops.

Bobbie stopped. "I think we'll set you up over there and we'll have a podium for you to use when you give a little talk about the book."

"I have to talk?"

She swatted at his arm. "Of course you do, like maybe a little tidbit about some of the photos. They're very moving, Tim. You have such a gift."

"Thanks." He'd had such a gift. Past tense. Unless you counted the bootleg pictures of Angie which he wasn't.

"Then, if you're willing, you can take questions from the audience, and after that sign books. I'm expecting a pretty good crowd, with all the tourists around and the locals wanting to see a local boy done good."

"Jeez." Tim felt his face flush. "I'm not a local boy. I'm one of the summer kids."

Bobbie laughed. "It's funny how quickly you become a townie when there's fame involved."

Tim rubbed the back of his neck. "I guess."

"Besides that, you're a hero." She gently touched his arm. "People really want to thank you and support you."

His stomach started to churn. "I was lucky. The real heroes are the ones who were executed."

She shook her head and swallowed. "Those damn terrorists. I just don't get all that killing in the name religion."

Tim looked down at his shoes. He couldn't speak because of the swirling ball of acid clogging his throat.

"I'm sorry. I shouldn't have brought it up."

"No, that's okay," he croaked out. "It's over for me. I just pray that the hostages there now get freed." Actually, that was a lie. He'd lost any faith in a loving God once he'd touched ground in the Middle East.

Yet another thing he'd left behind in Iraq. "Are we done here?"

"Yeah. I'll text you if I have any other questions." Bobbie's face was filled with pity.

Jesus, he had to get out of there. "Awesome. Thanks, Bobbie."

"Thank you." She followed him to the entrance of the store. "See you later!"

He stepped out into the sunshine. It burned so much gentler here than in Iraq. Still his hands began to shake. "Yep."

Maybe he should go take a sail. Or get a drink at Murphy's Bar. He squinted up into an ominous gray sky.

Murphy's it was. As he approached the bar's door he saw the two men from the Sea Crest Inn. He supposed he should have expected the press would find him at some point, but he wasn't going to make it easy for them. With one last regretful thought about grabbing a beer, he headed toward his car to go to the Yacht Club.

****

The five-to-six-feet waves slapped at *Fantasy*, the chop thick and brutal. Tim reefed the main sail and flew his smallest jib sail. His arms ached as he wrestled with the tiller to keep the boat on course.

It began to rain soon after he cast off, big, fat bullets of water pelting him. He should have turned back the minute that happened, but he didn't.

The first flash of lightning hit the water about half a mile to starboard, and even he wasn't foolish enough to tempt that particular fate.

The salt-filled air rumbled around him as well as crackled with electricity. Mother Nature threw just about everything at him. As he battled the elements on his little boat, he let everything else slip away, leaving just him and the sea.

Another streak of lightning landed way too close to the boat with a screaming sound and heeled the boat too close to the waves. The spreader broke and the mast fell with a sickening series of cracks.

He shook the water out of his eyes and groped his way along the lifelines to the radio to make a mayday call. That done, all he could do was sit and wait in the pitching sea and hope that the Coast Guard got there sooner rather than later.

The rain sluiced down his face in stinging icy sheets as he cut the mainsail away and off the mast. He gritted his teeth against the elements. The effort to keep the terror from having water slam him over and over caused his muscles to cramp in tight spasms.

Through the wind and rain, he thought he saw a helicopter bearing down on him. Coast Guard.

He shook with relief. They lowered a harness down to him so they could haul him up. The chopper's rotors sent the water in circles around the boat, and a spotlight bathed the scene in bright, white light. He managed to get the harness over his head and tugged on the line to let them know he had it on. It nearly dislocated his shoulders as they winched him up and in.

One more giant wave, and the *Fantasy* disappeared into the bay.

"Are you okay?" One of the rescue crew helped him out of the harness and handed him a towel. "We'll get you to the E. R. right ASAP!"

Tim didn't take his eyes away from the churning sea. "I'm fine," he said as he shook his head. "I don't need the emergency room."

"You might not have a choice. You're lucky to be alive. What made you think going sailing by yourself today was a good idea?"

Sighing, Tim toweled away the moisture on his face. He couldn't tell if it was from the rain or from his tears of frustration and outrage.

Chapter Twenty

Almost at the end of her shift, Angelique filled the salt and pepper shakers in her section of the dining room at the Sea Crest Inn. She'd been doing well enough at breakfast and lunch so they were going to give her a chance to work dinner, when the tips were much better.

She wanted to replace the shoes her little adventure on the high seas ruined.

She hadn't seen Tim since the day the reporters had been at the Inn. She heard about his little run-in with the Coast Guard. She'd been scared out of her wits and was really sure she would never set foot on another sailboat.

"Angie! There you are, me girl. I need you to run some food over to the bookstore." Birdie McCorkle bustled into the room.

"Okay. Sure." Angelique could use a bit of fresh air.

"Good. Come with me to the kitchen to fetch the goodies. Bobbie's having a local author in for a book signing." She clucked her tongue.

Angelique followed her. She'd only been to one signing when Lucien dragged her along to an event where he signed his cookbook and hawked his special L'Enfer spice blends. She'd been bored out of her mind.

She and Birdie boogied on over to the walk-in. On a shelf stood a dozen huge take-out boxes. "Here you go, dearie. Just carry them over to Cliff Notes. There's a likely lass." Birdie beamed at her.

"I don't think I can take them over all at once."

"Of course you can't. But, sure and it's not such a long walk. Take all the trips you need." She left.

Oh, well. Long walks in the fresh air were good, right? Many walks in the fresh air had to be better. Or not.

She should just get on with it. She grabbed two boxes and hoisted them on her shoulder.

The hotel and the bookstore shared a parking lot, paved with the usual crushed quahog shells. Even though she had on ugly, read sensible, shoes, she still had a problem with balance as she crossed the space between both buildings.

She pulled the boxes off her shoulder, now carrying them in a pose that could only be called 'two pizzas to go.'

She had trouble keeping the boxes flat. Obviously, given the frosted pastries in one of the boxes, tipping them would totally wreck the icing.

God, her arms hurt. She rolled her shoulders back and front, but it didn't help. She had two choices. She could make six trips with two boxes at a time, or struggle with more boxes and make fewer trips.

Arghhh. Math. It had to be math.

She hated math.

Who didn't?

Tim probably loved math. Lived for math. Knew exactly how long it would take a train going 40 miles per hour to get to the station as opposed to a car that started thirty minutes earlier, going 20 miles per hour.

Beyond math, she just flat out hated school.

Detested it. X = Pain in the butt.

And, thank God, she closed in on Cliff Notes. The door was open so she didn't have to put the food down in order to deal with opening it.

"Oh, let me help you with that."

Angie looked around her boxes to see Bobbie Darling standing in front of her. She happily surrendered the food to the bookstore owner. "I'll go and get some of the others."

"Are there a lot?"

"It'll take me a few trips to haul them all over. But it's no big." Angelique swore she could feel her nose grow longer.

"It's a very big favor to me. Let me get someone to help you." Bobbie set the boxes down on the checkout counter, looked around, and motioned to one person stacking books to come over. "Sadie will help you."

Sadie bopped on over. "What do you need?"

"Go with Angie here and bring the food for the book signing. Please." Bobbie smiled at Sadie.

Sadie nodded. "Of course."

"This book signing seems to be a big deal," Angie said as she crossed the parking lot back to the inn.

"Oh yeah. One of the local authors has a new book out. He's kind of a celebrity. T.L. Baldwin."

"I've never heard of him."

"He was one of those reporters who got kidnapped over in Iraq. He won a Pulitzer Prize for some of his photos back in the Middle East."

"Really?" *Le bon Dieu.*

"Yeah." Sadie tugged on the ponytail holder in her

hair. "He got rescued, of course, right before they executed him."

"Oh. Well, good." Angelique didn't really care about all that terrible stuff happening in the Middle East. Too depressing. Her life was depressing enough.

"It doesn't hurt that he's incredibly hot." Sadie fanned herself with her hand. "Like movie star handsome."

Soon she and Sadie were carrying the rest of the food across the parking lot to the bookstore. Angelique was more than a little curious to see this local legend.

The bookstore was filled to the brim, all the customers buzzing around like so many bees in a hive. Angelique and Sadie fought through the crowd to get the food to the signing area.

There, behind a table stacked with books, stood Tim Baldwin. Clad in jeans, a blue silk tee, and a darker blue, lightweight blazer, hair tousled, cheeks and chin stubbled, he looked good enough to eat.

"See? I told you he was hot," Sadie whispered to her.

Behind her dark glasses, Angelique blinked as she put it all together. Tim, her neighbor, was world famous journalist T.L. Baldwin.

World famous, Pulitzer Prize winning, Photojournalist.

She turned wide eyes up to his face. He had a deer in the headlights look to him, but after a second, he gained his composure, she guessed.

She followed Sadie and helped unload the food. In the meantime, Bobbie'd introduced Tim and he started to talk.

Her ears buzzed and spots danced in front of her

eyes. Tim Baldwin was a damn photographer.

The man she'd almost bared her soul to took pictures for a living.

He stole souls.

Her breath froze in her lungs. She had to get out of there.

She pushed her way through the crowd, desperate for air. Once outside, she sat on a bench against the shop and put her head between her legs, breathing carefully in and out. The spots in front of her eyes disappeared slowly and the clanging in her ears went away.

"Are you okay?" Angelique heard Sadie and felt her put a hand on her shoulder.

"Yeah," Angelique said as she sat up. "There were so many people in there, and I couldn't breathe."

"Okay. You sure you're okay?"

She stood. "I am." She had to get away from there. "I better get back to the inn or else Birdie McCorkle will come after me."

Sadie grinned. "We can't have that."

Angelique nodded. "Thanks."

She ran rather than walked back to the Sea Crest Inn. She just wanted to get home and hide.

Especially from her esteemed celebrity neighbor, T.L. Baldwin. She knew the T stood for Tim and for sure, the L stood for liar.

She did not see the media people from the Inn watch her leave, nor did she see one of them follow her out.

****

Tim hadn't expected so many people to show up. People jammed into every corner of Cliff Notes. The

130

seats Bobbie had put out for the signing were already full and now the crowd was standing room only. With the door open letting the warm air in, the heat began to build in the room. He should probably take his jacket off.

He certainly hadn't expected to see Angie there. From the look on her face, he could tell she didn't understand what was going on.

Tim fought the urge to run after her and told himself he'd give her some time to cool off and then show her the book. He'd confess that he couldn't take pictures anymore.

He would not confess that the only pictures he could take were ones of her. At least not yet.

Portraits of Despair was the furthest thing from any photography she was used to. He'd get her to understand.

Because if she didn't understand about the pictures in the book, she wouldn't understand how horrible it was not to be able to do the job he'd lived for.

Still lived for.

And he might as well admit it. Her good opinion of him mattered to him. It squeezed him like a spandex shirt that was two sizes too small.

Tim didn't want to examine his feelings. He had enough on his plate to deal with. He really didn't want to bare his soul to her in order to make her feel better.

But he would if he had to. He had too much loss in his life lately. And he realized he needed her in his life.

The thought terrified him.

In the meantime, he plucked up a copy of *Portraits of Despair* to give to her. If she wouldn't talk to him, he'd just leave it in her mailbox or on her back patio.

Hopefully she'd be curious enough to look through the book.

Then she'd see his heart. She'd see what drove him.

If she didn't? It just didn't bear thinking about. He'd lost so much. For some reason, he couldn't stand to lose her as well.

****

Angelique ignored the maniac knocking at her front door. She had a pretty good idea who that maniac was.

She had nothing to say to him. He had nothing to tell her that she wanted to listen to.

A photographer. A freaking, damn photographer.

She was totally made of stupid. Worse than that, the stupid came with a huge side dose of gullible.

Touching the scar on her cheek, she went to her kitchen and poured herself a glass of water. This being summer, she didn't have to turn on the lights.

Oh, for God's sake! She would not sneak around in her own house when she wanted to go into the kitchen and get a damn drink of water.

Okay. It was Lucien's house, but the principle was the same.

She'd been reactive rather than proactive and it didn't look good on her. Where was the Angelique who grabbed men by the balls and squeezed them until they yelped?

Stuck hiding out in Lobster Cove, slinging hash and cleaning up the messes of the great, unwashed masses.

Well, okay. They did bathe. She'd picked up, among other gross things, enough of their used and discarded towels when she had to chambermaid at the inn.

Oh, check out the word sucker in the dictionary and you'd see Angelique's picture right next to the entry.

No more.

She was so done with that.

Listening with care, she realized he'd stopped knocking. A tiny, hypocritical piece of her heart was disappointed.

Forget it. She'd played better men than T. L. Baldwin like a fiddle. Like a freaking Stradivarius. He'd crawl to her, begging for forgiveness.

It would be a beautiful thing.

Chapter Twenty-One

Tim hadn't seen her for three days.

Day one, he'd been upset by her act of defiance. Day two, he'd started to get a little annoyed. Day three, frustration nipped at his temper in sharp little snaps.

He owed her an explanation. She owed him to listen to it.

Damn woman.

She had him tied up in knots and he didn't like it. Not at all.

He grabbed a beer and walked upstairs to the patio off his bedroom. A brisk wind blew in from the sea, carrying the scent of the ocean with it. It ruffled the floor-length white sheer curtains covering the open doors. Thoroughly unsettled and grumpy, he plopped down onto the chaise lounge on the balcony and stared out over the water.

He could feel a storm brewing somewhere out in the distance. Black clouds would race in soon and he welcomed them, as they matched his mood.

Just then, he saw Angie come out onto her back deck and down the stairs to the beach. The wind whipped her flowered dress around her legs and played with the ends of her long dark hair. She raised her hands over her head and turned around and around in a circle.

He went and got his camera and started to snap. He

just couldn't stop himself.

She played like a child by the sea, twirling as the rain started to fall slowly, big fat drops that landed with extravagant plops on her and on the beach. Turning her face to the sky, she laughed with abandon.

That was the money shot he thought as excitement raced through him and made his heart pound. That exact moment when she faced the sky.

Lightning cracked out on the horizon, a long straight spear into the sea. The rain fell harder now in needle-like drops that would sting when they hit her.

With one last longing, joyful look to the darkening sky she went back into her house.

He had to have her. He craved the taste of her, to run his greedy hands over her soft, silky skin. He wanted to gather her hair in his grasp and learn her scent. His body got hard just imagining it.

He took a deep breath. First, he had to get her to talk to him.

****

Angelique had never, ever done anything like dance by herself in the rain. She'd just felt the urge to go out and celebrate.

Celebrate exactly *what* she didn't know. Being alive, maybe. Or the intense feeling of freedom she'd just realized.

She finally saved enough money to replace the shoes she'd ruined when she went sailing with Tim. Nobody else gave her the money. She'd earned it.

She laughed with the power of it.

Then she heard the knock on the door and knew absolutely who it was. Mr. T. L. Baldwin.

She glanced through the book he'd left in her

mailbox. It moved her beyond anything else she'd seen in her life. She wept for the lives of those miserable, lonely, terrified faces, especially the children.

What he'd seen through his camera lens humbled her. It wasn't intrusive. It wasn't exploitive.

It was breathtaking and beautiful, heartbreaking and sad.

She'd wanted to make him pay for lying to her. After seeing the pictures in his book, she didn't have the heart for it. She didn't have the heart to be a ball buster anymore.

Plus, if Bobbie Darling and Sadie were to be believed, he'd been kidnapped and tortured. That kind of made a stint in a French prison look like a walk in the park.

Emphasis on the words 'kind of.'

She went and answered the door. "Tim."

He pushed past her into her living room. She shut the door behind him and turned to face him.

And trembled at the intensity in his eyes.

"I saw you dance," he said in a low growl that rasped along every nerve in her body.

"Yes." It came out on a breath that felt like a prayer.

One second he was standing there, the next he snatched her up into his arms and crashed his mouth against hers.

She made a noise of distress and he immediately stopped the kiss. "Tell me you want me to kiss you. That you want me to touch you."

She sucked in a small sip of air. Did she want him to kiss her?

God help her, she did. "Yes."

He bent his head and claimed her mouth again.

This time his lips were as gentle as a whisper, teasing and coaxing hers to let him in. She opened up and let him in.

Connected by a fire within both of them, they sparred with lips, teeth, and tongue, not gentle anymore.

With every pass, she felt the greed, the desire for this man rise up in her. So she plundered as good as she got.

The two of them ripped at each other's clothes, Angelique desperate to connect skin to skin.

Tim's hands raced up and down her back, finally landing on her butt. He squeezed each perfect peach of a cheek and hauled her against him, rocking his erection against her tender flesh.

She moaned. This drive, this maelstrom was so beyond her knowledge and her experience. All she could do was grab the tiger by the tail and hold on tight.

The two of them struggled against each other until he dragged both of them down to the floor. Once there, he used his teeth to nip at each tight, aching nipple one first, then the other, then back again.

He kept on alternating like that, sucking one rosy nipple as he plucked the other with his wicked clever fingers.

She could barely breathe for the wash of pleasure breaking over her.

She'd never felt passion as all-consuming as this. Every synapse she had snapped, crackled, and popped at every touch of his hand.

She fisted her hands in his hair as he ran his mouth up and down her neck. That sexy stubble on his chin rubbed and scratched against her tender skin, adding to the thrill of it all.

Still he kissed her as he moved down her body, laving her belly button with his tongue. His hands squeezed her butt as he pulled her legs over his shoulders and brought her sex up to his mouth. He used his tongue to tickle and tease her clitoris.

"Ohhhhhh." All she could do was moan and ride the waves of pleasure that lifted her higher and higher. He wrapped his lips around the hard button and sucked and she came apart.

She screamed as her body pulsed over and over. Her heart beat erratically and she couldn't breathe.

He brought her down slowly, kissing her intimate flesh softly, slowly, chasing each shudder to completion.

"I need to be inside you now," he growled. After finding the condom he'd brought he sheathed himself with trembling hands. In one quick move, he positioned his hard, erection against her soft flesh and buried himself in her to the hilt.

She moaned as he claimed her, the sensation of being so totally filled by him. He began to move, plunging in and out, each thrust harder and deeper than the one before. Miraculously, she felt a climax to start to rise up in her again, powered by Tim's back and forth.

"God, you're so tight." He changed the angle of his penetration and managed to make her spasms build even faster. "Come for me."

That pushed her over the edge one more time and she keened as she fell. While she pulsed around his driving erection, he groaned long and low. "That's it, baby. Jesus!" He exploded in three long, hot bursts.

He dropped his head and captured her mouth and kissed her long and hard then rolled off of her, breathing hard, his chest heaving with each labored breath.

****

"God, I'm sorry! I acted like an animal." Tim had never been so rough with a woman in his life. "My only excuse is that it's been so long for me." He managed to push himself up to lie on one side. "I really came over to talk to you about me being a photographer."

"I liked it."

He closed his eyes. "You're sweet." He tucked some stray strands of her silky hair behind her ear. "I usually have more finesse."

She licked her lips. They were pink and swollen from his kisses. "Maybe you can show me some of that finesse the next time."

His heart about stopped. "There's going to be a next time?"

She smiled. "I hope so. Maybe in a bed?"

He wished for that with all his might. His stomach jumped at the thought of it. But—"I have to tell you, I'm really damaged. You need to know that."

She rose up to her knees. "Tell me in bed."

He stood with her and let her take his hand.

"Come with me. Let me take you to bed."

He had no choice but to follow where she led.

Her bedroom was so feminine. A couple of big, fluffy pillows adorned the flowered, worn quilt. Lace curtains billowed at the open windows. The walls were painted a soft shade of primrose. The white wicker furniture also held soft pillows, a darker shade of pink than the walls.

Against one wall, a high set of bureau drawers, also white, was topped with several pretty bottles, probably filled with perfume, and a vase holding a riot of wild summer roses.

The storm raged outside, with driving rain, cracks of lightning, rolls of thunder. "You should close your windows."

She dropped his hand and moved to turn down the bed. "Not yet. I like the fresh air and the scent of the storm." She sat on the bed and patted the space next to her. "The sound of the waves. Come here."

Who was he to disappoint a lady? Not Mama Baldwin's baby boy. He rolled onto the bed next to her, rolled onto his back, and pulled her on top of him.

She sat up and rubbed her soft, wet, girly parts against his still-interested cock. Then she brought her hands up and cupped her breasts, running her thumbs back and forth over her pretty rosy nipples.

He couldn't breathe. He didn't dare breathe.

"What you thinkin' 'bout *cher*?" Her accent had thickened and now dripped with the music of the South.

He swallowed hard and took a beat. "You. Just you."

"Good." She leaned down and rubbed the tips of her breasts over his chest.

He thought she was going to kiss him, but she pulled back at the last second. She swept her amazing breasts over his body in slow figure eights.

"Like that, *cher*?"

"You know I do."

"Hmm. That's good. I do, too."

She had her eyes closed as she moved against him, a small smile on her face. "You know, *Grand-mère* warned me about boys like you."

"Oh really?"

"Yeah, all because I was too flighty and men too clever and willing to take advantage of girls like me."

"Is that right."

"Mmmmm." One more pass of her fingers over each nipple. "She did."

He closed his own eyes. "We men are wicked creatures."

"You are! But you know what?"

"What?"

"I'm wickeder than ten men put together."

"Praise the Lord."

Her eyes opened slowly. "You're a praying man?"

"When the circumstances call for it."

"Then get ready to call up to your Maker." She took her hands away from her breasts, planted them on his chest, and kissed him, smartly, right on the lips.

She rose up, took his now massive erection in her hand, and sank down on it, covering him with her warm, wet, willing flesh.

"Sweet baby Jesus."

She swiveled her hips. "Didn't I tell you you'd find God?"

He was beyond power of speech. He'd lost control of himself the minute she'd let him kiss her.

Magnificent, like a dark haired Aphrodite, she caught his gaze and held it as she moved that amazing warm heat over and above, slow and sultry, in the slow, syrupy rhythm of the South, up and down his rock hard erection.

After his imprisonment, he never thought to feel like this again. He thought he'd left his sexual self back in Iraq. Angie had certainly brought his sex drive back to life.

In spades. Desperate, he thrust up all the way into the heart of her.

He wanted to lose himself in her, to pour all that was good in him into her warm receptive body. He'd find healing there.

Somehow, she was the key to solving his life. Discovering the person he was meant to be. Not solitary, not left to drift by loving, but disinterested parents, but one part of a whole.

The other part being Angie.

"You didn't tell me," she fired at him, her eyelids hooded. "Do you want to meet your maker?"

He thrust up into her. "What do you think?"

She swiveled again. "I think it might be an amazing trip."

"God, Sparky, take me there."

"Count on it, shoog." She moved her hips in ways that defied human anatomy and physics.

Nirvana was over-rated.

This was bliss, feeling her in charge, giving himself up to her.

Putting her in charge of the love. Could he do it?

He had to let her call the shots, because she was intent on taking him to heaven.

He intended to appreciate every step on the journey.

He hoped to find another step she'd never imagined. No worries. He'd imagined it enough for the both of them.

And then he couldn't think at all.

He thrust up into her, desperate for the clasp of her

heat, for her invitation.

He would take that invitation for all it was worth.

Chapter Twenty-Two

Angelique awoke to find that Tim was a total bed hog. He also was a very restless sleeper.

The storm had passed and now the moon gilded the room through the window. Unable to go back to sleep, she studied him as he lay there bathed in the moonlight.

His face didn't look peaceful in sleep, more like a warrior than the man who'd taken all those amazing pictures in his book.

His body was toned and fit, including six pack abs. His chest was lightly furred with a happy trail leading down to his penis, which was pretty impressive, to say the least.

She smiled remembering how he'd filled her so wonderfully. She still felt little aftershocks of the pleasure he'd given her.

He began to murmur and mumble as his arms started to twitch. In the blink of an eye, his body bowed up in a rigid curve and he screamed.

Angelique scrambled off the bed, totally at a loss of what to do. Her heart pounded against her ribs like a bird trapped in a cage. "Oh my God! Tim! Wake up!"

She got her robe off the peg she hung it on and threw it around herself. Not knowing what to do, she turned in a circle looking for something, anything, to wake him up. She should shake him, she thought, but he was flailing in violent waves.

"Noooooo!" He jerked up violently into a sitting position and didn't seem to know where he was. Sweat poured off him as he dragged air in and out of his lungs.

He shook his head like a wet dog and threw his legs over the bed to the floor. Bracing his elbows on them, he hung his head in his hands.

She touched his shoulder with a tentative hand. He flinched.

"Don't touch me."

"Okay." She leaned against the bedroom wall. "Can I get you anything?"

"In a little bit. I need to catch my breath." His hands shook in visible tremors. "Did I hurt you?"

"No, no you didn't. What happened?"

He heaved a sigh. "A nightmare. I get them sometimes. It takes me a minute to come back."

A minute seemed like the epitome of understatement. She bit her lip. She wanted to help him but she had no idea what to do.

"Just give me a second and I'll go home. I'm not real steady right after them." He hung his head. "The nightmares, I mean."

"Did I hurt you?" Her stomach fell to her feet.

"No. The panic, it goes away in time." He twisted some facsimile of a smile on his face.

Her hands trembled as much as his did. This was so far beyond anything she'd ever dealt with. If he'd only tell her what to expect.

He braced himself as he stood. "I have to get home."

"No." The thought of him being alone in his current condition appalled her. "You need someone to be with right now."

Another sigh. "Trust me, I don't."

"Let me be the judge of that. You want to tell me about the nightmare?"

"No, but I should. That way you can decide whether you want to continue on with—" he waved his hand in front of him "—this. We probably should have had this conversation before we fell into bed. I owe you the truth."

"You do."

"Let me put some clothes on."

"Your clothes are downstairs. I'll get them for you."

"Thanks."

Angelique hurried down the stairs, grabbed his clothes, and bolted back up. "Here."

Taking them from her, he stood, slipped on his jeans without putting on his underwear, and only did a few buttons of his fly then sat on the bed.

Ahem. Angelique found it very distracting.

God. He looked terrible, like he'd fought thirty devils and barely made it out alive. She'd never seen a more ravaged and tortured face in her life. She sat on the bed next to him, being very careful not to touch him, even though she longed to.

"So you found out I'm a photojournalist." He glanced at her then turned his head to stare into the space in front of him. "What I do is nothing like what the paparazzi does. There are very important stories to tell. Things Americans need to know. Not just America. The whole western world." He swallowed. "My job took me to the worst places in the world. Honestly? Hell would be a vacation to these people. So much violence in the name of whatever religion you claim is right." He gave a mirthless little laugh. "Death to the infidel, in this case, me. The epitome of the God damn infidel.

"I'd been charmed, good enough to get the money shot, talented enough to catch the emotion in the event. Then my luck turned."

He faced her. "I got kidnapped by one of those insane groups. I spent months in captivity, often with a hood over my head. I didn't know if it was day or night. The only thing I knew was that there were times when one of us were taken out of the concrete cell they kept us in and never came back."

"Oh, God. I'm so sorry."

"Don't be. I'm one of the lucky ones. Right before I was set for execution, some SEALs raided the compound and I was rescued.

Angelique watched as tears gathered in his eyes. He blinked them away.

"I didn't deserve it. So, yeah, I have bad dreams from time to time. It's a small price to pay, since I'm alive and Josef's not. You're going to want to say you're sorry. Don't. Sorry's just a word. It doesn't make it better."

She took a chance and ran her hand down his bare back, still moist with the cold sweat of despair. "I will say I'm sorry, but not for what you think. I'm sorry for jumping to conclusions about T. L. Baldwin. I meant it when I said I was so moved by your work."

He snorted. "And there's the rub. Since I've come back to Lobster Cove to heal, I haven't been able to take a single photo." His eyes darted left as he said that. "Who am I if I can't be T. L. Baldwin, wonder boy genius with a camera, anymore?"

147

"I don't know. How can I answer that question when I don't know how to be Angelique Durand anymore?"

"What?"

She took a deep breath. "My name isn't Angie Doucette. It's Angelique Durand."

"I don't understand." His hands shook and he clenched them together.

"I'm Angelique Durand. You know. The model?" How did he not know who she was?

"Sorry. I've been in the Middle East for a long time."

Now this she hadn't expected. She was going to have to spell it out for him.

"I was a model. I got arrested in Paris for something I didn't do and spent some time in jail." She swallowed. "My brother pulled some strings and got the charges dropped but on the way out of the police station I nearly got trampled over by a crowd of reporters and photographers and I got struck hard in the face with a camera." She touched the scar. "That's how I got this. No more modeling for me. And no more pictures of me. Ever."

He looked at the floor for what seemed like a million years. "What did you get arrested for?"

"Something I didn't do. Someone planted a fortune in diamond jewelry in my bag after a runway show for Chanel. When security checked my things while I was trying to leave, they found the jewelry and called the police." She shuddered, remembering. "It was the worst night of my life."

He looked at her then and touched the scar on her cheek. "I hate the thought of anyone hurting you. I'd go through everything all over again if it'd keep you from getting hurt."

Angelique did one thing she rarely did. She thought before she spoke.

His world was so far away from anything she'd known. He'd done important work. He would go on to do more. She'd put on clothes and looked good in them.

She had a scar on the outside. He had so many more on the inside, so many more that no amount of makeup would cover.

Angelique flushed hot while she compared the two of them. How trivial and less than nothing she felt when he'd faced death, serious death, like deader than dead, dead.

She had absolutely no experience helping someone else through his feelings. Her whole life had been about Angelique and only that.

The time for that was way over. This wasn't about her. It was about him.

She went for broke and put her hands, one on each side of his face. "There was nothing you could have done." She kissed his stiff, rigid mouth.

They stared at each other and she hoped she could in some way take the pain away. She did what she knew.

She kissed him. She poured all she was into that kiss, trying to say all the things she wanted to say to him. To give him…what?

What did she really have to give?

She had no clue, not even an inkling.

So she went, for the first time in her life, for the truth. "I don't know what to say," she repeated.

He tipped his head and rested it against her

forehead. "There's nothing you can say. But damn it, I need you to be here with me."

Tears did spring to her eyes. "I'm right here, and this is where I want to be."

"It's going to be a rough road. You have to know that. I never know what's going to trigger a flashback or a nightmare."

She smiled. "I guess having sex with me pushed you over the edge."

He pulled away and braced his hands against her arms. "You did no such thing. It might have been the storm or…or…shit, I don't know. It's random. I never know when it's going to hit."

"I don't care. If nothing else, I'm your friend. I'm here for you." And that surprised the hell out of her. She had never been for anyone else. Just herself. Only herself.

She tried on this new unselfish Angelique and she liked the way it fit. "I'm not very good at this, but I want to help you through this, as much as I can. I want to be there for you."

Tim's head bowed as his chest heaved once, twice, three times as he sucked in air. "I don't think you can fix me, but I want to have you around."

"Tim." Somehow, she didn't think keeping quiet was in his best interest. "Shouldn't you be like going to a therapist or something?"

"I can beat it on my own. Please, do this for me. I'm doing it for you."

"It's not quite the same thing."

"It is." He kissed her. "It is," he repeated.

Something inside her let go. "Okay. I won't say anything for now. But if you get worse, I can't promise that I'll stay quiet."

He nodded. "Fair enough." He lifted her hand and brushed his lips over her knuckles. "Fair enough. Now tell me all about Angelique Durand."

She felt her face flush. "Not much to tell. She grew up like I told you, on the Bayou, living with *Grand-mère* and my brother." She sighed. In for a penny, in for a pound. "Who is Lucien Durand?"

"Lucien Durand. You mean the Chef King, owner of the L'Enfer restaurants."

"*Oui.*"

"Well, hell. I told you I ate in his restaurant in New Orleans."

She nodded. "You did. I couldn't tell you I was his sister then."

"Why not? You could have trusted me with that."

"I didn't know that then. I'm here hiding and figuring out what I want to do with my life. It's obvious I can never model again. Not just because of the scar but because of the arrest."

"Jesus."

"Here's the thing. You've done something with your life. Your book is just beautiful. Me?" She hitched up one shoulder. "I've been the most selfish person on the planet. I did a lot of things I'm not proud of. I was a true wild child. I went through men like they were Pez candies. There's even a sex tape out there, of me and Brock Nelson, the football player. But worst of all, I tried to sabotage Lucien and Hope's relationship, just so I could become a famous model. If karma is real, I really earned what happened to me." She cupped his cheek with one hand. "But not you. Never you."

He shook his head. "You made a sex tape with

Brock Nelson?"

Of course, he'd focus on that. "I didn't know we were being filmed. His brother Buck somehow managed the whole business. Can we talk about something else?"

"How about we don't talk about anything at all?" He held open his arms. "Come here and let me hold you."

She nestled herself against him and he closed his arms around her. "I like this."

Angelique smiled. "Me, too."

They lay there wrapped around each other in silence for a time.

Angelique counted Tim's heartbeats until he heaved a huge sigh. "I guess I should warn you," he finally said.

"About what?"

"Brock Nelson. Both he and Buck are coming up to do a football clinic for the high school team in August."

"What?" She blinked. "Why would two professional football players come to Maine to give a high school football clinic?"

"They're friends of Jeff's from Addington. Hey." He shifted underneath her. "Didn't your brother just open a branch of his restaurant in Addington?"

She forced herself to smile. The idea of Buck and Brock Nelson in Lobster Cove just didn't bear thinking about. "Yes. Suffice it to say, I'm not very popular in Addington, Massachusetts."

He frowned. "Because of the sex tape?"

"No." She disentangled herself and sat up, holding the sheet over her breasts. "Because I wasn't a very nice person."

He pulled her back down against him. "Let's forget about Addington for right now. We're here, we're safe, we're together. Let that be enough."

She flung an arm over his chest and a leg over his thighs and kissed his warm neck. "I can do that."

****

Tim knew he had to go home. The worst of the panic had dissipated and he had to take care of Chester. His little pup was afraid of thunder and lightning.

He should have thought of that earlier but he'd had other things on his mind. Okay. One thing.

Angelique.

"I need to leave."

"Are you sure?" She had such a hopeful look on her face. He hated to disappoint her.

"I've got to go check on the dog, or else I would happily stay right here."

"Well, of course. I'd forgotten all about the poor baby." She handed him his shirt as disappointment showed in her face.

Yeah, the poor baby was 110 pounds if he was an ounce. "I'm sorry. I'd stay if I could. You are amazing."

She smiled. "*Mais* yeah, shoog."

He shrugged into his shirt. "Do you want to get together tomorrow night? Go get dinner or something?" *Please say yes.*

She smoothed down the silky little robe she wore. "I'm working dinner tomorrow at the inn, so I can't."

"Dinner, huh?"

"Yes sir. I got a promotion, me." Her smile grew into a pride-filled grin.

"Good for you. Maybe the next night, then."

"Maybe. Is that Chester I hear barking?"

Tim heard it now, the distinct *Roo-Roo-Roo* call of the desperate Doberman. "I do think so. I've got to go before I have a big mess over there to clean up." He kissed her. "I'll see you later."

He bounded down her stairs and out of her house. He'd let her inside him and showed her his demons. He hoped that after she had time to think about it she'd call the whole thing off.

Not that he'd blame her.

She'd let him see her demons as well. He still couldn't wrap his head around what she told him. There were gaps, things she chose to leave out, and he couldn't blame her.

He should be mad at her for not telling her who she was, but he lied too and that leveled the playing field. He'd get the whole story out of her. She seemed eager to tell it once they made love.

No. Not true. If he hadn't had the nightmare, she wouldn't have told him who she was.

Whatever. He could forgive her since she could forgive him. They both had secrets that needed to stay buried. He'd trust her if she'd trust him.

No. He'd trust her no matter what. He didn't really know her, but he trusted his gut.

He could trust Angelique Durand.

Chapter Twenty-Three

"Angie! Pick Up!" Behind the line in the Sea Crest Inn's kitchen Alma rang the bell on the shelf above the heat lamps.

"Coming!" Angelique hurried into the kitchen and pulled down the four orders of steamed lobster, corn on the cob, and salt potatoes. Now to find the finger bowls, lobster bibs, nutcrackers, lobster picks to get out the hidden meat, plus a shrimp fork, and a special bowl for the shells.

She filled the finger bowls with water, slipped them onto an under-liner plate covered by a doily, and garnished the whole thing with a lemon wedge and stabbed four more lemon wedges on the shrimp forks. Hopefully she had all the things she needed to give the four-top in her section.

She had the smallest section, with only four tables. It felt like a million tables.

She got there without dropping the extra heavy tray only to find that she hadn't cleared their salad plates yet. Heavy sigh. "I have your lobsters, but let me pick up your salad plates."

"Miss, we'd like to order a second bottle of the Rising Tide Riesling," said diner number one.

"I'll order it right away." Salad plates cleared, she put the whole lobster shebang on the table.

"Can we have some more lemon, please? And

155

more water." This from diner number two.

"Sure thing. Coming right up."

"Where's the drawn butter?" Diner number three scowled.

"I'll be right back with it."

"Bring one extra. I like a lot of butter."

"Absolutely."

She remembered to go to the bar to order the wine.

"We're out of the 2012. We've still got some 2013 left," the wine sommelier told her.

"Go for it." She just didn't care.

Racing back to the kitchen, she muttered "Butter, butter, butter." Once there, she scrambled to fill four ramekins with it. No, wait. She needed five.

"Angie! Your oysters are up!"

"Be right there!" After traying the butter, she hoped over to the raw bar section of the kitchen.

The two platters each held half a dozen oysters on the half shell. She grabbed two seafood forks and did the lemon routine again. She remembered the cocktail sauce, though she thought it an abomination. Lucien always said that if the oysters were fresh they didn't need any adornment.

Except maybe an injection of vodka.

And wouldn't Lucien laugh if he saw her right now. He'd guffaw like he was a boss. Which he was.

Never mind.

She dropped the butter off then moved to the party of two who ordered the oysters. "Here are your oysters."

"We didn't order any oysters. We're waiting for our chowder," the gentleman informed her.

Dear God. "I'll be right along with your soup."

She delivered the oysters to the correct table and zoomed back to the kitchen to grab the clam chowders. And wasn't it her luck that she spilled hot soup on her left hand as she battled with the ladle.

She did remember the doilies on the under-liners and the packages of oyster crackers to go along with the chowders.

As she went to her section, she noticed another duo had been seated. *Oh freakin' no.*

She could also hear the four-top giving the sommelier a hard time because the Riesling wasn't the 2012 vintage and that the 2013 was simply unacceptable.

She guessed she could kiss the tip on her biggest check of the night good-bye. Clad in stoic resignation, she went to greet her new table.

And what to her wondering eyes did appear?

Her brother Lucien and his wife Hope. *Holy crap.*

How the hell did The Great One know she was working her first dinner shift ever?

Never mind. He was Lucien Damn Durand. The world ran on his timetable.

Of course, he would show up on her first night in the major leagues. She pulled her big girl panties on and pasted a smile on her face. "Hello. I'm Angie," she widened her eyes to punctuate her point, "and I'm your server for the night."

The devil danced in Lucien's eyes. "Hello Angie. Nice glasses. It's a good look for you. What's good tonight?"

If she could have set him on fire, she would have. "Everything. But tonight we're featuring Chef Alma's very delicious Lobster Bisque. The fish of the day is monkfish, and, of course, the whole menu is available. May I bring you something to drink?"

"Is the monkfish locally caught?"

Lucien grinned at his wife. If he'd been sitting next to her, he'd have slapped her on the back, congratulating her.

Angelique had no idea. She went with her usual Plan B. She lied. "The monkfish? Of course."

Hope smiled as if she was Mother Theresa without the mustache. "That's great."

Lucien grinned. "I'll have a Sazerac cocktail." He looked at Hope. "Do you want something, *chère*?"

"Hmmmm." Hope studied the wine list. "Ooo. Can we get a bottle of the Bar Harbor Cellars' Rising Tide Riesling? The 2012 vintage."

Angelique ground her teeth. "We've sold our last bottle of the 2012. The 2013 vintage is lovely."

Hope's eyes sparkled. "Is it comparable?"

"What?"

"Have you tasted it?"

"I'll get the sommelier for you and he can answer your questions. In the meantime," she ground out, "may I get you something else to drink?"

"Just water for now," Hope said with a cheerful smile

"Great. I'll let the sommelier know you want to talk to him and be right back," she tilted her head at her butthole of a brother, "with your Sazerac and Hope's water."

****

"You want a what?" Hank, the bartender looked at her as if she her skin had just turned green in front of his very eyes.

"A Sazerac cocktail."

"I guess I may have heard of it but I've never made one. Let me check the book and pray we have the right ingredients."

"I know that this customer is very particular." A big understatement to say the least. "Thanks."

"No problem."

What to do next? Go to the kitchen. Surely there was a crisis there she had to deal with.

Sammy caught up with her. "Your four-top is done with their lobsters and wants to know about dessert."

"I'll get to them as soon as I can."

"I can clear the table for you if you want."

"That would be awesome! Thanks Sammy!"

The chowder table needed their salads. The oyster table needed the same.

Dessert would have to wait a minute.

She threw the salads together and splashed some of the house dressing on them and went on her way.

Appetizers cleared, salads delivered, she took dessert menus to the four-top and promised to bring them coffee.

Taking a deep breath, she went to deal with Lucien and Hope.

"Are you ready to order?" She smiled so big her face hurt.

"Yes." Lucien pursed his lips "The oysters. What kind are they?"

Really Lucien? Oh please. "I'm not sure. I can find out."

"Please. How is the monkfish served?"

That she knew. "As a kabob, with peppers, mushrooms, and onions on a bed of rice pilaf with the vegetable of the day."

"Which is?"

"A summer squash and zucchini mélange."

"Where did the vegetables come from?" The perennial question from Hope. Angelique wanted to tell her "the ground."

But instead: "I don't know but I can find out."

"Thank you."

They both looked at her with eyes full of expectation. No, change that. Lucien looked at her with the same look in his eyes when he put bait worms in her underwear drawer that lifetime ago on the bayou.

Why couldn't she have been an only child?

"I'll be right back," is what she said instead.

She imagined they were going to run her ragged all night and she guessed she had it coming. Still—

"I hear Lucien Durand is seated in your section. Is it true?" Alma pounced on her the minute she walked into kitchen.

"Yep. Lucien Durand in the flesh. He's got a few questions."

"Oh my God! What does he want to know?"

"What kind of oysters are we serving?"

"Taunton Bay. What else?"

"Where does the produce come from?"

"I don't know! I take whatever my supplier gives me."

"I'll just say from area farmers." It wasn't as if she hadn't lied to Lucien and Hope before.

"Anything else?"

"I don't think so."

"God, I'm going to have a kitten and a half. Lucien Durand!"

Yep, Angelique thought as she left the kitchen. A kitten and a half.

And she wondered why he and Hope had come to Lobster Cove. She guessed she'd find out.

****

"So, did he like his meal?" Alma looked about ready to crawl out of her skin.

"Yes." Lucien hadn't hated it, Angelique thought. "He thought it was lovely."

"Do they want dessert?"

"Yes. A Blueberry Pie à la mode and an Indian Pudding." Although Lucien had taken exception to the fact that the ice cream wasn't made on the premises.

"That's good. Tell him dessert is on the house."

"Will do."

She prepared and plated the desserts and took them out.

"Here you go! Indian Pudding and Blueberry Pie. Would you like your coffee topped up?"

"Yes, please," Lucien said. "Hope?"

Hope nodded. "Please."

"Coming up. Why are you here?"

"I'm checking up on you." Lucien picked up his dessert fork.

"I'm fine. I'm good."

"Not bored?"

"I'm too tired to be bored." She decided not to mention her sexy next-door neighbor. But—"Where are you and Hope staying tonight?"

"With you, at the summer house. Is that a problem?" Lucien skewered her with a glance.

"Uh, no. Of course not. It's your cottage after all." She mentally counted how many clean towels she had.

161

She hoped Tim would stay home tonight. She didn't want Lucien to know about him yet. Time to change the subject.

"Chef Alma knows you're out here and is off-the-wall excited. Is it okay if she comes out to say hello?"

"Of course."

"Awesome." Angelique smiled. "I'll let her know and get your coffee."

To her way of thinking, Lucien and Hope were here to do more than check up on her. She was on pins and needles until they let loose with it.

Chapter Twenty-Four

Tim missed Angelique. He looked down at his dog. Chester missed Angelique, too.

The two of them were just pitiful. They needed to get a grip. The grip kept slipping beyond their grasp.

As much as a dog had a grasp.

In his upstairs office, he saw the glare of headlights turning into Angelique's driveway. Finally. She was home.

He stood and went to the window facing her cottage.

Angelique wasn't alone. Actually, was Angelique even there? A tall dark-haired man and a very petite red-haired woman got out of the car.

Well, this was interesting.

He ignored the stab of panic the sight gave him. Who were those people?

Chester erupted in a barrage of sharp barks, the kind he used when someone came to the door. Tim hurried down to find out who was there.

He opened his door to find a very frazzled Angelique on his porch.

"Can I come in for a minute? I can't stay long."

He stepped back to let her in. "Does it have something to do with the two people who just went into your house?"

"Yeah." She blushed and looked down at the floor.

163

"Okay." He closed the door. "What's up?"

"I don't want you to take this the wrong way, but they're my brother and sister-in-law come to check up on me. So, can you, damn this is hard." She swallowed. "My brother has a problem with me and the men I date. He wants me to find who I really am and what I want to do for the rest of my life, something that doesn't involve a man."

He knew where this was headed. "So?"

"It's nothing about you, it's about me. So, can you stay away for a couple of days? Just until Lucien is gone?"

A ball of rusty nails lodged in his throat. He harrumphed around it. "Why? Because I'm damaged goods?"

She shook her head. "No, of course not. Bottom line, Lucien can be a jerk about me and men. Please don't get mad. I'd tell him if I knew he wouldn't blow a gasket."

He felt the bones of his spine stiffen and line up. "Of course. If that's the way you want it."

"I don't want it that way; it's just that it has to be that way for now." She raised her hand to touch his cheek.

He flinched. He didn't mean to, he just did.

She dropped her hand. "I'm sorry. Please understand."

"Sure. You better go. Your brother is probably wondering where you are."

She sighed. "Good night, then."

"Good night."

He didn't move until she was out the door.

Chester whined and pushed his muzzle against

Tim's leg. "Well, big guy, looks like it's just you and me."

"Woof."

"I couldn't have said it any better, buddy, couldn't have said it any better."

****

"That was very sweet of you to say all those nice things to Alma. I think you made her day." Angelique poured boiling water into a teapot. "Her year even."

Lucien merely shrugged. "The bisque was excellent."

"The inn is in a great location," Hope said. "And I'm happy that Alma is going local when she can."

Or maybe not so much. That thing about the vegetables? Yeah. What Hope didn't know wouldn't hurt her. "The local seafood is very good."

"The Taunton Bay oysters were a revelation. I might explore getting them for L'Enfer Addington."

Hope rolled eyes. "There are plenty of local oysters you could use."

He patted her leg. "You're so cute."

Angelique sighed. "Why are you here, Lucien?"

"I haven't heard from you in a couple of weeks and I was worried about how things were going."

"You mean you want to make sure I'm not screwing up." She realized her fists were clenched by her side and made a concerted effort to relax them.

"No. I think you're done with that all on your own. And I do have to say that I was very impressed by how you kept going on with a smile on your face even though there were things going wrong."

"Alma said it was your first dinner shift as a waitress." Hope smiled.

"They only gave me a four table section until I can get into the groove."

"I'd let you work for me," Hope told her.

Okay. That was laying it on too thick. Hope hated her and for good reason, the biggest one being Shane Baker, her sous-chef and Angelique's last victim. She'd treated him dreadfully. No way. Hope wanted her to work with Shane. "Wow. Thank you." Still, you didn't look a gift horse in the mouth.

"It's hard work, *ma soeur*," Lucien said. "And you did a good job." He loosened his tie. "What about the rest of your life? Making any friends?" He frowned. "I'm afraid you're spending too much time hiding out on your own.

And there it was. Her brother asking her if she was making time with a guy or two when she wasn't slinging hash. Okay. It was expensive hash, but hash nonetheless. But they wanted to know about the people she'd met? Jeff and Beth totally fit the bill. "I have actually. There's a couple here who actually grew up in Addington."

Hope leaned forward. "Oh, who?"

"Beth and Jeff Myers." No way Hope could know either of them, right? "Is the tea ready yet?"

Hope looked at her watch. "Yeah, I think it's steeped enough. I'll pour." Hope brought the teapot to the table and poured two cups, one for her, one for Hope.

Lucien Durand did not drink tea. He wanted black coffee, strong enough to strip paint off the walls.

"So how did you meet Jeff and Beth? I know Jeff, of course, since he worked for me on some catering gigs back in the day." Hope continued as she poured. "I never met Beth, but I know Andi Kelly sings her praises from dawn 'til dusk."

"Who's Andi Kelly?"

Lucien's face turned to stone. "You know her brothers. Buck and Brock Nelson."

"Oh." In that case, to hell with Andi Kelly. Shivers ran up her spine at even the mention of the twins' names, pansy ass bitches that they were. Time to change the subject. "Beth is very nice. We've had lunch at Maggie's Diner."

Lucien cocked an eyebrow. "How's the food there?"

She sighed. Lucien never disappointed. "It's good for a diner. But," Angelique chuckled, "they've something they call a Lobster Burger on a toasted brioche that's very nice."

Now Lucien leaned forward. "What's it like?"

"It's fresh lobster with a loose breading, and lime pickled jalapeños. Since my palate is deficient, I couldn't pick out any other flavors."

"Lime pickled jalapeños." He looked at Hope as if Angelique wasn't in the room. "What do you think?"

Hope stirred what passed for sugar in Angelique's kitchen in her tea. "I think we're going to stop at Maggie's Diner for lunch tomorrow."

Which begged the question: "How long are you staying?" Here's your hat, what's your hurry?

"I persuaded Hope to take a few days off and check out the seafood up here. She also wants to do some winery tours."

"A couple of days, anyway," Hope said as she blew over her steaming cup of tea. "I've got to get back. Shane is good, but he's not me." She grimaced. "I'm

167

sorry. I didn't mean to bring him up."

"It's fine." She swallowed then took a deep breath. "I was the dumper, not the dumpee." In for a penny, in for a pound. "I treated Shane dreadfully and I don't have an excuse. Shane's a good guy, he deserves better than the likes of me."

A silence bomb exploded in the room.

Hope cleared her throat. "He's seeing someone else now. A new waitress who works for me and who tends bar at The End Zone." The End Zone was a sports bar in Addington.

"And I thank God for it every day." Lucien took a sip of the bourbon he was drinking.

Hope laughed. "I'll worry once you start to wear garish shirts."

A wave of regret swamped Angelique. Back when she'd dated Shane, she'd done everything she could do to get him to forget the loud, often tacky shirts. He'd held firm.

Now she knew that you couldn't always tell about a man by the way he dressed.

Hindsight was always twenty-twenty.

Hope snapped her fingers. "You know what? I remember Jeff's best friend Tim Baldwin. I catered a lot of events at the Baldwin's home. Boy, there was a lot of money there. They had a huge house, almost a mansion, and if memory serves me well, they even had a beach house in Maine." Her eyes widened. "Right here in Lobster Cove. That's how we found out about this house."

Aw, crap.

"It appears to be a very small world," Lucien said.

And getting smaller all the time. "I've met Tim."

Lucien snorted. "That's where you were when we first got here, *n'est-ce pas*? Warning him about us? What don't you want us to know?"

"Oh dear, Lucien," Hope said before Angelique could answer. "This guy is the photojournalist from Addington who got kidnapped by ISIS. The one who got rescued right before he got beheaded? Remember? I told you all about him. T.L. Baldwin."

Angelique stood and went to her bedroom where she'd last put Tim's book. The best way to know Tim was to look at his pictures. She hugged it to her chest as she brought it to show her brother.

She handed it to Lucien. "This is Tim Baldwin."

He took the book from her while Hope went to look over his shoulder. She gasped as they uncovered the first image.

Lucien turned the pages in silence. He stopped and lingered on some of them. Angelique had known him all her life and had never seen him so still, so engrossed. She almost thought he'd stopped breathing.

Hope sniffed and rubbed the back of her hand across her eyes.

"You okay there, *pichouette*?" Lucien closed the book and tilted his head to see her.

Hope nodded. "The pictures are so tragic and so beautiful at the same time."

"*Oui.*" He sat in silence for a moment then flicked a glance to Angelique. "Why didn't you want us to meet him?"

"Well, geez, Lucien! You've only hated every man I've ever been involved with. Tim is different." Her palms began to itch and she clenched them in front of her. "I didn't want to take the chance this early on that

I'm dating him."

"Ah. I see." He gave Hope the book and stood facing Angelique. "*Ma petite.* I have loved you from the moment you were born. Perhaps even before that. All I have ever wanted is your happiness." He gathered her hands in between his own. "It makes me sad to think that you will still hide your life from me. I understand about the past, but I thought that time was over."

Whatever she'd expected, it wasn't that. "Lucien—"

"Shhh. I'm not finished. I'm proud of you. But you're still my baby sister and I still have to look out for you. Tim Baldwin has eyes to see and skill on how to bring it to life via the camera. He's a very brave man. Does he know about your problems?"

Angelique nodded. "*Oui.* He knows. He's also got problems of his own. His ordeal in Iraq has taken away his ability to take pictures. We're quite the pair. A former supermodel who won't let anyone take pictures of her and a photographer who can no longer take pictures."

"I hope there's a way to meet him before we go back to Addington."

"He lives next door. I'm sure it can be arranged." However. "You'll be nice to him, won't you?"

Lucien gave her a grin that would make a shark proud. "*Mais oui.* Of course."

Angelique had seen that smile before, usually right before he did something to tease her. "I mean it. Be good."

"I'm always good."

Giving into impulse, she wrapped her arms around

him and hugged him tight. Tears built up behind her eyelids. "Of course you are. And I wouldn't have you any other way."

Chapter Twenty-Five

Tim threw Chester's slobbery tennis ball across the beach. "Go get it, buddy! Go get it!"

The dog took off at a furious pace, chasing after that ball. Tim would usually be amused but not today.

Not today.

He'd gotten no sleep if you didn't take the couple of times he'd briefly nodded off into account. At least he hadn't had any nightmares.

Chester bounded back with the shabby ball in his mouth then dropped it at Tim's feet. He sat on the sand, tongue lolling out of his mouth, one ear up one ear down, his stump of a tail wagging for all it was worth.

"Okay buddy." Tim picked up the ball and tossed it again down the beach. "Go get it!"

Chester ran off after the ball, sand churning in his wake.

"That's some dog you got there, him."

Tim looked over to the man standing on Angelique's back patio. Her older brother, the great Lucien Durand. Man.

"Yeah, he's pretty awesome."

Lucien had dark hair, the color of Angelique's. His arms were ripped, probably from hefting all those heavy pots and pans. He held a steaming mug of coffee, if Tim didn't miss his guess. Even dressed casually in jeans and a designer polo shirt, the man was the poster child for wealthy, powerful men.

"Do you live here?" He sipped his coffee. "Nearby?"

"You could say that." He motioned with his head. "I'm the next cottage over."

Lucien's eyebrows rose. "So close and a little big to call it a cottage." He put his coffee down on the patio table and walked down the stairs to the beach. "I guess we're neighbors." He held his hand out for Tim to shake. "Lucien Durand."

"Tim Baldwin," he said as he shook Lucien's massive paw.

"You look very familiar to me." Lucien jumped a foot back as Chester pounded up to them, slobbery ball and all.

"I guess I just have one of those faces." He threw the ball in the other direction and the dog scrambled after it.

"That must be it." Lucien squinted out into the horizon. "This is an amazing piece of the planet. I guess you must be used to it."

Tim followed Lucien's gaze. "You never get used to it."

It was the truth, but only because the sea's nature was ever changing. High tide, low tide, high wind, no wind, sun, and rain. The weather could change on a whim and often did.

He loved that.

"I suppose you've met my sister."

Oh, shit. "Your sister?"

"*Oui.* The young woman living alone in my beach home. You must have seen her."

Okay. This was odd. Angelique had made it very

clear that he was persona non grata as far as her brother was concerned. He'd honor her feelings, but damn, he didn't know how to answer that question. "I've seen her around."

"I just bet you have."

"What do you mean by that?"

"My sister showed me your book last night."

"She did?" So much for keeping their relationship on the down low.

"She didn't tell me willingly, but I got it out of her. She says that she told you what happened to her. So here's what you need to know." Lucien looked Tim straight in the eyes. "Hurt her and I'll kill you."

"I've got no intention of hurting her. She's a remarkable woman."

"She tells me that you can't take pictures anymore. Your book, by the way, is impressive. You know that she is camera shy now."

Tim could figure out where this was going. "Yes, I know."

"Then I can trust you to honor her wishes in that regard."

"Lucien!" Angelique called as she walked to the beach. "You behave." She kissed her brother on the cheek then smiled at Tim. "I see you've met my brother."

"I have." And now color him confused. She'd been really clear last night about not wanting her brother knowing about them.

She wore a pretty blue sundress and had left her hair tumbling down around her shoulders. It didn't matter what reason changed her mind. He was just glad she had.

He returned her smile, which was the best he could do as he'd just lost his power of speech.

"Would you like to join us for breakfast? Hope's cooking a traditional Irish breakfast."

"Yes," Lucien said. "Please join us."

Tim didn't trust the smile on Lucien's face. He also realized that he didn't have a choice. "Thanks. I'd love to." He prayed to get out of there alive. "But I can't." He shrugged and motioned to Chester with his head. "Another time." He just couldn't do it right now.

Not even for Angelique.

"Let me walk you home," Angelique said.

****

"So what changed?" Tim asked as Angelique walked him back to his house via the beach.

"What changed? Lucien changed." Angelique touched Tim's arm.

He shook his head. "Come again?"

"He figured out that I was seeing you. Don't ask. It's a special Lucien skill, and at first, he was dead set against it. So I showed him your book."

"You showed him my book."

"*Zut!* Is there an echo on this beach?" She elbowed him in the ribs. "I did. I told him that the way to get to know the real you was to look at your work. He was very impressed. The pictures made Hope cry.

Holy shit. No wonder all the warnings about picking up his camera and taking a few shots of Angelique.

Too late.

He should regret it but he didn't. He'd figure out a way to help her see the beauty in the pictures. He'd have to let his work speak for him. It was his default setting for everything having to do with photography.

But instead, he said, "Hope cried? You're making that up."

"I am not, you beast. It's God's own truth." She turned to stand in front of him and clasped his hands in hers. "She cried. Your pictures are that moving. I wouldn't make that up."

What an effing dick he was. If Angelique said something, she meant it. Tim, on the other hand—

He had to plan his revelation very carefully. How could he tell her about the snapshots when he didn't understand the whole thing himself? "Thank you."

They'd gotten to his bulkhead stairs. "Do you want to have dinner with me tomorrow night? Lucien and Hope are staying tonight, but the next night works out because I'm not working."

"I could take you out."

He saw her shiver and try to hide it. Damn.

"I'd rather cook for you. I'm nervous about those reporters at the Sea Crest Inn. I managed to avoid being in the staff picture, but I don't want to push my luck, especially after I saw them at your book signing."

Tim frowned. "I didn't see them." And that was a problem.

"I've got Lucien's recipes for gumbo and oysters." She preened. "I did a good job with the beignets, you must admit."

God she was adorable. "Yes, you did." He looked around to see if Lucien was watching and after ascertaining that Lucien was nowhere to be seen, pulled Angelique into his arms and kissed her.

"I've got to go," she said as she leaned away from him. "Duty calls." She grimaced. "I'm working on the lookout terrace today and I hate heights." Shuddering, she continued. "I was leaning out a second story window waving at the garbage men one time when I was two and the screen gave way. The garbage man caught me."

"Poor baby."

She pouted. "I know! But about tomorrow night? Is seven o'clock okay?"

He kissed her forehead. "Sounds great."

"See you then." She turned and left.

He watched her walk away. He had to figure out a way to stop her from walking away from him once she learned about the pictures he'd taken of her.

Chapter Twenty-Six

"Fresh okra?" Helen Troy scratched her head. "We don't get much call for okra."

Angelique fought back a sigh. She'd planned to make *Grand-mère's* recipe for gumbo and okra was crucial.

"Not even frozen?" It wouldn't be gumbo if it didn't have okra.

"Sorry. What else do you need?"

"*Crème Fraîche*?" She needed it in order to pull off Lucien's Oysters Hope.

"Don't have any of that either. Is it like sour cream? 'Cause I have sour cream."

"I guess." She bit her lower lip. "I also need fresh tarragon and chives."

Helen smiled. "Those I have, right over in produce. But you know, out on millionaire's row, you should plant an herb garden."

What the hell did Angelique know about planting an herb garden? She imagined Hope would plant one if they needed it. "Thank you." Angelique trundled over to the veggie section.

She'd already put in an order at the Fish Market for shrimp and oysters. At least she could find all her seafood needs there.

She'd have to call Lucien to find out what were adequate substitutions for the ingredients she couldn't find in Lobster Cove. At least Lucien had brought her some of his *filé* powder when he and Hope visited the other day.

She was crazy. She didn't even have the proper pots for everything she wanted to cook. But given the choice between cooking and going out where the media lurked, ready to pounce on her, there really had been no choice.

She could do this. Millions of people cooked a meal several times a day. She could do this. They'd have a lovely meal and a romantic evening afterwards.

Providing she didn't poison him. She crossed her fingers.

****

Tim shifted the bouquet of freesia he'd picked up at Flowers In Bloom to his left hand so he could knock on Angelique's door with his right. He cleared his throat and knocked.

Why the hell was he so nervous? It was just dinner at her house. Except that he'd met her brother and that took things up a notch. Bam!

Doh! Wrong New Orleans chef.

She opened the door and he just about swallowed his tongue.

"Hey, *cher*. Where y'at?" She gifted him with a saucy grin. "Pretty flowers."

"They're for you." He held them out to her, feeling more awkward than a pimply boy handing a bouquet of dandelions to the prom queen.

She took them and buried her nose in the blooms. "I love the smell of freesia." Stepping aside, she motioned with her head. "Come on in."

As he had the last time, he found her cottage so

feminine. All pink and green, a touch of lace here, some ribbon there, pillows strewn all around. Fat rose-colored candles rested on every tabletop.

Look up the word girly in the dictionary and a picture of this room would be in there next to it. He wondered what Lucien thought about the décor.

"Smells good."

"It's *Grand-mère's* recipe, the gumbo that is. The oysters are a dish Lucien invented when he met Hope. I could tell you what goes into the dish, but then I'd have to kill you."

"Oh, really."

She poured him a glass of white wine. "I know you usually drink beer, but Lucien would never forgive me if I let you drink beer with Oysters Hope."

He took the wine. "My lips are sealed."

"They better be, Skipper. Now, sit down while I bring out the oysters. While I'm working on this, would you open the bottle of champagne I've got chilling in the fridge?" Angelique nodded in the direction of the refrigerator.

"Sure." Tim was glad to have something to do. He pulled out the bottle and worked the cork out with a little *thlippp*.

"The glasses are over on the counter."

"Will do." The glasses were very cute, hand blown and twisted into the shape of calla lilies. They were more fanciful than cute.

He brought the bottle as well as the two crystal champagne flutes to the table.

"Thank you!" She gifted him with a warm smile as she held her glass up. "To oysters!"

He thought oysters were weird things to toast, but

when in Rome...he clinked his glass up against hers. "To oysters."

She expertly cleaned the oysters and slipped them under the broiler. While they cooked and their shells opened, she whisked together some sour cream, champagne, and some fresh herbs. After she pulled the oysters out of the broiler, she discarded the top shell and spooned some of the sour cream and champagne mixture over each oyster.

"Here, try this. It's my brother's special oyster preparation that he made to honor Hope, then his girlfriend, now his wife." She winked. "I think he just wanted to get her into bed." She laughed. "I think it worked." She smiled. "Let me know what you think."

He took the cream-covered shell along with the seafood fork she offered. Without another word, he popped the cream-covered oyster into his mouth.

The champagne sizzled against his tongue as the sour cream mixture calmed the burn. It shouldn't have been delicious, but it was, very much so. "Mmmmm, it's good. What's in there?"

"Champagne, obviously. I can't tell you the rest."

"Or else you'd have to shoot me?"

"I've got the table set out on the patio. Let's move out there and have my *Grand-mère's* gumbo."

"Bring it on." He got all warm when she turned that million-dollar smile at him.

"Right this way, *cher*."

She didn't have to tell him twice.

****

This was going well, Angelique thought. The Oysters Hope tasted pretty much the same as they did when Lucien made them.

And she had double-checked. There wasn't a single piece of shell or grit in any of the oysters. She hoped she hadn't messed up the gumbo.

Although, could you call it gumbo if it didn't have any okra in it? Even so, she kept her fingers crossed. At least she'd been able to find Abito beer here in the great wild North, the only thing to drink with gumbo.

"It smells great." Tim sniffed into the air, like he was Chester scenting hamburgers cooking on a nearby grill.

She put some saffron rice into each bowl then ladled the gumbo over it. It smelled pretty much like *Grand-mère's*.

"Go ahead," she told him. "Let me know what you think." She held her breath.

He dipped his spoon into the soup then brought it slowly to his mouth. He blew over the spoon and slid it past his lips.

His faced turned red and he started wheezing. He looked like he was having a heart attack.

Oh my God! What did you do for someone having a heart attack? She had no idea, so she went with the basics.

Call 911.

She scrambled back into the house to get her phone. She punched the numbers.

"This is 911. What is your emergency?"

"My friend is having a heart attack! You've got to come quick!" Angelique started to hyperventilate.

"Please calm down, ma'am. What is your address?"

"Fifteen Seagull Lane. Hurry!"

"The E.M.T.s are on their way."

"Okay! Thank you!" She clicked the phone off and turned to run back to the patio and try to keep Tim from dying out there.

She froze. Tim stood in the door from the deck. "What are you doing there? You're supposed to be dying of a heart attack!"

"Sorry to disappoint you. It wasn't a heart attack."

"It wasn't," she squeaked.

"Nope. That gumbo is pretty spicy."

"Spicy! Spicy? I thought you were having a heart attack! I called 911!"

"Um, about that…are those sirens I hear?" He coughed. It might have been to cover up a laugh.

Since he wasn't having a heart attack, she might have to kill him with her own bare hands. "Oh, no." She groaned. "Can they put you in jail for calling in an emergency when there wasn't one?"

He grinned. "I don't know. Maybe."

"Great. Just great. Lucien can never, ever find out about this."

The E.M.T.s were pounding down her door. "I'm coming," she hollered as she went to let them in.

They burst into the room lugging a small fortune in electrical equipment and a gurney. "Where's the victim?"

Tim waved from the door. "Right here."

The first guy in the door stopped short. "You don't look like you're having a heart attack."

Angelique stepped up and turned the charm up to eleven. "I'm sorry," she said in a drawl that would make Scarlett O'Hara prickle with envy. "I thought he was having a heart attack and I guess I panicked." She actually fluttered her lashes.

"What happened?" the E.M.T. demanded, the very picture of pissed off.

"Gumbo," Tim said, with a sorry shake of his head. "Gumbo."

"Yeah. Ms. Doucette makes a very spicy gumbo. I wasn't expecting it and I guess it looked to her I was in cardiac arrest or something."

Yeah, she was going to have to kill him. Angelique, in the kitchen, with a carving knife.

"If that don't beat all." The E.M.T. glanced at Angelique.

"Like I said," she said, in a tone of voice dripping of corn pone and grits and as much sex appeal as she could manage, "I didn't know. I'm so sorry. I'll know better next time."

"Okay." He looked over to Tim. "Do you want an EKG before we go? Can't be too careful."

"No, I'm good. Thanks for coming so fast."

"Then we'll be on our way." He nodded to Angelique. "Don't be so quick to touch the panic button next time."

"Yes, sir." She resisted the urge to salute the E.M.T.

Finally alone, she turned on Tim. "You jerk!"

"Sticks and stones. I'm sorry I worried you."

She wanted to slap him silly. He wasn't the least bit sorry. "No you're not."

"Yes, I am." He walked toward her. "I just didn't expect the gumbo to pack so much heat."

She brought her hands up in front of her in order to push him back. "It was barely spicy."

"Maybe not for someone born on the bayou." He moved another step forward. "We northerners are a bit more sensitive."

"Sensitive, my Aunt Yvette! *Cochon!*"

He laughed. "So I'm a pig, am I?"

"The worst of all the pigs in the world. In the universe!"

"I am, I really am." He pushed aside her hands and put his hands on her hips and pulled her in close to him. "But you wouldn't have me any other way."

"Yes, I would," she whispered. "I really—"

He silenced her with a sweet, intoxicating kiss that left her boneless and whimpering.

"Now, this," Tim whispered against her mouth, "could really give me a heart attack."

She gulped in as much air as she could. He smelled lovely, of the wind and the sea, and of soap and of, of, well, of Tim. That unique scent that belonged to him alone.

She was burning up, being held so close to his body.

"You hungry? We don't want that gumbo go to waste."

Gumbo? "What?"

"I thought we'd go and have a bite to eat, if you promise to not call 911 again."

She was melting in his arms and he wanted to eat gumbo. She'd begun to think her bedroom would be their next destination. "You want to eat?"

His eyes glittered. "You're right. I'm hungry, but not for gumbo." He pulled at her right ear with a scrape of his teeth and a lick of his tongue. "I think I want to head upstairs and make a meal of you."

"I'd like to head upstairs with you," she whispered barely above the beat of her heart.

He swung her up into his arms, just like Rhett Butler. She nearly swooned as he carried her upstairs.

Really, who needed spicy gumbo to get hot?

Not Angelique.

All she needed was Tim.

Chapter-Twenty-Seven

Tim laid Angelique on her bed as if she was made of spun sugar, all gossamer and fragile and precious. He hadn't come over here in order to make love to her.

Okay. Who was he kidding? He'd come over with sex on his mind but had wanted to woo her properly.

Then she called 911 and all he wanted to do was eat her all up with a spoon.

Or, wait a minute. Who needed a spoon? Not this guy.

He knew all kinds of other ways to eat her all up.

Tim toed his Topsiders off and lay on the bed next to her, on his side so he could see her amazing eyes.

He found her staring at him, her eyes huge and dark. They lit a fire deep inside of him, but instead of a huge blast of heat, this one smoldered low, waiting to be fanned into an all-consuming bonfire.

Wanting to wait a bit before he unleashed the bonfire, he made sure his hands were gentle as he reached over to smooth over her body.

She gasped the minute he touched her. He kept his touch feather light, like a whisper of a prayer as he reverently explored her. He kissed every inch of her silky soft skin.

"Tim," she moaned, "what are you doing to me?"

He bent his head and nipped at her generous lower lip. "Ssshhhh. Close those pretty eyes and just let me

187

love you."

She sighed and invited his touch. He slowly slipped off her clothes, one piece at a time. He kissed every inch of flesh he bared.

He took his time until she was panting and writhing underneath him, then slow didn't work anymore. He left the bed just long enough to tear off his own clothes and drag on a condom.

He knelt on the bed and dragged her ankles to sit upon his shoulders. With very little finesse, he plunged into her.

They both groaned as he made them one. She let her eyelids flutter shut. "No, dammit. Look at me. You just look at me."

She opened her eyes and stared wildly at him as he began to move in and out of her. Jesus, she was tight around him and hot, so hot. He tried to keep his body under control, but the fever to come drove him to keep on thrusting forward and back. Because he wanted her to orgasm with him, he reached down to where their bodies were joined and rubbed the little bud of her slippery clitoris and stroked it, circled it.

She flew apart on a scream, her inner muscles squeezing him relentlessly, bringing forth his own climax. The rush was pure heat and a scalding release.

He flopped over her, resting his weight on his elbows, which were at either side of her head. She trembled beneath him, her chest rising and falling in short, sharp bursts.

"What was that?" Angelique dropped her head back against her pillow.

"If you don't know, then I did it all wrong." He shook his head as he rolled off her to lay sideways next to her.

"Fishing for compliments?" Her smile held all sorts of promises and mysteries.

"Maybe." He reached out and cupped one perfect breast in his hand.

She laughed. "Okay, then. You were magnificent."

"And don't you forget it." He dipped his head to kiss her.

"I won't." She changed her position and pressed her backside to his groin so they spooned.

He wrapped his arms around her snugging her even more closely to him. He smiled, closed his eyes, and fell into the deepest sleep he'd had in a long time.

****

Angelique lay pressed against Tim, wide-awake and listening to him breathe. He was such a puzzle to her, one moment loving and gentle, another moment as turbulent as a summer storm, still another moment distant and closed off.

And it could all change in the snap of a finger. What had she gotten herself into?

She already felt far more for him than was wise. He was such a tortured, wounded soul and all she'd ever done was break and twist a man into what she wanted.

She simply couldn't do that to Tim.

But what could he do to her? The old love 'em and leave 'em Angelique Durand was gone and here was Angie left in her place. For the first time in forever, her heart was on the line.

She didn't like it. Not one little bit.

She closed her eyes and willed herself to relax the muscles in her body, to feel them melting into the mattress.

He murmured something she couldn't make out and banded his arms around her. She sighed and settled back against him.

How could something so wrong feel so good?

Answer? It couldn't. Being with Tim felt all kinds of right.

When next her eyes fluttered open, she noticed the sun streaming through the windows. She looked over to the pillow where Tim had laid his head, laid, as in past tense.

Angelique sat up and listened for any evidence that he was anywhere in her house. She got out of bed and threw on her robe, but she knew he was gone.

She should have known he'd leave, probably because of Chester, but she wished with all her heart that he'd woken her up before he left.

She refused to pout, as she knew it would do no damn good.

What should her next step be? She had absolutely no clue.

Chapter Twenty-Eight

"I heard you had a heart attack," Jeff said as he slipped into a booth in Maggie's Diner.

Tim swore. "I guess word gets around."

Jeff grinned. "That it does."

"Just shut it, okay?"

"Sure. I don't want to get your blood pressure up with you having a heart condition and all."

"I may have to shoot you in the face yet." Tim cracked open a menu, but he barely read it.

Sally sauntered over to their table. "Hello, gentlemen. Can I get you guys a drink before you order?"

"Moxie, please," Jeff said.

"I'll have a coffee, please." Tim looked up and gave Sally a small, polite smile.

"I'll make yours decaf, Tim. Don't want all that caffeine to make your heart race, what with that heart attack and all."

Tim gritted his teeth. "I didn't have a heart attack, so regular coffee will do me just fine."

Sally winked at Jeff. "Okay, a coffee and Moxie coming right up."

Tim grunted then looked up to see Jeff grinning at him. "What?"

"What nothing. It's just that it's rare for a guy your age to have heart problems."

"You're gonna have heart problems if you keep this up." Tim muttered

"Okay, okay, I'll stop. You've got to admit it's pretty funny."

"I'll admit no such thing." His brow furrowed. "And nobody should give Angeli...uh, Angie a hard time about it, or I'll rip their guts out."

"Getting a little serious, my man?"

"No!" Tim yelled then grimaced. "Maybe."

"That's great, bro! She's a nice lady and it's obvious by the scar that she's gone through some bad stuff."

Tim immersed himself in reading the menu again. "What're you going to have?"

"My usual, the Lobster Burger." Jeff rubbed his hands together. "I hope they have tomalley."

Ugh. Tim had never gotten the big deal about tomalley. As far as he was concerned, tomalley was green, gloppy lobster liver. "I'm leaning in that direction, only without the green stuff."

Sally came back to the table with a bottle of Moxie, a frosted mug, a coffee, some creamers in a ramekin, and two napkins wrapped around place settings. She set all that down on their table. "Here's your drinks. Do you know what you want?"

"I'll have the Lobster Burger with tomalley if you have it." Jeff nodded.

"And for you, Tim?"

"I'll have the Lobster Burger, too, only without the green stuff."

"Are you sure you want a Lobster Burger? They're pretty spicy."

"Yes, Sally. I'm sure." Tim's temper started to stir.

"All righty then. You're the boss." She looked like she was holding back a laugh. "I'll get these orders right up in the kitchen."

She left.

There was a God. Maybe.

"So, tell me what happened and don't leave anything out." Jeff grinned as he poured the Moxie from the bottle into the glass Sally left.

"Not much to tell. She cooked some gumbo, wanted me to try it. It was a little bit spicier than I expected. I might have wheezed a little bit." Tim glared at Jeff, daring him to smile. "She over-reacted, thought I was having a heart attack, or something, and called 911. I just had a reaction to the gumbo. That's all."

"Must have been some wicked hot gumbo."

"It was. Then she really felt bad and I had to comfort her."

"Of course she needed your kind of 'comfort.'" Jeff shook his head.

Tim felt a smile grow across his face. "She did indeed."

"Trust you to land on your feet." Jeff took a careful sip of his Moxie.

Tim stirred sugar into his coffee and frowned. "It wasn't like that. I shouldn't have said anything. She just felt really bad. I like her, Jeff. I like her a lot, but she's not part of the plan. I came here to heal, not start a new relationship. I don't want any of my mess to touch her."

"Yeah, I can see that." Jeff sat back in his seat. "When I first found out about Danny, I never thought it would end this way—Danny, Beth, Cookie, and me being a family. There was a lot of stuff for us to wade through, but we got through it."

"This isn't the same thing. You and Beth had a history. Me, I've got enough shit to carry. I won't subject her to it." Tim lifted his coffee cup.

"From where I'm sitting, it's clear that you can't stay away from her. You either go for it or let her go."

"Yeah, that sounds about right." Letting her go was the right thing to do. He just couldn't do it.

Sally sidled up their table. "Two Lobster Burgers right here." She put one in front of Jeff, the other in front of Tim. "Enjoy! Oh, and Tim, you've got nothing to worry about. We have a defibrillator back in the kitchen, so let us know if you start having palpitations."

"Sure thing, Sally." Jeff laughed.

"It's not that funny," Tim grumbled.

Jeff unwrapped his silverware. "Whatever." He took a bite of his Lobster Burger. "Have you thought about joining the town softball team? Julia's been nagging me to ask you."

"Sure. It'll be fun." Tim scowled. "As long as everybody lays off the heart attack jokes."

"Absolutely. We'll all be as serious as, well, as heart attacks."

"Do I have to beat you up to stop the jokes? Because I'm so up for it right now."

"All right, I'll stop. No more jokes." Jeff took another big bite of his sandwich.

Somehow, Tim just didn't trust Jeff at all, regarding the jokes. He might as well get used to it.

The next couple of days were going to be long ones.

****

"I don't know much about softball," Angelique told Beth as the two of them made their way up the

194

bleachers aside the softball field.

"There's not that much to know." Beth sat on the hard metal bench. "The pitcher throws the ball, the batter takes a whack at it, and everyone runs either after the ball or across the bases." She shrugged. "I wasn't much for sports back in the day."

Angelique sat next to her. The bench was already hot from the sun. "Me either." That was an understatement. The closest she'd gotten to sports had been sleeping with Brock Nelson, and look what good had come from that.

Nothing good. Just a sex tape. How stupid she'd been.

And how common. Ordinary. Trivial.

She so regretted that.

Beth's son Danny scrambled up the bleachers, his face smeared with chocolate ice cream and a huge ketchup and mustard splotch on his T-shirt. There was a mystery stain that Angelique didn't want to speculate about.

Beth sighed and pulled a container of wipes out of her purse. She handed a bunch of them to Danny. "Did you eat any of that food or are you just wearing it all?"

The kid rolled his eyes and swabbed at his mouth with the wet wipes, missing most of the chocolate. "Can I go to the football field with Ben?"

"You don't want to watch your father play softball?"

Danny grimaced. "Softball's boring."

"Too bad. You're staying here." Beth took the wet towelettes and cleaned Danny's face as best she could. The kid was a wiggly mess.

Angelique watched Beth and Danny and for the

first time ever she wondered what kind of mother she would be.

The question took her a little aback. The words "Angelique" and "children" had never been uttered together, even when she'd been a child. Her father had treated her like she was a really short adult.

She always thought she hated kids. They were messy, loud, germ factories. Never mind the havoc having babies would inflict on her body.

No. Nowhere in her wildest imagination had she seen herself as a mother.

"Hey! Dad!" Danny stood on a bleacher and windmilled his arms over his head to get Jeff's attention.

Jeff turned, looked up, and grinned as he waved back to his son. Angelique could feel the love and joy between the two.

It was, perhaps, the most touching thing she had ever seen. An arrow, it's aim true, split her heart so all these strange longings, feelings she never felt before, spilled out of her. She placed her hand over her stomach as she imagined carrying a life within her. Rubbing her midsection, she could almost feel a child kick against her hands.

The hairs on the back of her neck stood up and she glanced down at the field to see Tim staring at her. Or at least she thought he was, as he was wearing sunglasses and she really couldn't tell for sure. Her breath hitched and her skin actually burned underneath his scrutiny. She put her hand over her mouth, helpless to look away from him.

A shout from the Lobster Cove bench had both Tim and Jeff looking away. Jeff gave Beth and Danny one last wave. Tim barely nodded before the two of them jogged off to join the team.

"Ahem."

Angelique turned to see Beth watching her. "What?"

"That was some slow burn between you and Tim."

"How could you tell?"

Beth smiled. "Body language. Tells me all I need to know about burns, slow and otherwise."

Angelique sighed. "I guess it was."

"Tim's a great guy, you know. Jeff thinks he might have real feelings for you."

"I don't know. I guess I'm afraid to know. So far we've only been about sex."

"I've known him ever since high school. You know that. He was a spoiled little rich boy back then." Beth smiled. "That spoiled little rich boy has grown up to be a remarkable man. If you can't return his feelings, after what he's been through, please don't break his heart. I don't think he could handle it."

"Nobody's said anything about love yet." *And, hey! I've got my own issues!* "I don't know how I feel and I don't think he knows how he feels."

"But, don't you think you can take a chance on him?" Beth's forehead wrinkled. She looked well and truly baffled.

"I'm a mess, Beth. I don't have anything in me worth sharing. Nothing worth counting on." She didn't confess that the only thing she had to give was her body.

And sex with Tim would only go so far.

"I think you're wrong, but I don't want to pry." Beth looked out over the field, shielding her eyes with

197

her left hand. "If you want to tell me, you'll tell me. But from a person who kept a huge secret for ten whole years, don't let it paralyze you." She jumped up as Jeff hit the ball with a resounding crack and ran for first base. "Go, baby, go!" she screamed through a megaphone she made with her two hands around her mouth.

Angelique stood with the rest of the Lobster Cove fans. The excitement of the crowd carried her up to her feet.

Beth had given her a lot to think about. If she examined her conduct so far, she'd see, most likely, that her running hot and cold for Tim turned her into a tease.

Again.

She couldn't do that anymore. She couldn't be that person.

So, she'd follow her heart and decide how much she could give Tim and do just that.

Chapter Twenty-Nine

"So for my Fourth of July party, can I impose on you to make gumbo?" Tim slapped a long-handled stainless steel spatula into his left hand.

Angelique snorted. "Only if you're man enough to eat it, *cher*."

He grinned. "I'm not going to eat it. Jeff is going to eat it." He couldn't stop enjoying the vision of Jeff all red faced and gasping for air. "Matter of fact, Jeff really loves spicy food, so maybe you could add a little bit more of the hot stuff."

He bet Jeff wouldn't be laughing so hard at him then. It'd be sweet to bring him down a peg or two.

He wished he could take a picture of it.

"I'm sure gumbo isn't part of the Fourth of July festivities up here in Maine. I've been thinking it's all lobster, all the time." She pursed her lips.

He trembled with the urge to plant a kiss on that come-kiss-me-you-know-you-wanna mouth. "Maybe you can make us change that."

"I think not." She pulled up one strap on her sundress, which kept falling off her shoulder. "I think the best I could do would be to get them to make lobster gumbo."

The morning light gilded her and surrounded her in soft, golden sunbeams. The mild breeze flirted with her glossy dark hair and spread the silken strands around

199

her face and shoulders. She wore an old-fashioned style dress, with tiny straps and a full skirt. In honor of the day, the dress was blue and spread with red and white stars.

Sometimes she was so dazzlingly beautiful that he lost the ability to breathe, never mind think. She brought a fragile loveliness, a glow into his very dark life.

He could almost believe there was goodness in the world and that he would find it and live in it.

"I'm going to take a walk on the beach before I start whipping up some extra hot gumbo. Do you think Chester would like to come with me?" She reached down to pet the dog's head. The dog flashed his most polite and beguiling smile and whimpered a little.

Oh, manipulator, thy name is dog. Tim shook a finger at Chester. "Sure, if you want him with you. Just don't let him run away and barge in on anybody's cookout searching to score a hamburger or a hotdog, like he's just some starving doggie who gets no love."

Angelique clapped her hands a couple times and beamed at Chester. "C'mon, buddy. Let's go for a walk."

Tim watched and waited several very slow seconds as Angelique and Chester took off down the beach. When he knew she couldn't see him, he ran into his cottage to grab his camera.

He hurried down to the beach and found Angelique and Chester in his viewfinder. He adjusted his lens to telephoto to get both woman and dog more up close and personal.

A furious drive to take pictures washed over him. Driven, every synapse he possessed cried out to keep on going. This long-dead hunger he had for the perfect shot sang with the joy of being set free.

A lesser man would close his eyes and enjoy the connection to the world via his camera.

No. He couldn't close his eyes. He had to drink up and revel in the feeling that he was back in the game.

A wave of guilt splashed over him. Tim knew she didn't want to have her picture taken.

He should regret breaking her trust, but he didn't. He just rejoiced that she had brought his gift back to him. There had to be a way to make her understand.

****

Angelique laughed as she watched Chester scamper down the beach. He'd run away then stop and look around for her. After knowing where she was, he came flying back to her, tongue lolling, panting in joy.

She gave him praise for coming back when she called. Chester looked behind her and gave a happy woof. She tried to see who he was woofing at, but the light was in her eyes.

Nothing seemed unusual or out of place.

But why couldn't get over the feeling someone was watching her?

She shrugged. She needed to head back to her cottage because she had some gumbo to make.

Chapter Thirty

Angelique got back to Tim's just as the party was getting underway. Tim stood near the grill, beer bottle in hand, probably waiting for the coals to get hot enough to cook over. Beth was setting out big bowls of potato salad and who knew what else. Jeff, Danny, Cookie, and Chester played a very noisy game of tag down on the beach.

"Hey! You made it!" Beth hurried over to Angelique. "Let me take that from you. Does it need to go on the stove?"

Angelique nodded. "On low, I guess." Really. What did she know?

"It smells delicious! Can I get you a drink? A glass of wine or a beer? We've also got iced tea and lemonade for the kids."

Angelique surrendered the pot of gumbo to Beth. "A glass of red wine sounds lovely."

"You got it." Beth trundled off into Tim's house.

Angelique frowned. Her back straightened at the familiarity and ease with which Beth had taken on the mantle as Tim's hostess. For some unknown reason, it bugged her.

She should be the one to trundle into Tim's house, not Beth.

Wait? Could this be jealousy? Angelique didn't know. She'd never, ever felt that emotion.

Tim crossed the patio to give her a kiss. "Hey."

She held back a sigh. "Hey."

"I'm happy you're here."

God. How could she think when he looked her that way?

"Oh yeah? Looks like you and Beth have everything under control."

"Looks are deceiving." Tim's voice lowered to a purr.

God, that deep I-am-Batman voice just rasped along every nerve she had and buzzed some nerves she'd forgotten about.

She shivered as he nuzzled her neck. The man had the most sexy pair of lips in the world.

Maybe even the galaxy.

Or maybe the universe.

Upshot? The guy had a killer mouth, one designed to drive a girl crazy.

She liked that in a man.

He lowered his head to kiss her again.

"Hey, Romeo," Jeff slapped a hand on Tim's shoulder. "Those coals hot enough to start cooking?"

"Go away," Tim said. "Far, far away."

Jeff laughed. "The kids are getting hungry and those hot dogs and burgers aren't going to cook themselves."

"Whatever." Tim pressed a quick kiss on Angelique's nose. "Be right back."

"I'll be here."

And to her surprise, there was no place else she'd rather be.

****

Tim and Jeff had gotten a bonfire going on the

beach as the sky turned bright shades of magenta, fuchsia, and apricot. At least, those were the names Beth and Angelique called the colors. Pink, red, and orange worked just fine for Tim, even though he was supposed to be some big shot visual artist. The driftwood crackled, sending yellow sparks up into the sky. The scent of wood smoke permeated the air.

Jeff and Beth's children, Danny and Cookie, were shrieking and running up and down the beach, fueled by S'mores and excitement about the coming fireworks. The kids had even exhausted Chester, who flopped at Tim's feet.

Tim expected that Chester would run along home to hide once the fireworks started. Loud noises weren't his dog's favorite thing. In fact, he usually hid when Cookie was around, as her high-pitched voice could pump out ear-splitting noises only dogs could hear.

"Penny for your thoughts." Angelique sat on the sand next to him.

He took her hand and pressed a kiss into her palm. "You smell good."

She nudged him with her shoulder. "That all?"

"You're pretty, too."

A smile bloomed across her face. "Thank you, kind sir."

"The gumbo was a success. I think Jeff will stop with the jokes."

She sighed. "I still feel so stupid about that."

"You're cute when you're embarrassed."

"I must be really cute, then, because I'm still really embarrassed about the whole thing." She wrapped her arms around her middle and shivered.

"Are you cold?"

"A little bit."

"Do you want me to get you a jacket or something?" He might have something of his mother's in the hall closet.

"Would you mind? The wind is kind of picking up out there." She obviously tried to hide the fact that her teeth chattered.

"Not at all. I'll bring a blanket out, too."

"Thank you." She gave him another sweet smile to carry with him as he gladly went on his mission.

He found a navy blue Spinnaker Sailing and Yacht Club sweatshirt in the front closet, exactly where he remembered it was. He grabbed a red tartan blanket off the top shelf and whistled on his way back to the beach.

Angelique sat where he left her, arms wrapped her knees, while she listened intently to Cookie. His heart lurched with an out-of-the-blue longing for Angelique and a child.

His child.

Six months ago, hell, just last month, the thought of bringing a child, children, into this piece of shit world was the most irresponsible thing he could do. He'd never counted on the innocent tableau Angelique and Cookie made to tug at him so sharply.

"Hey, you two." He dropped the blanket on the beach and handed Angelique the sweatshirt as she stood.

"Oh, thank you." She sighed. "It's getting cold."

Cookie nodded. "It's why I gotta wear my Sharks hoodie." She frowned. "Sharks are scary. I like Barbies better."

Tim spread the blanket and helped Angelique down onto it before sitting beside her.

"I like Barbies better, too." She scrunched her nose at Cookie while the little girl climbed into Angelique's lap.

Tim didn't know what astonished him more: Angelique liking Barbies or Cookie sitting in Angelique's lap.

"Does your scar hurt?"

"It did at first, but not anymore." Angelique ran her hand down the little girl's blonde curly hair.

Cookie lifted up her hand then pulled it back onto her lap. "Can I touch it?"

Angelique's breath hitched. "Sure." She sat absolutely still.

The child barely touched the scar, with a fragile and tentative hand. She bit her lip as she traced her fingers up and then down the injury. Done, she sat back. "I think you're really pretty, even though you've got a scar.

Angelique sniffed and Tim knew without a doubt that she was choking back tears. "Thank you."

"Everything okay over here?"

Tim looked up to see Beth looking at them. "Yeah, I think we're good."

Beth smiled that Lady Madonna smile she'd perfected. "Fireworks are going to start soon, Cookie. Why don't you go to the bathroom before they start?"

"Can Angie take me?"

If Beth was taken aback, she didn't show it. "Of course. But Angie might have something else to do. And you've been going to the bathroom by yourself for about five years now."

"I don't mind." Angelique stood. "It's no problem. I'm happy to go with her." She shrugged. "I should use

206

the bathroom myself." Tim stood to help her up.

The two went hand in hand into the house, Cookie skipping all the way. Tim couldn't have looked away from them even if someone held a gun to his head demanding he turn his attention elsewhere.

"I hope Cookie didn't say anything to upset Angie. She's like any other kid. She doesn't have the greatest filter." Beth sighed. "And sometimes it's like she's channeling her mother. We both know that Katie isn't the most generous person."

"No," Tim said, "She isn't." He slipped his arm around Beth's shoulders. "But you're doing a great job with her regardless of Katie."

Beth shook her head. "Jeff and I just love her." She shrugged. "I know she can act really selfish and Lord knows Danny can be a handful when he plays Captain My Way or the Highway." She sighed. "It's never easy, but love is the key." She glanced over to Jeff and Danny throwing a football around.

Tim followed the shift of her eyes and had to admit his best friend had found true happiness with this woman and his two children.

Jealousy stabbed him right in his heart. He wanted what Jeff had. He wanted a family, a place to settle down, work that didn't send him haring all over the world, documenting the worst of the cruelty of men.

Angelique and Cookie laughed as they came out of his house, the sound sweeter than any other he'd ever heard. Cookie, carrying two popsicles, raced over to Jeff and Danny to give Danny his frozen treat. Both the kids sat right down in the sand to consume the popsicles.

Jeff jogged over to Beth and Tim. "Those two are

about to launch higher than any rocket." He sat next to Beth. "They've had so much sugar we'll never get them to sleep tonight."

"I'm sorry," Angelique said as she joined the rest of them. "Cookie asked so prettily I couldn't say no." Tim reached up for her hand and pulled her down next to him.

"What color are their faces going to be?" Beth leaned in to Jeff.

He grinned. "Purple."

"Ugh." Beth groaned. "For the first ten years of his life my son never had any kind of junk food. Now I put him to bed with a purple face." She elbowed Jeff. "You're paying all the dental bills. And," she added, "working to get the stains out of their clothes."

He kissed her. "Absolutely and without a single complaint."

Tim cleared his throat and turned his gaze to Angelique. She stared over the bay, her dark eyes unreadable.

He wanted to kiss her, right then and there. Better yet, scoop her up in his arms, carry her to his bed, and make love to her all night.

They'd make their own private fireworks. He liked the sound of that.

Truth to be told, he liked, more than anything in the whole world, the noises she made when she came.

The absolute best music ever.

Mozart wouldn't have even come close to replicating the amazingly awesome sounds Angelique made as he gave her pleasure.

"What?" Angelique turned her head. "Did I do something wrong?"

He brushed a couple of silken curls off her face and tucked them behind her ears. "I'm just wishing that the fireworks were over. While I love Jeff and Beth and their kids, I can't wait for them to leave."

"Why is that?" Angelique's dark eyes sparkled.

"Let's just say that I have some plans for dessert."

"We had blueberry tarts from Julie's Coffee and Sweet Shop," she pointed out.

"Not blueberry tarts." He shook his head as he took her hand and played with her fingers. "Something different."

"What then?" She pulled her hands out of his and poked him in the side.

"Let's just say we didn't use all the whipped cream for the tarts." He waggled his eyebrows up and down like a cartoon villain.

Her eyes widened. "That sounds, uh, intriguing."

"Doesn't it just."

"How long do these fireworks last anyway?"

"Too long, if you ask me."

"I did ask you, *cher*." Angelique snorted.

"See? You make me crazy."

"But you're enjoying every wild moment of it." She snuggled next to him and rested her head on his shoulder. He felt so warm and smelled of the wood smoke and salt air. "Mmmmmmmm."

Tim pulled her in closer. "You sound happy."

Angelique blinked. "I guess I am."

"Is that a problem?" He pressed his lips to the top of her head.

"I don't know. I'm not used to being happy."

"It's about time you get some more happy in your life."

"I think you're right." She sighed.

Sparkling bursts of color streaked into the sky followed by a loud boom.

"Looks like the fireworks started. Good," he murmured. "Once they're done the sooner I can work on making you all kinds of happy."

Tim didn't know all the kinds of happy there could be, but he was more than willing to find out for Angelique's sake.

Chapter Thirty-One

"I thought they'd never leave," Tim said after he closed his front door behind Jeff and his family. "I love them to death but tonight, not so much."

Time to get on with his happiness project. He crossed the room to get to Angelique, who stood next to the small fireplace on the far wall. He caught her face with both hands and dipped his head to kiss her.

Her lips were so soft underneath his lips. He coaxed her mouth to open and let him in for an outrageous French kiss.

She tasted so sweet, so rich. So Angelique. He couldn't get enough of her. His hands slid from her face to her shoulders in order to remove the straps of her pretty little dress. Thank the baby Jesus that she was not wearing a bra. He pulled down the top of the dress to bare the tight peaks of her breasts while he nibbled up and down along her neck.

He rubbed his thumbs over the hard, ruched nipples. She moaned and pushed her breasts into his palms. The sound skittered down to his cock and hardened him to the point of exquisite pain.

He needed to be inside her, like yesterday. He grabbed her butt and hoisted her up to his waist. She wrapped her legs around him. He turned and braced her against the wall.

He supported her with one arm as he used the other

to free his erection and push her thong panties aside. "Sorry baby. I just can't wait anymore." He fit the plump head of his penis to her warm, wet sheath and entered her in one brutal thrust.

She panted as she met him stroke for stroke. "Oh God," she keened and rocked her pelvis in small circles around him.

"God, that's so good baby," he groaned against her mouth as they traded rapacious kisses. "So good."

He felt the soft flesh of her channel begin to pulse against the hard length of him. The delicate muscles squeezed harder and harder as she went up in flames.

Damn, he was going to blow. With one long thrust he growled as he gave in to his own pleasure, pouring his seed deep within her.

****

Angelique slowly lowered her legs from around Tim's back to stand on her own. She wasn't exactly sure she'd be able to stay upright without Tim's help so she melted against him, relying on his arms to prop her up.

"I'm sorry, baby. I meant to go slow tonight, make it last."

She couldn't seem to form words yet, so she rested her cheek against his chest.

Against his heart, with its steady and reassuring thump, thump, thump. "Any longer would be like to kill me." She sighed.

"We'll have to put that to the test." He swept her up in his arms and carried her up the stairs.

She twined her arms around his neck and held onto the solid warmth of him. Her eyes drifted shut and she turned her head to run tiny kisses up and down his neck.

His evening beard rasped deliciously under her lips.

Tim laid her on the crisp white cotton sheets of his bed. "You wait here. I'll be right back." He kissed her.

"Wh-where are you going?"

He grinned. "I promised you whipped cream and I always keep my promises." He hitched his jeans into place and headed down the stairs.

Oh. My.

Wondering whether she should take off her clothes the rest of the way or just put them to rights, she realized she must look a sight. Instead, she fluffed up her hair before starting in on her rumpled, twisted sundress.

"No, you don't," Tim said from the doorway. He held a couple of cans of Reddi-Whip. "That's my job."

After setting the whipped cream on the nightstand, he went over to his bureau and lit three fat, fragrant candles then he slid onto the bed. "C'mere." He pulled her close and pulled her dress over her head.

She trembled where his hands roamed over her. He kept his touch feather light, raising goose bumps on her hypersensitive skin.

"You are so beautiful," he murmured. "I haven't taken the time to love you right." He kissed her and coaxed her lips apart with his tongue.

Her eyes drifted closed as he made exquisite love to her mouth, practically making her weep with pleasure. She mewed when he lifted his head.

"Don't worry, Sparky. There's a lot more where that came from." He reached behind him, grabbed one of the cans of whipped cream, and shook it.

"What are you going to do with that?"

"This." He popped the top and sprayed the

whipped cream over her tight, hard nipples. "Pretty." He lowered his mouth slowly to lick the cream off. "Delicious."

She couldn't catch her breath as he swirled his tongue over and around the taut peaks of her breasts. Her head swimming, she anchored her hands in his hair and held on for dear life.

"Hmmmmm," he said as he shook the can again. "I'm still hungry." He decorated her breasts again and drew a line down from her chest to her belly button.

Her muscles quivered as he lapped the whipped cream from her body. She writhed as he held her close and feasted. Pleasure spiraled through her with each pass of his tongue.

He continued to lick and lave her trembling skin as he moved down her body, to the soft lips covering the hard button of her clitoris. She screamed at the first intimate kiss he delivered to her melting core.

Pleasure rolled over her in wave after wave. She was drowning in it. Her hips lifted up to meet his hot, wicked mouth.

As she flew off the peak with the sharp release of her orgasm, he reached between them and joined their bodies with one long, hard thrust.

Her climax went on and on, her inner walls molten and squeezing the magnificent length of his erection. She met him thrust for thrust, desperate to bring him to the same amazing release he'd just brought her. Impossibly, she felt the tender spasms build again as he moved in her body.

"I'm close, so close, baby," he growled. "Come with me." He nipped her lower lip with his teeth.

With one last ferocious roar, he pushed into her

hard and deep and came in four strong bursts. She came apart along with him.

****

Air sawed in and out of Tim's chest as he came back to himself after the most profound climax of his life. He had totally lost himself inside this amazing woman. He didn't think he'd ever be the same again, as if some newer, better man had been born out of this insane physical connection he had with Angelique.

He rolled over and pulled her on top of him. "Are you okay?"

She shuddered on a wavering sigh. "More than okay. Amazed is more like it."

"Me, too" He stared into those big brown eyes of hers. So much of his new life came into focus, revealed in her velvety soft gaze.

She gifted him with one of her beautiful smiles, a lovely curve of her mouth that shot him straight in the heart.

Love for her washed over him in bright, pulsing waves.

Tim had always wondered how he would know when he fell in love. Never, in his wildest imagination, could he have predicted this mix of elation at how right, simple, and inevitable it was and sheer terror that Angelique might not reciprocate his feelings

That she now held the whole of his heart in her small, adorable hands.

She leaned up over his chest to kiss him. "You know what I'm thinking, *cher*?" Her eyes sparkled.

"Don't have a clue." It was the absolute truth to God.

She reached past him and snagged the can of

whipped cream and shook it. "I'm thinking turnabout is fair play."

He grinned. What a woman. "Bring it on."

Chapter Thirty-Two

"Pass the soap, please."

Angelique pursed her lips in light of Tim's demanding voice. "I dropped it." She sat facing him in the huge Jacuzzi that took up most of the space on his second floor balcony.

"Maybe you should try to find it, like feel around in the water and see what comes up."

She splashed him. "You'd like that, wouldn't you."

"I would enjoy that, yes." He splashed her back. "I could make it worth your while, too."

"You could?" Angelique shook her head. "Feeling pretty cocky right now, aren't you?"

"You say that like it's a bad thing." Tim reached over and pulled her on top of him. He kissed her as the warm water fizzed and twirled around them. The night sky winked down at them just like the fireflies bobbing around them on the deck did. The waves lapping on the shore provided the background music.

He'd placed bayberry candles into hurricane lamps and their luxurious scent filled the air.

He ran his hands up and down her back as he slipped his tongue into her mouth and deepened the long, sweet kiss. She trembled with desire as he worked his tender magic on her.

The kiss spun down and he sat up and turned Angelique around so she fit between his legs with her back to him. She turned her head to face him as he squeezed her shoulders. "What are you doing?"

He nipped at her earlobe. "Making you feel good. How'm I doing?"

She sighed. "You'll do, I suppose."

"Hmmmmm."

She felt the rumble of his chest against her back. Dropping her head back to rest on one shoulder, she gave in to his ministrations.

He began to make swirls and lines on her back with one finger. She giggled and squirmed.

The swirls and lines turned into letters, a T, an I, and an M. "You wrote your name on my back."

"Yep. I want everyone to know who you're with."

"That's silly."

"What can I say?" He used the flat of his hand to 'erase' his name. "How about this one? First word." He traced an I. "Second word." He traced an L, an O, a V, an E.

Oh, my. She stopped breathing.

"Third word." He took another nibble on her ear as he wrote a Y, an O, and a U. "Know what that spells?"

She got to her knees and turned to face him. He looked like a pirate with the beard stubble from his cheekbones to his chin. His eyes burned bright as he waited for her.

Where the heck was her voice? She cleared her throat. "I love you?" she whispered.

He smiled. "I do."

"Do what?"

"I love you, Angelique Durand, like I've never loved a woman before."

Oh God. She hadn't allowed herself to even dream

of this moment. Her stomach took a couple of dizzying loop-de-loops.

He stared at her, his gaze expectant but tinged with fear.

"Turn around," she told him.

He saluted. "Yes, Ma'am."

The skin of his back was warm and smooth, the muscles defined and powerful looking. She cracked her knuckles. "First word" She traced a lowercase I and dotted it with a heart. "Ready for the next one?"

"Bring it on."

She drew a big Valentine's heart and put scallops around it. "Got it?"

"Yep," he murmured.

She lightly bit the place where his neck met his shoulders. "Here goes." She sketched a great big ol' U and then the number 2.

He turned and pulled her in his arms "Are you sure?" He rubbed his cheek over the top of her head.

She wanted to be honest with him right out the gate. "As sure as I can be. I've never been in love before so I don't really know what it feels like."

"I haven't been in love either, but I think about you constantly, wondering how you are, hell, even where you are. We just made love and I can't wait to do it again. If that isn't love, I don't know what is."

As she listened to him, her heart pounded. She could say 'ditto' to everything he'd said. "Then, I do love you." She hadn't realized it until he drew the words on her back.

He kissed her hard. "Let's take this pool party inside. I can't do to you the things I want out here in public." He waggled his brows. "I have very private things in mind."

"Private things, huh?" She smiled. " I love the way your mind works.

She loved everything about him. She was giddy over it, over him.

No one would believe that flighty, queen of the flirts, fickle Angelique Durand had finally fallen in love, but she had and like the Grinch's, her heart had grown three sizes with the force of the realization.

She leaned in and kissed him. "Take me back in so you can tell me more about all those very private things.

He grinned against her mouth. "Atta girl."

Chapter Thirty-Three

"...so this event is very important." Betts Quinn slapped the manila file folder she held in her right hand against her left palm. She'd asked Angelique to meet her in the lobby of the Sea Crest Inn. "Alma tells me that you have an in with Lucien Durand."

Angelique stifled a groan as well as the urge to pound her head against a wall. "Not really."

"Oh." Betts was clearly disappointed. "Lucien Durand is such a celebrity, and it doesn't hurt that he's so handsome he makes your teeth ache."

Mais yeah, Lucien could make your teeth ache...ache with the urge to punch him right in that arrogant nose of his. "I never noticed."

Betts stared at her as if her skin had just turned snot green. "Maybe you should call the doctor and get an EKG. Or an MRI of your brain. Or buy some glasses."

Oh brother. "I guess he's just not my type."

"And is Tim Baldwin your type?"

Angelique could practically hear the stars in her eyes pop up. "He's a very handsome man."

Betts chuckled. "He is that. He's also near and dear to my heart. His parents are lovely people. Not stuck up like some of the other rich Bostonians who have summer homes up here. Not only that, anyone with eyes can see how much he adores that dog of his."

"Chester is a real character."

"All dogs are. I just love 'em. All animals really." She winked. "Better than most people actually. It's why I'm so anxious about this Applause for Paws fundraiser for the no-kill shelter in Bar Harbor and for April's rescue operation."

Angelique bit her lower lip. "I've never met Tim's parents."

"Oh, you wouldn't have. They left about a month ago, maybe two months ago, I forget, on a sailing odyssey from the St. Lawrence Seaway all the way to Key West. The leaf didn't fall far from the tree," Betts told her. "That boy loves to sail."

"I've gone sailing with him." She shuddered. "I spent the whole time in fear for my life."

"That boy does like to take chances. Truth to tell, sailing on Frenchman's Bay can get pretty hairy. But…kidding aside, all those years haring off to all those dangerous places, taking those violent, frightening pictures." Betts shook her head. "Risking his life to take those pictures. And then he got kidnapped and almost died."

Angelique knew better than anyone how much he still suffered from his time with ISIS, damn them.

"He doesn't talk about it much."

"At least he has a nice girl like you by his side."

Nice girl? No one who really knew her would call her nice. Selfish? Yes. Conniving? Absolutely. But nice?

Never.

"Are you sure you can't get Lucien Durand to attend the fundraiser?"

She sighed. "I can try, but I'm not promising anything." Who knew what Lucien would do?

Betts clapped her hands together. "Maybe he could do a signing at Cliff Notes. Alma adores his new cookbook, almost as much as she adores the sexy picture of him on the dust jacket. Bobbie would love to have him sign his new book and donate a part of the profits to the shelter."

"Maybe." Loyalty to Hope goaded her on to add, "He is married, you know. He's very much in love with his wife."

Betts harrumphed. "Well, a girl can dream, can't she? I'm going to talk to Bobbie right now about the book signing. I'm sure she's going to be thrilled."

"Remember, I'm not promising anything." Angelique told Betts, panic draping itself around her shoulders.

"Got to stay positive for those precious fur babies. Let me know what Chef Durand says!" Betts trundled off in the direction of Cliff Notes.

Angelique watched her leave, thinking that she should probably live up to the nice girl reputation and give her brother a call.

Because Tim really did deserve a nice girl. She could be that for him.

Even better, she could be that for herself. She deserved it, too.

****

"Hey, Chester! Who's a good boy?" Dylan Foster, vet at Lobster Cove's Old Mill Veterinarian Hospital, cooed to the Dobie. "Are you a good boy?"

Chester's tail thumped against the tiled floor while Dylan rubbed the top of his head. "He's doing great." She smiled at Tim. "You'd never know he'd gone through so much before you rescued him."

Tim sighed. The dog probably saved Tim more than the other way around. You couldn't eat a gun if you had someone to take care of, to talk you down.

Chester definitely needed to be taken care of. His talk you down vocabulary, however, amounted to woof and grrrr. "He's a good dog."

"Listen, I want to talk to you about this Applause for Paws fundraiser for the shelter in Bar Harbor. One of the things we want to do is introduce all the successful rescue adoption dogs and cats. Is that something you think you and Chester can do?" Dylan leaned against the wall of the exam room.

Why not? Tim shrugged. "Sounds okay."

"Great! Dr. Weaver will be so glad to hear that." Dylan beamed at him. "I'll give you a call when we've got more details. And don't forget the dog parade."

What the hell was a dog parade? "I'm looking forward to it." He took the leash from her then snapped it on Chester's collar. "Let's go buddy."

He ambled out of the vet clinic into the bright July sun thankful for Chester. He'd been counting his blessings a lot lately.

Angelique topped the list. He'd been working on the photos he'd taken of her. Almost done on creating a portfolio of them, he imagined he'd show them to her one day soon. He'd talk her into posing for him when he showed her how beautiful she still was.

Tim owed her so much. He hoped this tribute showed her just how much she meant to him.

Chapter Thirty-Four

"I'd like to take you somewhere special for dinner." Tim took Angelique's hand as they sat in the sand watching the sunset. "Somewhere out of town."

The evening breeze blew in gentle waves over them. "Mmmmm, I'd love that. Where?"

"Addington. It's been too long since I've been to the ol' hometown and I'd like to spend time with your family."

"You want to spend time with my family." She laced her fingers together until her knuckles turned white. "With my brother. Am I being punked?"

He snorted. "Yes. The man who loves you wants to spend time with your family." His eyes darkened. "But if it's too much of a big deal, we can find someplace in Portland."

Oh, no. She'd hurt his feelings. "It's not a big deal. You surprised me, is all." She'd rather have a hangnail and go without a manicure for six months than hurt him. "I think it's about time Lucien and Hope got to know you better."

His shoulders loosened a bit. "When can you leave?"

"I've got to get time off from work, of course. I don't think Birdie McCorkle will have a problem with it. If she does, I can always invoke the will of Betts Quinn."

"Betts?"

"*Mais* yeah. Betts wants Lucien to come up to Lobster Cove for the Applause for Paws event. If I tell her I need to go to Addington to talk to him, she'll pack me a bag and push me out the door."

"Did you tell her Lucien is your brother?"

"Oh no," Angelique said. "I'm not ready for that step. She thinks he's an old friend of the family."

She knew Lucien didn't want people to know who she was yet.

Angelique herself didn't know who she was yet. She was getting there, but not quite.

"So, here's what I'm thinking." Tim wrapped his arm around her shoulders. "We'll go on down, check into this B and B I know about, see the sights, then hit your brother's restaurant for dinner. That way, if he hates me, he won't punch me out in front of the customers."

She laughed. "Don't count on it. He'll be more than happy to punch you out and put an extra entertainment charge on the customers' bills." She bit her lower lip. "We might be better off going to Hope's."

He rolled his eyes. "I've eaten Hope Monahan's food practically all my life. I've only been to L'Enfer the once. Plus, you're not a chicken."

"I'm such a chicken, I cluck in my sleep. But, you're right." She grimaced. "L'Enfer it is. I have to warn you, though. Lucien might put extra spice in your food to see if you can handle it."

He looked aghast. "So, if I hear you right, my road to acceptance by your big brother is paved with spicy food?"

"The spicier the better. And if you didn't guess by now, Lucien isn't above dirty tricks."

"I kind of figured that. Any clues on how to handle him?"

"Oh *cher*," she shook her head. "No one handles Lucien Durand. I will say that complimenting Hope is the only way around him. Maybe we can tell him we're going to Hope's for dessert because you just love her apple tart."

"Can we get a to-go order of her shrimp in puff pastry? Those are really good."

"We can get whatever you want as long as you sing Hope's praises loud and long."

"Still, I think I better get my taste buds and stomach ready for all things spicy. What do you think I should do?"

"I don't know. Find a circus and get lessons from the fire eater?" She snapped her fingers. "I know. Tabasco shots. Lots of Tabasco shots."

"Cute." He kissed her. "Really cute. How about this? Let's go on upstairs to my bedroom and you can show me a thing or two about handling hot stuff."

She stared into those lovely green eyes of his. "Sounds like a plan." She shivered. The feeling like she was being watched skittered up her spine.

"You okay? Are you cold?" Tim's voice was husky with concern.

She shook her head. "No. It just felt like someone was watching me." Her skin crawled. "Must be an old reaction to always being followed around by cameras."

He looked around. "Maybe."

"Do you feel it, too?"

He waited a beat then shrugged. "No. I think we're

both a little camera shy."

Wasn't that the truth. "I guess." Still, she couldn't shake off the mood.

He leaned over to kiss her. "I'll see you later. Will you miss me 'til then?"

She stroked his arm. "You know I will."

He grinned and left, and she took one last look over the horizon before turning to go back into her own bungalow.

****

Tim stood and cracked his back. He'd been sitting at his computer for hours playing with the photos he'd taken of Angelique. Finally, it was complete. He'd toyed with retouching them to diminish the scar, but couldn't.

He loved the scar. The scar was a huge part of the woman he'd fallen in love with. Without it, she was untouchable, just too damn beautiful to be real.

Without the scar she was an unattainable goddess; with it she was a warm, wonderful, generous woman.

He picked up the picture he liked best, one of her walking backwards on the beach, laughing and clapping for Chester to come to her. The sea breeze tossed and tangled her hair. Her mouth curved up in joyful abandon as she focused totally on the dog.

Glad he finally finished the album, Tim could finally come clean and show her how lovely he found her, scar and all.

He could show her how she touched him, beyond the visual, even though she'd given him his gift of sight back.

He finally had a plan. After the trip to Addington when he'd make Lucien know that he was serious about

Angelique, whether Lucien liked it or not.

When he and Angelique got back to Lobster Cove, he'd show her the photos, get down on one knee, and ask her to marry him.

Maybe he'd jumped the gun, but he'd already bought the ring.

It seemed as if all his hopes and dreams were pinned on the next few days. He wished for two things; that his timing was right and that she was on the same page he was.

He brushed all thoughts of failure to the back of his mind. What had Jeff said? Faint heart never won fair lady.

Chapter Thirty-Five

The sign on the side of the road proclaimed "Welcome to Addington," but Angelique broke out in a cold sweat. She didn't know exactly how welcome she'd be.

She figured things at L'Enfer would be all oh-look-the-prodigal-has-returned, so that would be bearable.

The whole visit to Hope's had her arse over teakettle about a couple of things.

First, Beth and Jeff had nearly gone into swoons over the prospect of Hope's shrimp puffs, like they were manna from the desert. Hope didn't even like to make them anymore because of the unsustainability of shrimp, but if Lucien asked her to make them, she would bite the bullet.

The second thing had her stomach churning. Going to Hope's meant seeing Shane Baker again, something she did not look forward to.

She crossed her fingers. Maybe he'd stay in the kitchen. Or have the night off.

Angelique sighed. Color her the Queen of Denial.

"How long has it been since you've been back here?" Tim took a right onto Main Street.

"Centuries."

He reached over and put his palm over hers. "It'll be okay."

"Maybe. It'll be good to see Lucien." Especially if

he was the Lucien who'd shown up in Lobster Cove.

Tim squeezed her hand. "It'll be okay. I've been told by all and sundry that I'm a pretty presentable guy. I'll have your brother eating out of the palm of my hand."

She snorted. "Just remember this. Don't hate Lucien for being a jerk. He was just born that way."

Tim snickered. "Don't worry. If I can survive ISIS, I can survive Lucien Durand."

"Who do you think trained ISIS?" She sighed. "Sorry, bad joke."

"Hey, no worries." Tim murmured. "Sometimes it helps to laugh about it."

She tossed her hair over her shoulder. Time to change the subject. "We're stopping at the B and B first, yes?"

"Oh, yeah. That's best, don't you think? Or maybe you want to do something else?"

"No. It's a good idea to check in and refresh." Not to mention playing with her make up to make the scar less obvious.

How odd. She didn't care one way or the other going out and about in Lobster Cove with her scar on display. This would be the first time she'd gone out in Addington *après* injury. She could only imagine people would have two reactions—glee or pity. She'd earned the one but not the other.

"Then that's what we'll do." He faked an outrageous yawn. "Might need a nap, too. Spending some quality time on a bed with you will be a great pick me up."

"You have a one track-mind, but I like it. A quality nap it is."

She wondered if they'd actually nap.

She hoped not.

****

"Does my brother know we're coming?" Angelique asked as Tim maneuvered his car into the parking lot at L'Enfer.

"He knows a T. Baldwin has a reservation at seven o'clock."

She rolled her eyes. "So we're surprising him?" Not likely. No one surprised Lucien Durand.

"Yep."

"What if he's not here? Some nights he helps out at Hope's."

Aw crap. "Hope needs help?"

Angelique shook her head. "No of course not. But Lucien misses her. It's sweet enough to put me in a coma."

"Oh. Well let's hope he's here."

"You can hope he's here. I'm fine if he's not."

"If he's not here and he's not at Hope's, where do you think he'd be?" *Damn.* Tim really wanted to get this business with her brother done.

"He might be out at the site where he and Hope are building a house. Let's cross that bridge when we come to it." She squared her shoulders and sighed.

He took her hand and squeezed it, probably more for his sake than hers. He let it go to open the front door and usher her in.

There he stood just inside the lobby, the great Chef Lucien Durand. His eyes widened when he saw Tim with Angelique. After a beat of silence, he came around the host stand and pulled her into a hug.

"*Ma soeur,*" Lucien murmured. "Not that I'm not

happy to see you, but what are you doing here?"

"We have reservations," Tim crossed his arms across his chest.

Angelique pulled away from Lucien. She took Tim's hand. "Lucien, you've met my next door neighbor in Lobster Cove, Tim Baldwin." She smiled.

"Of course I remember," Lucien said, his tone of voice pretty frosty.

"We didn't really get a chance to get to know each other." Tim said. "We're here to rectify that."

Silence. Then, "You said you have reservations?"

"Yes, under the name Baldwin."

"I see." Lucien took a couple of menus from the goggle-eyed woman behind the desk. "I will seat my sister and her friend," he told her.

Lucien grabbed Angelique by the arm, leaving Tim to bring up the rear, and led the way to a table.

Jesus, what an obvious power play.

Heh. Let Durand play games. Tim was playing for keeps.

****

The small hairs on the back of Angelique's neck prickled from all of the people in the restaurant staring at her. She kept her game face on, sure as shooting, but this evening was turning out to be a trial.

Tim hadn't even spoken to Lucien yet about their relationship.

Lucien, of course, had taken over and decided they would eat all her favorite foods, not because he wanted to make her happy, but because he wanted to show Tim that he knew her better than Tim did.

Ten points for Lucien.

Tim, for his part, ignored Lucien's chest beating

and acted polite but not subservient. He manfully swallowed every overly spicy bit of food with no outside reaction.

Ten points for Tim.

Wait until Lucien found out they were heading over to Hope's for dessert.

They all still had yet to have "the conversation." Though she was not particularly religious, she sent a flurry of prayers out to whichever deity was around to listen.

"How did you enjoy your dinner, Mr. Baldwin? We always want to make sure that our famous clientele are satisfied." Lucien pulled up a chair at their table and motioned for a bus-person to come over and clear the dishes.

"Lucien," Angelique warned.

Lucien grinned all sharky-like.

Tim took one small sip of water, then another. "Very much. Your food lives up to your reputation."

"I hope you have room for dessert. Angelique never eats sweets, *tant pis*, but you can indulge."

"Actually," she said, "we're going to Hope's for dessert. I hope she's got her apple tart on the menu tonight."

Lucien looked from her to Tim and back again. "I believe dessert tonight at *chez* Hope is a peach cobbler made from the first crop from her own trees." He shrugged. "Or something cherry. So if you're looking for apples, you won't get them at Hope's."

Tim cleared his throat. "Peach cobbler sounds delicious. But as a born and bred son of Addington, I can't go back to Lobster Cove without some of Hope's shrimp puffs." He grinned. "I have orders to take some back for my friends. They'll run me out of town on a rail if I don't bring them any."

"Why are you here?" Lucien abruptly turned to Tim and changed the subject.

"I think that's kind of obvious. We're in love, Angelique and me, and we don't want to hide it from you."

Lucien threw Angelique a sharp glance. "He's a photographer."

She rolled her eyes. "I'm aware of that."

"What's going to happen when he goes back to his work?"

"What do you mean?" Angelique frowned.

"Are you going to go with him when he goes into all those dangerous places just to take pictures?"

"That part of my life is over," Tim interrupted.

"What are you going to do now?" Lucien turned his attention back to Tim.

Tim's hands fisted by his sides. "I'm not sure yet."

"So you're hooking your future to a man who doesn't have one," Lucien told Angelique.

"Things haven't gone that far," Angelique said. "Neither of us know what's next. We're just enjoying the moment."

Her answer didn't sit right with Tim, but she was right. Neither of them were in a position to talk about the future.

Lucien looked at his watch. "If you want to get dessert at Hope's, you should probably leave soon. She stops serving in about a half an hour, although she'd *sans doute* keep the kitchen open for you."

Of course, she would, Angelique thought. *He's going to call her the minute we're out the door.*

"Sounds like a plan." Tim said as he stood and came behind her to hold her chair. "Thank you for dinner. It was great."

"*Bien sûr*," Lucien said. "And Baldwin? Take very good care of my baby sister."

"I wouldn't dream of doing otherwise."

"Thanks, Lucien," Angelique said as she grabbed Tim's arm to pull him out of there. "Come on, Tim. We've got some peach cobbler calling our names."

Chapter Thirty-Six

"So, I need to tell you something." Angelique fiddled with her seatbelt. "There was this guy I dated and I treated him really bad."

"I remember." He had a good idea where this thing was going.

"Well, he works for Hope and there's the possibility we'll see him tonight."

"Okay." Really, what did she want him to say?

"We know for sure that Lucien was on the phone to Hope before we were out the door. Maybe she can persuade him to make himself scarce."

He grunted. "I don't need protection from ex-boyfriends."

"No question. No question at all." She pulled his right hand off the stick shift and brought it to her lips and kissed it. "It might be a little uncomfortable, is all."

"Nothing I can't handle."

She kissed his knuckles again. "Hope is really nice." She grimaced. "Too nice. Much nicer to me than I deserve."

He bristled. "Don't say that. You've taken your licks and done your time. If she's forgiven you and moved on then you should, too."

He kept his gaze on the road but could feel her staring at him. "What?"

"I just wonder what you see when you look at me."

"I see Angelique Durand, the imperfect woman I love." He worked to not look at her. "I see the beautiful woman who accepts the broken man I am."

"You're not broken. Bent a little, maybe, but not broken." She shrugged. "Us being in the same room with Shane is nothing. To me Shane is nothing but a huge regret." She looked away from him.

"You wanted to love him."

So much shame. "I didn't. I didn't care one whit for him. He was a diversion on the way to my ideal life."

She dropped his hand and looked out the front passenger window.

"We don't have to do this, you know. No amount of shrimp puffs is worth your discomfort."

She shook her head. "No. I need to do this."

Both were silent as he steered his car into the clamshell-covered parking lot of Hope's. Really, it was New England. Every parking lot and driveway was covered in clamshells. "Here we are."

She nodded. "Let's go."

"We don't have to."

"I know." She put her hand on his stubbly cheek. "But I don't want to see Jeff cry when we come back empty handed."

Tim took her hand, pressed a kiss into her palm, and closed her fingers over it. "Yeah, he's an ugly crier."

Her hand felt small and cold as he held it while they walked to Hope's entrance. Hope's front gardens were in full bloom and delicately scented the warm summer air.

Tim had never been in Hope's restaurant. She'd

catered every party his parents had thrown back before his father retired. Her food never failed to make his mouth water.

Angelique disengaged from his touch as they entered the restaurant's foyer. The hostess came forward, smiling. "Good evening, welcome to, uh—" Her eyes widened when she saw them then her face closed up in hostility.

Fortunately, Tim recognized her. "Renee Haven, is that you? How many years has it been?"

Renee barely spared him a glance, but a second later, her mouth turned up into a cautious smile. "Tim? Tim Baldwin?"

"In the flesh." Damn, Angelique had turned into stone right next to him. "How are you?"

"Good! How are you? I followed your whole story from over in the Middle East. Everyone in town did."

He swallowed. He hadn't expected this. He should have. "As you can see, I'm none the worse for wear."

Angelique still stood there, doing her statue impression.

"Do you think we can get a seat in the bar? Lucien promised us some dessert and I promised Jeff Myers I'd bring him back some shrimp puffs."

"How is Jeff? I heard he and Beth got married and have a little boy."

"They're great, really great. Happy. And if I show back up in Maine without shrimp he's going to make ISIS look like Romper Room." *See?* Tim could make a joke about it.

Renee motioned toward the bar. "Right this way." She craned her neck. "Oh. Maybe I should warn you…"

"Angie!"

The three of them looked in the direction of the excited howl that could only come from one source. Cookie Myers.

The little girl launched herself at Angelique. "Angie! Angie! Angie!"

Angelique caught her and gave her a big hug. Tim's heart expanded to see the sheer joy on his lady's face.

"Hi Uncle Tim!" Cookie grinned at him while clinging to Angelique like a limpet.

"Yes. Hello, 'uncle' Tim."

Katie. Of course. Where Cookie was, Katie couldn't be far behind. "Hi Katie. You look well."

"So do you, or as well as you can after all you've been through."

"Mommy! This is my new friend Angie! She lives in Lobster Cove with Uncle Tim."

"Does she really?" Katie turned her attention to Angelique. "You're the only person Cookie's been able to talk about since her last visit to Maine."

"Angie, as you can tell, this is Cookie's mother Katie. Katie, this is Angie Doucette, a friend from Lobster Cove."

"Hmmmm." Katie extended her hand. "It's nice to meet you. I do have to say that you look very familiar. Do you have ties to Addington?"

Angelique cleared her throat. "I have some family here."

"Really." Her brow creased. "Somehow I think it's more than that."

"Look, Mommy! Angie has a scar but I think she's really pretty anyway."

Okay, Tim knew that the jig was nearly up. If

anyone in the world could figure out that Angie Doucette and Angelique Durand were the same person, Katie was your girl.

Angelique had come to the same realization. "Actually, my name isn't Angie Doucette. My real name is Angelique Durand. Lucien Durand is my brother. I guess I didn't meet you when I lived here."

Tim could almost enjoy the sight of Katie's mouth opening and closing like a beached mackerel, if only Angelique hadn't looked so uncomfortable. Neither of them had thought this whole thing through. It was stupid to think they could slip in and out of Addington without people recognizing her.

"Did somebody organize a party out here and not invite me?" A very tall, very blond, very tan man wearing an orange, turquoise, and yellow Hawaiian shirt walked into the foyer.

And just like that, the other shoe dropped.

"Shane," Angelique murmured.

****

The only thing to fix her current reality, Angelique thought, was for the floor to open up and swallow her whole. How stupid could she be?

Let's go to Hope's, she'd said. Compliment her cooking. Lucien will love it, she'd said.

Living in Lobster Cove had totally lulled her into a false sense of security. Angie Doucette was accepted, even though she was a stranger. Here, in Addington, where her family lived, everybody judged every breath she took.

Then there was Shane, still tall and blond surfer boy handsome, still no taste in clothes.

Still in full possession of his knight in shining

armor complex.

"Angelique?"

Sighing, she met Shane's gaze. "Hi Shane."

"How are you?" He shoved his hands in his jeans pockets.

"Fine. How are you?"

Tim moved closer to her and put one hand underneath her elbow and offered the other to Shane to shake. "Hi. I'm Tim Baldwin."

Shane's eyes shifted briefly to where Tim had touched her then zapped up to Tim's face. "Shane Baker. You're that photographer. You know. From Iraq."

That photographer. Tim shook his head internally. Blondie there was an idiot. "Yeah, I know. I was there." He turned to Renee. "Can we just find our own way into the bar?"

Renee nodded. "Sure. I'll go let Hope know you're here. How many orders of the shrimp puffs do you want?"

"A couple, I guess. One for Jeff and one for Beth."

"Oh, isn't that charming," Katie blurted out. "You might want to tell Beth to lay off the shrimp things. They're fattening."

"Are you ready to go, Kate?" The deep voice of the newcomer into the foyer from hell sounded too familiar and definitely scary.

Buck Nelson, the architect of her infamous sex tape and twin brother to her co-star, was in the house.

"Absolutely," Katie answered him. "Buck, I know you must remember Tim Baldwin from when you coached him, but do you know Angelique Durand?" She lifted her left hand, which sported a sparkly rock the size of Connecticut. "We're getting married!"

Angelique's stomach lurched and churned as Buck said, "Yeah, Angelique and I go way back. Good to see you."

She wished she could say the same thing. "Congratulations. I hope you'll be very happy." Far away from her.

Katie peeled her daughter away from Angelique. "Come on, sugar Cookie. Let's get you home."

Cookie gave Angelique a quick hug. "Bye, Angie. See you next time I visit Daddy." She gave Tim a hug as well. "Bye Uncle Tim."

"Bye, doodle bug."

Cookie stamped her foot. "I'm not a bug!"

"We need to go now, sugar plum." Katie took Cookie's hand. "I hope you enjoy the rest of your evening."

Tim increased his hold on Angelique's elbow. "Let's go to the bar." He pulled her along with him.

"Hold on." She hissed the words at him. "Not so fast. I don't want either Shane or Buck to think I'm running away."

"Right." He slowed but his jaw clenched. "This probably wasn't the best idea we've ever had."

"No kidding." She sighed. "We're here now. We just have to tough it out. That peach cobbler better be really good."

The bar was all oak paneled walls and floors, buffed to a bright sheen. A stone fireplace took over an entire wall. In the winter, it would hold a roaring fire, but not in July. Antique wall sconces glowed with a soft, mellow glow, supplemented by candles in hurricane lamps on each table. Quiet and tasteful New

Age and Celtic music flowed from the speakers around the room. The atmosphere was peaceful and romantic.

A waitress with an elfin cap of sunny blonde hair and large eyes a misty color of green came to their table and put out coasters sporting Hope's logo. "Hi, I'm Faith and I'll be taking care of you tonight. May I get you anything from the bar?"

Tim adjusted in his seat. "Would you like a drink?" he asked Angelique.

"Oh yeah." She did want a drink, no doubt about it. "A Bellini, please."

"A Jameson's straight up and a Bellini, please," he told Faith. "Renee's getting us a couple of to go orders for shrimp puffs, but what's on the dessert menu tonight?"

Faith held her pencil over her order pad. "Hope made peach cobbler tonight and a minty rose essence ice cream. Of course the peaches are from her trees and the mint and rose petals from her garden."

"Oh, God." Angelique had truly forgotten what a genius with pastry Hope was. Her mouth watered. "We'll take one of each."

"Coming right up!"

Angelique first watched Faith walk away then turned her attention to Tim. "Sorry about that mess in the foyer. I really didn't think we'd run into Shane."

"Totally not your fault. You couldn't have predicted he'd show up while we were there. I mean, I'm good with it as long as you're okay."

"I am." She nodded.

"And there was no way I could have known Katie would be here with Buck Nelson. Jesus. I'm so sorry. Just one look at him made me want to punch his lights out."

"He has that effect on people. Don't worry about it. To tell the truth, I was every kind of stupid and felt flattered by it at the time. I mean, sex tapes put both Paris Hilton and Kim Kardashian on the map." She shook her head. "Between the two of them, they have the brain of a turnip. Back then, I guess I suffered from turnip brain syndrome, too, since while I felt violated, I also enjoyed everybody knowing my name. Pitiful, isn't it."

"You were young, it's done. Let's live in the now." Tim rested his forearms on the table. "We've got dessert coming that sounds insanely good. I don't think I've ever eaten rose petals."

"Really," she said, like everyone ate rose petals every day. He shook his head.

"Yeah. When Hope catered my parents' parties, she always put flowers on for decoration. I didn't know you could eat them."

She felt the first smile of the night spread across her face. "Who knew? But, really, when Luce and Hope were just getting together, she made him a rose petal dessert and blew him away."

"Your brother doesn't strike me as easily impressed."

"Here are your drinks," Faith stepped up to the table and placed the Bellini on the napkin in front of Angelique and the whiskey in front of Tim. "Hope knows you're here and will bring out your desserts when they're ready."

"Thank you so much," Angelique said. "This looks absolutely perfect."

"I know how you like your Bellinis, so I gave the

bartender a hand." Shane also came up to the table.

Faith stumbled clumsily to get away. "Let me know if you need anything else." She high-tailed it out of there.

Shane frowned for one second as he watched the pretty little waitress leave. "I just want to say that I'm glad to see you looking good. I did worry after I heard the whole story."

What? "Thank you." Time to change the subject. "You look good even if I still need to wear sunglasses to look at your outfits."

He pretended to be offended. "*Moi?* I have impeccable taste." He held his hand out to Tim. "I want to let you know how much I was moved by your work. You're a true hero."

Tim gripped the table with white knuckles then stood to shake Shane's hand. "The true heroes are the ones who didn't come back."

"We need truth tellers in the world, and you are one of the best." A crash came from the bar area. Shane sneered. "You couldn't hire someone who knows how to tend bar could you?" he told Hope as she arrived at the table. "I need to have a talk with Faith. Again." He stalked away.

Hope sighed. "Don't mind Shane. He's been just like a bear with a thorn in his paw for a couple of weeks now."

Hope put the desserts on the table and extended her hand to Tim. "Why don't you sit down."

They shook hands and Tim sat.

"Whatever is bothering Shane has nothing to do with you." Hope pulled up a chair and sat with them. "He and Faith have been at each other's throats for days."

"I hurt him, Hope." Angelique used one very shaky hand to pick up her drink.

Hope's eyes slid over to where Shane argued with Faith. "I think I can safely say that it's not you causing him problems right now."

Instead of being insulted and overlooked, she rejoiced in the warm waves of relief that flowed over her. "Thank you." That's all she could think of to say.

"You're welcome. Now, eat up! The cobbler is getting cold and the ice cream is melting."

Tears pricked Angelique's eyes, tears of relief for herself and tears of joy for Lucien. He'd found an amazing woman to partner with.

Surprisingly, she wanted the same thing.

And she wanted it with Tim.

Chapter Thirty-Seven

"So what do you think?"

Tim waited for his taste bud orgasm to subside before he answered Hope's question.

He patted his hand against his heart. "I can now die happy."

"This ice cream is really delicious, Hope," Angelique said.

Hope beamed. "Glad you like it. I have to say I enjoy watching you eat it." Her smile dimmed a little. "Now, tell me why you're here. Lucien called me just before you got here and he spoke more French than English, which happens when he's upset." She shrugged. "Or pissed off."

Angelique winced. "Or both. I don't suppose you could convince him to stay at L'Enfer."

"What do you think?"

"I'm surprised he's not here yet."

Tim shook his head as he licked the last little bit of rose ice cream off his spoon. The two women really thought Lucien could call the shots.

Tim had other plans. Lucien Durand may be able to get women to dance to his tune. Too bad Durand was going to have to deal with him.

"Well, look at this. My two favorite women in the world."

Bow down, minion. The magnificent Lucien

Durand has entered the house.

Hope rolled her eyes, stood, and went on tiptoes to press a quick kiss to her husband's cheek. "You're here even faster than I thought you'd be."

"I hope there's still some of that ice cream left. I'm dying to try it." He went to Angelique. "*Ma soeur.*" He bent and kissed her cheek.

Tim stood. "Won't you join us?" Nothing like taking charge of the situation, right?

Lucien turned his head slowly, as if he was drawn to Tim's gaze like the Enterprise caught in a Klingon tractor beam.

"Tim."

"Lucien." He sat back in his chair. "So I imagine you have some questions. I'll let you know if I'll answer them."

"Oh, boy," Hope said. "Should I go get the first aid kit?"

"Of course not, *pichouette*. Us, we're not fighting here. We're just getting to know each other."

"In the Gospel according to Lucien, sometimes blood shed is a necessary evil," Hope said, her tone of voice dry as the Sahara.

"He never changes," Angelique said. "Lucien, I love you and I can never thank you enough for how you forgave me and supported me, but—"

"This isn't about you," Lucien told her. "This is all about me getting to know Mr. Pulitzer Prize, King of the Photographers."

Tim suddenly knew where Lucien was coming from. Lucien worried that he was another user photographer trying to make a meal of Angelique.

Knowledge is power. "It isn't about you, either.

Whatever is between me and Angelique is just that—between us. Why don't you just concentrate on your amazing wife and leave the rest of the world's love lives alone?"

"You don't scare easy, you. I admire that," Lucien said.

"I don't care if you like me or not, but Angelique is special," *more essential than breathing,* "and brother or not, I'm not going to let you interfere in our choices to be together."

Lucien didn't look at him, but Tim knew he'd taken control of the conversation, no matter what advantage Angelique's brother thought he had.

"I'm not done," Lucien said, tapping the forefinger of his right hand on the table. "You understand that you've outed her, *vrai?* That you're going to be hounded once you get back to Lobster Cove?"

Angelique frowned. "We've been careful. No one can figure out about me living in Maine."

"Oh." Hope put her hand in front of her mouth. "Katie and Buck."

"What about them?" Tim didn't like the sound of anything involving Katie.

"She knows you're in Lobster Cove and she's going to be doing a lot of media now that she and her bastard of a boyfriend are engaged. I wouldn't put it past her to mention it."

"That doesn't make sense." Tim couldn't see it. "Katie wouldn't welcome and reference to a connection between Angelique and Buck. It's all Katie, all the time in Katie Land."

"I hope you're right," Lucien said. "But I wouldn't count on it."

Tim cast a glance at Angelique and his heart clenched. Her eyes were focused on the table, her fingers playing with a napkin. The need to protect her rocketed through him. "I can handle anything Katie can dish out."

Lucien's lips barely lifted in a dubious smile. "I sure hope you can. You seem like an okay guy." He grinned. "I'd hate to have to kill you if you let anything happen to my sister."

"Understood." No one would feel worse than Tim himself if he couldn't protect her.

****

"I don't want you to worry about Katie."

Angelique sighed as she looked out the window of Tim's car. They were making the long trip from Addington to Lobster Cove. "I'm not. Seeing Buck was a surprise, but I don't know Katie from a hole in the wall. I mean, I know about her from Beth but other than that?" She shrugged. "If she's half as bad as her reputation, then she deserves everything she gets from Buck." An awful idea hit her. "I feel sorry for Cookie. I hope everything is okay for her."

"I don't think much will change. Nelson is on the road with the Rangers for much of the year so he won't be around her a whole lot."

"Oh. Yeah, I suppose so." They'd just crossed the bridge from Portsmouth, New Hampshire into Kittery, Maine. After leaving Hope's they'd gone back to the Bed and Breakfast and just cuddled together in the big soft sleigh bed in their room.

He understood that she really wasn't up for sex after seeing Buck, so he'd taken her into his arms and held her close while she slept.

So much of their relationship had been about sizzling hot sex. This new phase seemed from out of a fairy tale, with all the romance and the comfort.

It was so foreign from anything she'd ever known when it came to men.

No. Not true, she admitted. Shane had given her the same kind of attention Tim gave her now. She hadn't wanted it.

Water under the bridge, she supposed. It had to be. She wished Shane all the happiness in the world. He deserved it.

"It's a cliché, but a penny for your thoughts."

She smiled. "Not much. Just that Shane deserves to be as happy as I am right now."

Tim's face softened. "You're happy?"

"Happier than I have a right to be."

"Me too. Happier than I have a right to be."

He didn't play coy and make her admit that he was the reason she was so happy. He was open and honest and didn't play games with her. She trusted him, trusted him with her whole heart.

For her it was nothing short of a miracle.

Chapter Thirty-Eight

"I'll be right back with your lemon," Angelique told the party at table 18. "Is there anything else I can bring you?"

Her customers murmured several shades of no and didn't bother to thank her. What else was new?

As was typical for a late July evening, the inn was full and the dining room packed. She was really proud that she hadn't gotten into the weeds yet.

Yay!

As she trotted back to the kitchen for 18's lemons she noticed table 5 had two stylishly dressed, perfectly-coiffed and made up women who were whispering feverishly to each other.

They were staring at her.

Her insides went cold. She'd been recognized.

Every instinct she had told her to go to the kitchen and walk right out the back door and never come back, but she just couldn't leave Alma, Betts, and Birdie in the breach.

Why had she ever wanted to be famous? Her *maman* must have just dropped her on her head when she was a baby.

Angelique grabbed the lemon wedges and headed back through the dining room. After delivering them, she headed to clear some salad plates from table 12 but as she'd feared, one of the women waved at her, clearly trying to flag her down.

She had a couple of choices. She could ignore them totally. She could take care of her customers and then go over. She got a minute's reprieve when table 5's waitress went to take care of them.

The reprieve didn't last long. Just after Angelique dumped the dirty salad plates, Christine, table 5's waitress and the queen of loud, came up to her. "Table 5 thinks you're a world famous super model. I told them I didn't think you were but that I'd ask." She rolled her eyes.

All conversations stopped on a dime. She guessed the jig was up. Angelique sighed and wished she could just disappear. "I don't model anymore," she looked around the kitchen, "but I used to. Tell them I'll be over when I get a chance," she told Christine. "I'm probably not the person they think I am."

"I told them your name is Angie Doucette but they seem to think that's an alias and that you're Angelique Durand, you know. That model who went to jail and got her face messed up." Horror creeped slowly across Christine's face as she looked at Angelique's scar.

Angelique plodded her way to the kitchen and picked up the dinners for table 12. She left the kitchen with her head held high. After delivering the food, she squared her shoulders, swallowed hard, and made her way to her fans.

"Hello. Christine said you wanted to meet me?"

"Oh my God, it's you isn't it? You're Angelique Durand!" The woman looked like to swoon.

"Yes, I am. And you are?"

The woman poked her equally star struck friend in the ribs. "I'm Eleanor and this is Antonia. We're huge

254

fans of yours! And we love your brother's restaurant."

"Thank you. I appreciate it and I'll let Lucien know."

"Can we get your autograph?"

"Of course." She pulled a pen out of her apron pocket. "Do you have something to write on?"

Both their faces turned red behind their expensive foundation as they frantically emptied their purses on the table.

"I have an order pad right here. I'll sign a couple of dupes for you." She got their names, wrote casual, personalized notes, and handed the papers to them.

"This is so lovely of you to do. Thank you."

"You're welcome." The hairs on the back of her neck rose. She needed to get back to her tables.

"It really is so nice." She turned to her friend. "I'm going to have to apologize to Katie. I didn't believe her when she told us Angelique Durand was hiding out in Lobster Cove."

"Katie? Katie Myers?" Soon to be Katie Nelson.

"Yes! Do you know her?"

Now she did, a little too late, but oh yeah, she knew Katie. "No. I know her daughter and her ex-husband, but I don't know her." Needles prickled up and down her skin. "I'm very happy to meet you, but I do have to get back to my customers."

"It's such a shame you had that accident. So unfair, to go from being one of the most beautiful woman in the world to...to a waitress in a small tourist town. Although, you do a good job with make-up to hide the scar."

Angelique might yet throw up. "Thank you. Please let Christine know if you need anything else."

She hurried off to check on table 18 but found every person in her section with food in front of them and staring at her.

Tears pricked at her eyes. Apparently, even though she'd lied to every single one of her friends and colleagues here at the Sea Crest Inn, they'd picked up the slack.

She made it to the kitchen. "Um, thank you for helping me out with my tables. Where can I pick things up?"

"I'll have entrées up for 14 in a sec," Alma said.

Christine put two chocolate brownie sundaes on a tray. "These are for 18."

"Thank you." What was going on?

"No problem, Angie." Christine took her hands and squeezed them before she could pick up the tray. "We're all a team. You'd do the same for me."

"I would." *In a heartbeat.*

"Better get those desserts out before the ice cream melts."

"Thanks!"

"Get right back in here to take this food out," Alma yelled.

"Okay! Be right back."

She felt a huge grin blossom across her face. None of her friends and co-workers cared about Angelique Durand, but they did care about Angie Doucette.

Of all the gifts she'd ever been given, this was one of the biggest.

****

"So, Angie is Angelique Durand and someone totally not like who she appears to be."

Tim ran his hand over his hair, to keep from

punching Jeff's lights out. "She is who she appears to be. Someone who's gone through a real bad time and wants some peace and quiet. She just wants to be left alone. Unfortunately, your ex-wife is telling anybody who will listen that Angelique Durand is hiding out in Lobster Cove, working as a waitress."

Jeff grunted. "My daughter loves her. How do I tell Cookie that Angie isn't Angie?"

He wanted to karate chop Jeff in the neck. "Angelique is Angie. If you ask me, Angelique is a better influence on Cookie than Katie is."

Another grunt. "You've got a point. Still. How do you know she's not leading you on?"

"Are you kidding me?" Tim felt like he might burst a blood vessel. "You're not usually this stupid."

"Settle down. Given the choice between Katie and Angie, I'm Team Angie all the time." Jeff's eyes got hard and bitter. "I'm not real happy about Buck Nelson being Cookie's step-father, especially now that I know about the whole sex tape thing." Jeff clenched his fists. "I need to check with my lawyer." He shook his head. "If I could find a way to cancel next month's football clinic, I would in half a heartbeat."

"You do that. In the meantime," Tim pinched the skin on the bridge of his nose, "I really want to kill someone and I can't. Hold me back. Please."

"Absolutely. You'd do the same for me."

"You got it. Listen," Tim started. "Katie sicced those women on Angelique. What do you think she has to gain?"

"To be the first with the news. To show me she'll always have her tentacles into my relationship with Cookie." He nodded. "And straight up, old fashioned

Doreen Alsen

jealousy. You told me Cookie treated Angie like a member of the royal family. That had to make Katie crazy. Beyond crazy. And having a piece of really juicy gossip that elevates her to queen status?" Jeff shrugged. "Protecting that is totally in her wheelhouse."

"Awesome." Tim felt weary, so much so that his bones could barely hold up his skin. "There's no way I'm going to let Katie and Buck get any closer to Angelique. I think I'll arrange for us to be out of town during that football camp."

"Good plan. I wish I could send Danny with you, but he would not understand. I've hyped the twins as being the equivalent of the second coming. I've invited them to stay with us, but they're only staying for dinner and heading back to Addington afterward."

"Is Katie coming with them?"

"Oh, you know she is. That's another problem. If Katie decides to go on the road with Buck, there's no way I'm letting her take Cookie with her. I'll sue for primary custody and bring her here to live."

"Sounds reasonable. It's no life for a kid on the road." Tim knew firsthand how hard it was to live out of a suitcase. And he'd been a grown up.

"It does sound reasonable. That's why Katie will fight it tooth and nail."

"If I can help you out at all, just let me know." Tim did not envy Jeff's relationship with his ex-wife.

He hadn't envied their relationship back when they were still married, either.

"I still don't know what to say to Cookie about Angelique. We've made a big deal with her about not lying." Jeff scratched the back of his neck.

"You don't have to say anything. Let her talk to

258

Angelique one on one about why Angelique lied. She can take ownership of the lie and show Cookie how to deal with this kind of thing."

"What kind of thing?"

"Owning up when you've done something wrong, like lying, then coming clean, and asking for forgiveness."

Jeff stared at the ground then looked Tim in the face and nodded. "Sounds like the lesson we want Cookie-girl to learn. We'll set it up next time she's here."

"Sounds like a plan."

"You're really into her, aren't you?"

Tim looked his best friend in the eyes. "Yeah, I am. Go figure."

"That's cool, bud. It's about time you found a woman and settled down."

Tim hadn't thought of his bond with Angelique that way. After he decided not to hide away from her for her own good, he planned on fun and games. He hadn't planned on finding someone and settling down, as Jeff put it. At one point, really, just last year, the idea of staying in one place far from the action and the danger would have been laughable.

Now? Not so much.

He sure didn't want to fly around the globe to find the next new war zone. He did want to fire up the ol' hot tub, get naked, and relax with a bottle of champagne and his lady.

Thing was, he wasn't the marrying kind.

Or was he? He'd already been checking out diamond rings in the store windows downtown.

Maybe for Angelique he could be.

Chapter Thirty-Nine

"Angie, do you have a minute?"

Angelique closed her eyes for all of a second, took a breath, and after pasting a smile on her face, turned to deal with Birdie. "For you I have two."

Birdie slapped a hand over her heart. "Aren't you sweet, dearie? I'm after asking you for some help with my makeup and hair for the animal shelter party."

Of all the things Angelique expected to hear, that was not it. She cleared her throat as she took in the whole vision that was Birdie McCorkle, nuclear crimson hair topping the list. She crossed her fingers behind her back. "You look beautiful as you are."

Birdie heaved her considerable bosom. "Please. I'm after looking different, you know, make a splash with a new style. I looked you up and you were," she cleared her throat, "are, very beautiful. And it's so much style you have. I thought maybe you could help me." She smiled ruefully and shrugged. "I want to turn some heads." She fluffed her impossible red colored hair. "I'm not getting any younger, if you know what I mean."

"You don't look a day over thirty-five." Angelique still could lie with the best of them.

"Oh, get on with you, dearie! I look sixty if I look a day. I'm of a mind to change the color of me hair. Marge does a lovely job, that she does, but I'm fancying something more flashy."

If Birdie's hair color got any more flashy, people would mistake it for the ball they dropped at Times Square on New Year's Eve.

"Actually, I think if you change to a quieter color, you might attract a bit more attention." *Hmmmmm.* A thought hit her. "Is there someone whose attention you're trying to snag?"

Birdie's faced turned a charming shade of fuchsia. She shrugged all casual like, but Angelique thought she saw a glimmer of something in her eyes. "Oh, no. Mr. McCorkle was the one man for me, bless his soul." She made the sign of the cross. "I just want to shake things up."

Yeah, and Angelique was Mother Teresa. She'd let her have her secret. And then she thought what the hell? She knew makeup and hair. She could work with Marge to give Birdie a makeover. "Why don't you make an appointment at Hair's the Thing and I'll go with you."

"I wouldn't want to hurt Marge's feelings."

"Of course not. I can give advice without it looking like I'm taking over." A very new skill she'd learned.

Birdie sighed. "May all the saints and angels smile upon you, lass. It's grateful I am to you." Her beeper went off. She looked at it and grimaced. "I've got to check in with laundry. We'll talk soon, aye?"

"Aye. We'll talk soon, Birdie."

She grinned. "It's a darling accent you have there." She gave a small wave and walked away.

Angelique smiled and stuffed her hands into the pockets of her khaki shorts while she watched Birdie walk away. This whole nice person thing was turning out to be pretty fun!

****

"It's just insane!"

"What? That all the women in town want beauty advice from you?" Tim and Angelique sat in his hot tub under the stars. Unusually balmy and sultry for summer in Maine, it was a night for moving slow and easy.

"Well, yeah. I've had at least ten people call me for advice once it got around I was helping Birdie McCorkle."

"Helping Birdie was a gift to all of mankind." He shuddered just thinking about her old hair color and style.

"Stop it." She lightly batted him on his shoulder. "That's not where the story ends. Marge has offered me a small space at Hair's the Thing so I can take appointments for makeup and consultations on wardrobe choices and things like that."

"Sounds like it's more your thing than waiting on tables and cleaning hotel rooms."

"You'd think." She took a sip of the crisp, with a hint of apricot, Rising Tide Riesling from Bar Harbor Cellars and swallowed.

Tim watched her take another sip of her wine. Tonight was the night he'd show her the photos he'd taken of her.

He had it all planned. Food from Evelyn's, caterer extraordinaire, dessert in the hot tub, then he'd take her to bed and show her the album. She would understand.

She had to.

He had a whole speech written out. He'd practiced it in front of his bathroom mirror for the past four days. It reminded him of how he worked to perfect his pitch to Jenny Warner when he asked her to the prom.

Luck had been on his side. Jenny said yes.

He hoped with all his might that he would have the same success with Angelique.

A whole hell of a lot more than getting lucky in the backseat of his father's car was at stake.

He'd put off the portfolio part of the evening's entertainment, but he couldn't hold it off forever. It was time.

"Should we take our little party back inside?"

Angelique slid so that the warm frothy water covered her shoulders and gave him a sassy grin. "What's your plan?"

"I've got something to show you."

Her eyes widened as she glanced at his groin and stiffening erection. "I think you've shown it to me already."

He snickered in spite of himself. "Something else."

"Oh," she pouted.

"I promise you'll like it." Though the jury might be out on that point for a little while, as he pleaded his case. He got out of the tub, grabbed a couple of bath sheets, and wrapped one around his waist.

"Here, let me help you out." He offered her his hand to help her out. That accomplished, he gave her the second towel.

"Thanks." She covered herself with the huge white towel and secured it over her breasts.

"Why don't you go on in while I grab some things from the kitchen? I scored some chocolate dipped strawberries from Julie's."

"Oh, yum! Hurry back." She stood on tiptoes and kissed his cheek.

"You know it," he said as he led her through the

door into the house.

His heart thumped hard as he bounded down the stairs to the kitchen. Not much was at stake, he mused.

Nope. Only the damn rest of his life.

****

Angelique sighed as she settled back against the plump pillows stacked up on Tim's bed's headboard. Drowsy from the spa tub, she closed her eyes and sank into the soft bed and crisp linens.

Tonight could literally be counted as one of the best nights of her life. She couldn't help smiling with the happiness welling up inside her.

"Hey."

She opened her eyes to find Tim standing in the doorway laden down with strawberries, chocolate, a bottle of champagne, and, oddly enough, a photo album. "Wow."

He set the things down as he sat on the bed next to her then leaned in and kissed her. "I have a surprise for you."

She shimmied up the headboard, keeping the sheet over her breasts. "Ooooh. I love surprises!"

His eyes turned very serious. "I hope you'll like this one." He reached for the photo album and handed it to her.

She blinked. "What is this?"

"Open it up and see."

She rubbed her hand over the front cover of the book, awash with a sudden wave of apprehension. She glanced at his face.

He nodded. "Go ahead. Take a look."

Her fingers trembled a little as she opened the cover. Her eyes widened and she forgot to breathe.

The album showed pictures of her, pictures from the past few weeks.

Pictures she hadn't known about being taken.

They captured so many moments of her celebrating her freedom and her newfound confidence and identity.

Who took these?

Tim? No. He couldn't have. She'd told him how she felt about this kind of thing. He knew.

A harsh prickling rushed over her body. Alarms rang off in her ears like air raid sirens.

Tim knew how she felt and took secret pictures of her anyway. "You son of a bitch," she hissed as the blood drained from her head.

Tim winced. "I can explain."

"I'm sure you think you can." She closed the cover of the album.

He reached for her hands but she pulled them away. She didn't want him to touch her right that second.

He held his hands up in a hand's off kind of way. "I first saw you when you were walking on the beach in front of the Yacht Club. I was at Jeff and Beth's wedding and really feeling sorry for myself because I'd lost my ability to take pictures. Then I saw you and I don't know, maybe I fell in love with you at first sight, or something."

"Oh, please." She snorted, fighting the urge to hit him over the head with the photos.

"Okay, maybe not love, but I felt something good for the first time after coming home from Iraq. Then when I found out you lived next door to me—"

"What? That it would be real easy to spy on me and take pictures I didn't know about. God! I didn't even know you were there and you were spying on me!" She thought she might throw up.

"No, it wasn't like that at all. I saw you and I couldn't help myself. You are so beautiful and real and…and…I could see you. Really see you, right down to the heart of you. Look at the photos. You'll see."

Bile rose in her throat at just the thought of looking at more pictures. "I don't want to." She started to shake. "I've got to get out of here." She stood, wrapping a bed sheet around her and pushed past him.

"Don't go. Please. I love you. Let me make you understand."

"I can't talk to you right now."

"We'll talk tomorrow then." He stepped in front of her, blocking the way to the door.

"I don't know. I don't know if I can ever trust another word you say. Please let me by."

Tim's nostrils flared as he stared at her. For a brief, dizzying minute, she thought he wasn't going to move, but then he did. She brushed past him, not even going into his bedroom to get her clothes. She headed straight down the stairs and right out the door, running to the safety of her own home.

How could he have fooled her like that? How stupid had she been, thinking he loved her for the person she was? Instead, he'd been all about taking advantage of her and turning her back into an object for people to leer at.

She hiccupped, a painful spasm of her diaphragm. Even worse, he was exploiting her very flawed, scarred face.

She tore off the towel she'd wrapped around her, pulled on some yoga pants and a huge T-shirt. After finding a duffel bag, she threw some clothes into it, stuffed her feet into a beat up pair of flip-flops, and left her house.

She didn't know where she was going but the urge to run away nipped at her heels like an angry dog.

She revved up the engine of her cute little white VW and pulled out into the street. She didn't spare a glance at Tim's house as she sped off into the night.

Chapter Forty

Before Tim could get dressed so he could run over to Angelique's, he heard her car fire up.

He made it to a window to see it peel out.

Damn.

Where the hell was she going? How could she leave without listening to him?

Yeah, what he'd done was wrong, but she had to give him a chance to make it right.

Running away never solved anything.

Except for one big ass ol' huge thing.

Wasn't he running away and hiding here in Lobster Cove, trying to outrun ISIS and the ghosts of his beheaded colleagues?

No, he decided. It wasn't the same thing. Not at all. Once he got past his photography block, he could leave Lobster Cove, if he wanted to.

Right now, he just didn't want to.

In the meantime, he had to find Angelique, to make sure she was safe. She was too upset to be driving around out there all by herself.

If something happened, he would never forgive himself.

So where would she go?

Her only friends were her co-workers from the Sea Crest Inn and Beth. Maybe he should call Beth.

Beth was a good friend. She'd take Angelique in

for the night and help her calm down.

But he better check that was what happened. Then he'd go over there tomorrow and plead his case again. She couldn't tune him out forever, because hadn't she told him she loved him?

Cold sweat trickled down his back. What if she didn't love him? What if using her as his muse to court back his gift stripped away all her love for him.

What an arrogant ass he'd been trying to keep both Angelique and his talent for taking the perfect shot, when all along it had been either slash or…

If she didn't forgive him, he would have nothing, not her love, not his talent.

He'd be nothing.

Despair pulled at him like a riptide destroyed the beach. He had to make this right. He had to make a choice.

Tim chose Angelique, if she'd still have him.

Failing with her would kill him, tearing his soul into tiny, rusted, ragged pieces. He'd never come back from that and he couldn't blame it on ISIS.

It was all on him.

****

"What do you mean she's not here?" Tim threw up his hands as he paced across the floor of Jeff and Beth's living room.

"What I said. Angelique isn't here. What I want to know is why you think she should be here." Jeff took a sip of his coffee.

Tim threw himself into a chair. "We had a fight last night and she left. I guess I thought she'd come here because she's friends with Beth."

"Why didn't she just stay in her own house?"

"I don't know."

"You must have really made her mad. What did you do?"

Tim swallowed. He'd dreaded this moment for so very, very long. "I haven't been quite honest with everybody. Something happened back in Iraq."

"Yeah, you nearly got killed, which, by the way, I'm glad didn't happen."

Might as well just spit it out. "I lost my ability to take pictures."

"What?"

"I try to take a picture and my finger freezes on the shutter and I get this panicky feeling. Sometimes I puke my guts up. I always can't breathe."

"Jesus, Tim." Jeff put his cup on the coffee table and leaned forward in his chair. "Are you talking to anybody about that?"

"Obviously not. The thing is I can take pictures as long as Angelique is in the frame."

Jeff didn't say anything for a beat and a half. "Holy shit. And didn't I tell you to go get help!"

"And can you not lecture me until I tell you the whole story? So I took pictures of her, knowing that she didn't want her picture taken, that she didn't even know I was taking pictures of her. I just couldn't help myself. It was like having my soul back, you know? So, I was going to tell her last night and show her this album I made, and, you know, let her see how beautiful she is in my eyes and ask her if she'd pose for me." He didn't tell Jeff he was going to ask her to marry him. It was just too humiliating.

"What'd she say?"

"Let's just say she didn't react the way I hoped she

would. I tried to explain, but she wouldn't listen. Like ran away rather than talk to me."

"Man. You really screwed the pooch on that one." Jeff shook his head.

"Yeah, I know." Tim stood, shoved his hands in his pockets, and started to pace again. "I've got to find her so I can make her see why I kept it a secret."

"Why did you keep it a secret?"

"I don't know." He shrugged. "Total stupidity. Because I'm a coward? Pick one. Pick both."

"Well, she didn't come here. Maybe Betts or Birdie McCorkle might know."

Tim chuffed out a breath. "I guess I should swing by the Sea Crest Inn."

"That's what I'd do."

"What if she's not there?"

"I don't know what to tell you, man. Start at the Sea Crest and go from there."

"Yeah, I suppose. Listen," Tim stopped pacing. "If she calls Beth, can you let me know?"

"Depends on what she tells Beth. I'm not going to go behind Beth's back."

Tim sighed. Sometimes Jeff being a stand-up guy really pissed him off. "Right. Well, the sooner I get going, the faster I'll find her."

"Good luck."

"Thanks."

Tim had the sneaking suspicion he was going to need it.

Chapter Forty-One

Angelique stood at the end of a deserted pier watching the gray sea churn in big rolling waves. The color of the sky matched the water, so it was difficult to see where one stopped and the other began. The wind whipped stinging salt spray around her.

She wore old jeans and they were a little tight, because of the five or so pounds she'd put on since she'd stopped modeling. Her stomach boiled just like the water. She stuffed her hands into the pockets of her Lobster Cove Sharks hoodie and let her mind go.

Her white canvas Keds were soaked and the cold from the rain migrated upward through her body.

Lucien wanted her to go back to Addington, but she didn't want to go there. She had to solve this on her own.

Which meant she had to go back to Lobster Cove and face Tim.

She couldn't believe that he had lied to her, especially as he knew all her issues. *Dieu,* issues was such a weak word for what was wrong with her.

She was no one's ticket to salvation. Tim needed more help than she could give him. Exhibit A was his last brush with death while sailing, needing to be rescued by the Coast Guard and fighting them on it. It was only days until he took delivery of a new boat, then it was back to the races for him.

She couldn't sit by and watch him self-destruct. She loved him too much.

Angelique didn't understand about the whole inability to take pictures thing, but maybe if he could make her understand, she could forgive him.

But she wouldn't get back with him until he got his act together. Someone had to be the grown up in the room.

She sighed. She had to go back to Lobster Cove soon as she couldn't keep hiding out here on Cape Cod. She'd made promises to Betts and Birdie and a host of other people and she was not about to let them down.

Maybe it was time to pack up and go home.

Home to Lobster Cove.

****

It wasn't the first time Tim wished that ISIS had killed him dead.

Angelique had been gone for two weeks.

Two very long miserable weeks.

No one knew where she was, with the exception of Birdie McCorkle and Birdie wasn't tweeting, no matter how hard he begged.

Actually, she wasn't talking to him at all. She wouldn't even acknowledge his presence as he was having breakfast with Jeff and his family at the Sea Crest Inn.

The terminally perky waitress who took their order managed to bring Jeff and Beth's coffee with no problem. She apparently forgot Tim's and went back to the wait station to fetch it.

Tim watched while she poured the cup and left it there on the station to do something else. When she did finally get around to delivering the damn coffee, it had gone stone cold.

He didn't complain, just glugged it down and pretended it was the most delicious beverage ever.

She came back to the table to see if anyone wanted a refill, and he told her yes. She sniffed, lifted her nose, and trotted off, walking past the wait station and into the kitchen.

"You're pretty popular around here," Jeff said in between bites of his cheese Danish.

"Yep." Tim hadn't a clue that anyone at the Inn knew about Tim and Angelique's relationship. "I'm a real superstar."

"Do you want me to ask around, see if I can find out where Angelique went?" Beth handed Danny a wet nap. "I think you're wearing more blueberry pancakes than you ate," she told her son.

Danny's face split into the biggest grin ever known to mankind.

Oh, did Tim ever want to know, more than anything. He longed for news about Angelique. Instead, he shook his head. "No use chasing after her. She'll get back in touch with me when she's ready."

"When's the last time you slept?" Beth said.

He shook his head again. "I sleep." If you counted snoozing off in catnaps on his couch that lasted about twenty minutes. He hadn't gone back to his bed since Angelique left.

And then there was the fact that the re-enactment nightmares were back.

"Okay, let me re-phrase the question. When was the last time you slept an entire REM cycle?"

He sighed. "I'm fine." She opened her mouth to say something but Tim headed her off at the pass. "I am. I appreciate the concern, I really do, but you need to leave it alone."

Beth clearly didn't agree with that, but she didn't say anything else. The waitress showed back up with a cup of piping hot coffee and put it in front of him. "Can I get you anything else?" Her face dared him to ask for something.

"No thanks," he said, feeling drenched in weariness and failure. "I'm good."

Or at least he might be. One day.

Chapter Forty-Two

"Hey, you're back! Does Tim know yet?"

Angelique turned to see Birdie McCorkle lumbering across the kitchen of the Sea Crest Inn toward her. "I haven't run into him yet."

"The poor lad's been miserable while you were away. You need to forgive him and give him a second chance."

Tim was miserable?

Good.

Time to change the subject. "When did you schedule your makeover?"

"Marge has me down for Saturday at two in the afternoon. I made sure you have the time off."

"Oh." She blinked. "Good. At Hair's the Thing, right?"

"Aye! Marge is looking forward to getting some tips from you."

Mon Dieu! "I'm not a hairstylist, so I hope I don't disappoint her."

"Sure and you won't disappoint her." She sighed. "Remember what I said about Tim. You two are adorable together." She clasped her hands together in front of her. "Meant to be."

Angelique rubbed a hand over her stomach as she watched Birdie walk away.

A notorious matchmaker and believer in Destiny

and happily ever after, of course Birdie would say that she and Tim were meant to be.

Somehow, she didn't think Destiny had gotten Birdie's memo on that subject.

****

"Hey! Did you hear? Angelique's back in town."

Tim stopped rubbing wax on the keel of his new boat and slanted a glance up to Jeff. "Where'd you hear that?"

"Maggie's. Sally couldn't wait to tell me." Jeff picked up a terry cloth, scraped it across the jar of wax Tim had open, and rubbed it onto the keel in circular motions.

"I bet."

"So have you seen her yet?"

"No." Maybe if he punched Jeff in the mouth he'd shut up and just keep on helping him spiff up the boat.

He'd probably be left polishing the keel alone, so punching Jeff's lights out wouldn't be his wisest choice.

"What are you going to do?"

"About what?"

Jeff snorted. "About Angelique. And don't try to tell me that you're not jumping out of your skin at the thought she's back in town."

"I don't know. Seeing me might just send her scrambling out of town again."

"Maybe." Jeff dipped his cloth into the wax and gathered some up. "It's also within the realm of possibility that she's back to talk to you."

"If that was the case, she'd have gotten in touch with me by now." Tim attacked the hull of the boat with another cloth full of wax.

"So, you're just going to give up."

"I don't see as I have a choice."

"There's always a choice. And here's a clue." Jeff grinned. "It involves groveling."

"Groveling?"

"A lot of groveling. But it's worth it in the end."

"Easy for you to say." Tim grunted.

Jeff stared at him for a minute without speaking. "I never took you for a coward."

Yellow was his new favorite color. "I guess you don't know me very well at all."

"Bullshit." Jeff's tone of voice was heartfelt. "I know you better than anybody else on this earth and I know when you're fronting."

Jeff's comment brought heat to the top of his head. "Then how didn't you know that I couldn't take pictures? That I was so fucking relieved that you didn't ask me to take your wedding photos."

Jeff cleared his throat. "I needed my best friend to be my best man, not my photographer. It had nothing to do with pictures of the wedding. It came down to our friendship, bro, photos be damned." He stood and fisted his hands by his sides. "You mean so much more to me than your ability to see through a camera lens to take an awesome picture of my lady love."

He suppressed a laugh. "Lady love. Who do you think you are? Who do you expect me to be? Sir freakin' Galahad?"

"Are you kidding me? Women love that kind of stuff. Why do you think those Scarlette LaFlamme books are so popular?"

"Scarlette La Who?" He'd never heard of her.

" I told you. She writes these historical romance

novels. Beth is just crazy about them." Jeff chuckled. "Sometimes I think I need to write that woman a thank you note."

"TMI, buddy. T. M. I."

"What do you have to lose by just going to her house and hanging out until she talks to you?"

"If she wants to talk to me, she knows where to find me."

Jeff shook his head. "Dude." He turned his back on Tim and started rubbing wax onto the boat hull again.

Tim rubbed the back of his hand across his chin. He tried to get back into working on the Melges again so he could clear his head, but thoughts of Angelique lingered on the edge of his mind.

Just like they always did. She was the ghost that was always with him, teasing him on the wind, driving him crazy.

Jeff had a point. He couldn't go on like this. He had to pull out all the stops to get her talking to him again.

He needed to get her back, plain and simple. Without her, his life meant nothing.

Less than nothing.

****

"Did you see this?" Birdie held a copy of People magazine out to Angelique.

Uh-oh. "No."

"Take it and turn to the section called 'Found on the Beach.'"

She took it with all the caution one might use when reaching for a rattlesnake. Feeling her stomach roll, she swallowed back the bile that threatened to choke her.

The paparazzi had found her.

The photos were not the best quality. A picture of her setting up food at Tim's book signing. A grainy, long distance pic of the two of them on the beach.

Tim was easily identifiable in some of the photos. Angelique, not so much. Her glasses covered a multitude of sins. But her name was attached to the pictures and that was enough to bring the reporters and the crowds.

She heard a loud buzzing in her ears. It took a second for her to realize that Birdie was talking to her. "What?"

"I'm gathering all the copies of the magazine as I can and putting them out with the rubbish. I'll alert Bobbie Darling as well, so she can take them off the shelves at Cliff Notes."

"You can do that?"

"Hmmmmpf. This is Lobster Cove. We take care of our own."

One of Lobster Cove's own. Tears clogged her throat. She swiped at her nose with the back of her hand. In the short time she'd lived there, she'd become part of the family, as it were. "Thank you."

"You're welcome." Birdie looked around then pulled a room key out of her pocket. "Now, I want you to go on up to room 208 and relax away from all the prying eyes."

"But my shift isn't over."

"We're not busy and you'll be no good to us, as upset as you are. In the meantime, I'll go to your house and get you some clothes, some of your things. Make me a list." She pressed the key into Angelique's hands.

"Thank you." She blinked back the moisture welling up in her eyes. At the moment, all she wanted to do was run away and hide under her bed."

****

Tim was nursing a beer and flipping channels looking for the Red Sox game when he heard a clamor of voices outside Angelique's house. Thinking it had to be her, he ran to his kitchen door, poked his head out, and looked both ways for paparazzi. Seeing none, he slipped out and over to Angelique's back porch.

He shaded his eyes as he peered in the sliding glass door, hoping to get her attention. If God loved him at all, Angelique would let him in.

Imagine his surprise when Birdie McCorkle slid open the door. "And what is it you're wanting?"

"I thought you were Angelique."

Birdie snorted, the sound inelegant. "Obviously. So sorry to disappoint you."

"How is she?"

"Come on in," Birdie said. "We don't want the vultures to catch wind of me talking to you."

He stepped through the door. Birdie shut it, locked it, and pulled the drapes across the glass. "Where's Angelique?"

"Impatient, are you?" She shook her head. "I'm not after telling you."

What the hell? "I've got to talk to her, Birdie. I've got to make her understand."

"I'm sure you do, but she's in a bad spot, some of it due to you, and unless she wants you to know where she is, I'm not going to tell you."

"Son of a bitch!" He kicked a nearby chair.

"Now, there'll be none of that."

He growled at her.

She chuckled. "I'm not scared of the likes of you,

lad. I've always liked you, and sure as the sun rises, you're one of Lobster Cove's own."

"Fat lot of good that's done me."

"'Tis true, you've had a rough time, none of it deserved. We're behind you, but right now Angelique needs us more. When she's ready, she'll get in touch with you."

"So I'm just supposed to wait."

Birdie smiled, but it was clear to Tim that her heart wasn't in it. "That's the long and short of it."

"Where is she now? Some place safe?"

"Aye, she's tucked away in a place tighter than a vault."

Tim resisted the urge to roll his eyes. Only middle school girls did that. "As long as she's safe. Can you give her a message for me?"

"You know I will."

He swallowed. Here he was, baring his soul to Birdie McCorkle, of all people. "Tell her I love her and I'll wait as long as it takes."

Birdie sniffed. "For whatever it's worth, me boyo, I'm as sure as I can be that she's in love with you, too. Wait for her. She's worth it."

Tim hung his head. "I know she is. I only wish I could be the man she deserves."

Birdie touched his shoulder. "I think you already are, Timothy. With God's good grace, you'll find your way back to each other." She sighed, her shoulders rising up to her ears like they were earrings. "I only had Mr. McCorkle for a short time in my life, but he was it, the only man for me. Now, it's not that another may not catch my eye these days, as I'm not dead, but I'll only give my heart and soul to Ian McCorkle." She made the sign of the cross. "May he rest in peace." She gave Tim the hairy eyeball. "He treated me like I was a queen made of spun sugar. Now you do the same with Angelique."

Tim swallowed. "I'll do my best, ma'am."

"Be sure that you do."

Chapter Forty-Three

Tim was in the middle of slapping a ham and cheese sandwich together when his phone erupted in his pocket. *Angelique!*

He fumbled with the phone. "Angelique! Where are you?"

"I'm at Birdie McCorkle's house." Her voice sounded thin.

His heart went zing! "I'll be right over."

"No! You can't."

"What? Why not? We need to talk." This made no sense.

"Yes, we do, but I can't risk being seen with you."

Huh? "I need to see you. To talk face to face and see for myself that you're all right."

"That's not going to happen." She sighed. "Have you seen People magazine?"

"Of course not. I don't pay any attention to that kind of stuff. What's that got to do with my seeing you?"

"The paparazzi have found you, and by extension, me. They've been taking pictures of you here, on the beach in Lobster Cove."

"Son of a bitch." A feeling of being watched settled over him.

"In some of the pictures you're with a mystery woman." She cleared her throat. "Me. If we're seen together, it's only a matter of time until they figure out I'm your mystery woman."

"I can protect you."

"No you can't." Her voice sounded sad and weary. "I can't be with you anymore."

"Yes you can!" If she wanted him to beg, he'd damn well beg. "I'll destroy every trace of every picture I've ever taken of you."

She sniffled like she was holding back tears. "It's not just about those pictures. I can probably forgive you for that. But I just can't take the chance that the paparazzi will find me. As long as my name is connected to yours, and they know where you are, I'm a target and it'll destroy me. I'm moving away, to some place no one can ever find me. I won't drag you down with me.

"Drag me down?" His heart thumped hard with each breath he took. "You can't drag me down."

She sniffled. "You can't even imagine the damage I can do."

"Please! Let me help you." Damn. He felt moisture well up in his eyes.

"No. Don't try to see me, call me, anything. I'm sorry."

He thought he heard her gasp as she ended the call.

Sliding down along the kitchen counter to sit on the floor, he rested his forehead against his knees and wept.

****

Angelique's vision blurred as she tried to read the directions on the box of hair dye she'd bought in Bar Harbor. She wouldn't be going to any Lobster Cove shops anymore.

She'd gone to Marge at Hair's the Thing after

business hours and had most of her long dark hair cut off. She now sported a short pixie with soft curls framing her face.

Well, as the commercial said, blondes have more fun. Now was her time to find out.

She had an appointment to see an eye doctor to get colored contact lenses in order to change her eye color. No one would ever be able to link Angie Doucette to Angelique Durand, as long as people kept their mouths shut and Katie Myers' Addington friends stayed where they belonged…in Addington.

She studied her reflection in the bathroom mirror, grimacing at how puffy her eyes were from crying. No more. She was done crying over Tim Baldwin. She'd meant what she said about being able to forgive him, eventually, for the secret photos, but more than that, it was just too dangerous for her to be around him.

It totally sucked large that she was in love with him. She didn't see herself getting over him any time soon. It would get better once she was able to move away from Lobster Cove and start over somewhere else.

She didn't want to start over somewhere else. Angelique loved Lobster Cove, which surprised the hell out of her. She'd made a place here. She belonged.

Sighing, she looked down at the box in her hand. Time to put Miss Clairol through her paces.

****

"Hey! T. L. Baldwin! Over here!"

Tim squinted against the sun only to see about five guys with cameras camped out in front of his beach steps. *Fuck.* He had to get rid of them before they found Angelique. "Go away! I have nothing to say to you!"

"Rumor has it you're dating Angelique Durand. Do you care to comment on that?"

"No. Go away before I call the police."

"It's a public beach," one of the paparazzi said.

He heard Chester growl from the patio door. Maybe he had a better solution than the cops to get rid of these clowns. "Okay. Have it your way."

He went to the door and grabbed Chester by the collar. The dog strained at his hold and punctuated his growling with some menacing woofs. His lips pulled up, revealing his dangerous Doberman teeth."

"Let me put it this way, gentlemen. You've got until the count of five to get out of here or I'll let my dog loose. We clear?"

"But—"

"One."

The idiots with the cameras got the message and scrambled away. Tim gave a quick thought to letting go of Chester, but decided against it. "S'okay, buddy. Good boy," he crooned to the dog until he felt Chester relax into a riff of low energy growls. "I think you earned a soup bone tonight."

Chester sat and his stump of a tail thumped along the deck. "Woof!"

"I couldn't have said it any better myself." He glanced over at Angelique's house hoping for a glimpse of her.

No such luck. But it was terribly clear that she was right. Being around him made her a paparazzi target. He'd have to figure out what to do about that, pronto.

Chapter Forty-Four

"Come on, Birdie. Tell me where she is." Tim faced down Birdie McCorkle in his quest to get some face time with Angelique.

"She feels strongly that being with you is dangerous for her." Birdie fisted her hands on her hips, clearly ready to do battle with him.

"I've got the paparazzi problem all taken care of. As long as Chester's around, they're not going to bother her."

Birdie sniffed and stared at him, making him feel like a disgusting, slimy specimen on a lab slide.

"Please."

"Oh, and it's lucky you are that I've a soft spot in my heart for you." She rolled her eyes. "I've got her making up the rooms these days, so those damn reporters can't find her." She smiled. "She's up on the third floor of the main house. Don't blink. You might miss her." She chuckled as she walked away.

Don't blink? What the hell did she mean by that?

He shook his head. Birdie McCorkle had one very strange sense of humor.

****

Angelique pushed dirty linens into a bag to haul down to the laundry. Her lower back ached in throbbing waves as she stood to stretch and massage it with her hands. As she rolled her shoulders backwards and forwards she heard footsteps coming down the hall. She bowed her head and willed herself to become as invisible as possible.

"Excuse me," the person said as he passed by her.

"Tim?" She spoke before she thought.

Tim stopped dead in his tracks. "Angelique?" His eyes widened and rounded. "What have you done to yourself?"

She ran a hand through her new short, blonde hair. "Like it?"

"It's different."

"I changed things up now that the paps are on the hunt."

He closed his eyes and shook his head then let it hang down. After a moment, he raised his eyes and stared at her. "I need to talk to you."

It was her turn to shake her head. "I've said all I have to say. Now, if you don't mind, I have work to do." She turned her back to him.

"I'm seeing a therapist."

She froze. "That's good."

"I haven't had any nightmares for a week now. And I'm not going to do dangerous things anymore."

She barely dared to breathe. "I'm glad. You've got a lot to offer the world. I'd be afraid to lose you."

"Would you? I mean, be afraid to lose me?"

Her hands began to tremble. "Yes," she whispered.

He put his hands on her upper arms. "Then be with me."

"I don't know if I can."

"You can. We can face anything as long as we're together."

"I still need time."

His hands dropped away. "Angelique."

"I mean it. If you love me like you say you do, you'll give me what I need."

"How much time?" Impatience flared in his gaze.

"I don't know! Just a little while longer."

"You can't make me wait around forever. I'm not like one of your old boyfriends that you can just keep on a string until it's convenient for you."

The sudden stab of pain made her gasp. She wrenched away from him. "Is that what you think?" she demanded as she faced him.

His mouth softened. "No. I don't think that. I shouldn't have said it."

"No, you shouldn't have. Are you going to bring that up every time we have a disagreement?" She felt like she could shoot fire out of her fingertips.

His shoulders slumped. "No. I don't even know why I said it this time. I'm sorry."

"I think you need to go. I've got work to do."

"Okay, but I'm not giving up. We belong together, Angelique."

"Please go." She refused to cry.

She didn't turn around until she was sure he'd left.

****

"Did our Timothy catch up with you?" Birdie walked into the Sea Crest Inn's laundry room where Angelique was folding and stacking towels.

"Yes." She really didn't want to talk about Tim.

"So, are you going to give him a second chance?"

Angelique hugged a towel to her chest. "I don't know. It all feels so complicated. I should just pick up and go somewhere else to live."

"Don't you dare!" Birdie gasped. "You belong

here!"

Her head felt too heavy on her neck. "I don't want to leave, but everyone knows who I am now. I'll have no privacy at all."

"Things will die down after a bit and they'll find someone new to focus on. You'll have all the privacy you want. With Tim."

Angelique shook her head. "There's no more me and Tim."

Birdie stared at her. Angelique tried not to flinch.

"I had one great love in my life," Birdie finally said. "Ian McCorkle. He was a fisherman, but so full of grand plans, he was. 'Birdie, me girl,' he'd tell me, 'one day we're goin' back to County Clare, you dressed in the finest silks and shiniest jewels, and everyone will know our ship came in.'" She sighed. "My Ian could spin a tale longer than the day. I loved him with all my heart and soul. Now mind you, me parents didn't want us to marry so young and to move so far away, but we didn't hear anything else but what we wanted and dreamed about."

"Oh, Birdie." Angelique's heart had just ripped in two jagged pieces.

"Don't you dare pity me, Angie. I lived more in the time I had with my Ian than most people get for a lifetime. I thought I died when he did."

"If you don't mind me asking—"

"The boat he worked on went out in a gale that turned fierce, hurricane fierce, in a matter of an hour. They floundered and crashed against the cliffs. All that was left was debris until the bodies washed up." Birdie swallowed but remained dry eyed. "They'd been in the sea for several days, so identifying them was a difficult matter. We were able to tell my Ian by his watch. It was still ticking."

"I'm so sorry." Since Birdie wasn't teary, Angelique didn't dare let a single drop fall. "I just need some time."

"So here's me best advice. Don't waste a second. When a man looks at you like Tim Baldwin does, you pay attention. Don't throw love away with both hands. Give him another chance, Angie. He deserves it." Birdie patted her on the cheek. "You deserve it."

"Do I? I've not been the nicest person in the world."

"You couldn't prove that by me. Besides, it seems Lobster Cove is a place where people come and find true love. Don't fight it. True love is a wonderful thing. As is forgiveness."

A wave of love washed over her for this woman, who had horrible hair and not one single lick of style. She put her arms around Birdie's neck, squeezed her eyes shut, and hugged her tight.

She finally had a best friend.

Chapter Forty-Five

"Oh, Chester looks just bee-yoo-tee-ful, Uncle Tim!" Cookie clapped her hands and jumped up and down like a fist full of Mexican jumping beans.

At Cookie's suggestion, they'd put one of her many tutus, the rainbow one bedazzled with sequin butterflies, on Chester for his costume. Topped with a sparkly tiara that had lights that blinked on and off and played Happy Birthday to You whenever you pushed a button on the crown, which they'd Macgyvered to stay on the Doberman's head, the dog looked flat out ridiculous but resigned to his fate.

"He looks very festive," Tim said.

"He looks stupid," Danny said. "I still think we should have dressed him up as Mega-Mole." Mega-Mole was a character in Danny's favorite comic book series, The Adventures of The Refractor.

"He does not look stupid!" Cookie vehemently stomped her little sandal clad foot. "Don't listen to him, Chester. You look pretty."

"Yeah. Pretty stupid."

Tim's temples started to throb.

"That's enough out of you, Danny." Beth sent her son one of the hairiest eyeballs Tim had ever seen. Danny grinned while he made a zipping motion across his lips.

The kid was a pistol. Tim loved that about him.

Cookie was clouding up, a Nor'easter about to blow in. "Chester looks awesome, Cookie girl. No other dog will look as good."

She stuck her tongue out at her brother. The pair of them were priceless. Chester did the doggie version of rolling his eyes.

Other pet owners gathered on the expansive lawn in front of the Yacht Club. Keen Quinn dragged his German Shepherd Guda, dressed as a policeman, over to the staging area. Eve Darling led her Bichon Frisé, Cupid, as the angel winged god of love.

Tim shook his head. Where did people come up with this stuff? He looked down at Chester who was patiently letting Cookie fluff up his tutu. He guessed he shouldn't talk.

Alice Dalton carried around a huge Maine coon cat dressed up in a dog suit.

Yikes.

"Hey, Tim." He turned around to see Tracy Novak and her pup, who wore a brown doggie sweater with darker brown spots on it. Around his neck she'd put a collar that looked like a chocolate chip cookie with a big bite taken out of it.

"Nice costume," he said.

Tracy grinned. "My Cookie's dressed like a cookie."

Danny's ears perked up. "Your dog's name is Cookie?"

"Sure is." Tracy knelt beside the dog and adjusted his collar.

Danny cracked up and pointed at his sister. "You're named after a dog!"

"I am not!" she screeched. "They call me Cookie

because I'm cute and sweet!"

Danny only laughed some more and barked at her.

Beth closed her eyes and counted to ten. "That's enough, Danny. Come on. Let's go get some ice cream." She dragged the two kids away.

Tracy stood and frowned. "Oh dear. I hope I didn't cause too much trouble."

Tim scratched Chester behind his tiara. "Danny looks for ways to cause trouble for Cookie. It's his solemn duty as an older brother."

She laughed and patted him on the arm, maybe a little bit longer than was just between acquaintances. "I'm sure you're right."

"I hope I'm not interrupting anything." A very cool, Southern-flavored voice came from a few feet away.

Angelique stood there all cool and calm, hands clasped in front of her, a serene smile on her face. Her eyes hid behind dark glasses.

Interesting. Very interesting.

He didn't think he'd ever get used to the short blonde hair and the perennial dark glasses.

Tracy looked from Angelique to Tim then back again. "I'm going to take Cookie here over to the parade stage. I'll see you there. Hi, Angelique."

"Hi," Angelique said back, her voice dripping ice chunks. Dare he dream?

She was jealous. Jealous of him and Tracy.

It was either a dream come true or wishful thinking.

He picked dream come true, being the optimist he usually was not.

Angelique straightened her shoulders and turned up

the wattage on a bitterly tight smile. "Friend of yours?"

He fought the urge to do his happy dance.

Well, if he had a happy dance, that is.

"Yeah, I've been friends with Tracy for a while." He scratched his temple. "Actually, we go way back. She's a hometown girl and we hung out when I'd come up here for the summer."

Angelique sniffed, much like a semi-mollified queen would. Chester whimpered and she looked down at him. "Oh, you poor baby! Mean daddy dressed you up like this."

"Mean daddy?" Tim scoffed. "I beg to differ. Chester loves his costume. Cookie made it for him."

Chester's body language said otherwise, but Tim ignored him.

"Well, if Cookie made your costume, you good boy, you best boy," Angelique crooned to Chester, "then you need to go for it, baby."

Chester woofed.

"Angelique! There you are!" Betts Quinn bustled up to them. "Helen Troy had to drop out of judging the dog costume parade and I need you to take her place."

Tim wanted to scream in frustration. He had Angelique here, with him, talking to him, maybe jealous of him, all good things as far as he was concerned. He took his Wayfarer shades out of his shirt pocket and shoved them onto his face.

"Me? I don't know nothing 'bout judging no dog parade," Angelique said.

"It's easy. Just come with me." Betts grabbed Angelique's arm and dragged her away.

Tim watched the two stumble up to the Yacht Club patio and frowned. He hoped this was a good sign.

Chester chuffed out a little bark. "I hear you, buddy. We've got a parade to join."

****

Angelique allowed Betts Quinn to drag her across the lawn to the Yacht Club veranda. The lawn was soft from an earlier rain, and her three-inch heels sank like spikes into the dirt, causing her to stumble along behind Betts.

She gritted her teeth. Those Jimmy Choos were her new favorites.

"Now here is the judging criteria. It's not rocket science." Betts smiled and handed her a clipboard. "All the dogs will get a prize, but you just have to work here with Dylan to decide which dogs get what prize." She turned to Angelique and pointed her in the direction of Lobster Cove's veterinarian, Ms. Dylan Foster and the owner of April's Animal Rescue, April Showers.

Apparently, April's parents had quite the sense of humor.

Betts looked around the grounds with a self-satisfied little smile. "It looks like all those press kits we sent out and the ads we ran in the papers besides the Anchor did some good! Hopefully we'll get a lot of donations because of it." She gave a general wave in the direction of all the media types milling around.

Angelique shivered and turned away from the crowd. People were here for the dogs, right? They wouldn't think to find her at an event like this.

Dylan gave Angelique a little wave. "I'm taking care of the health/appearance thing. You're judging the cuteness/creativity factor."

Angelique looked over to the lineup of dogs. There was just too much adorableness. In particular, a small dog dressed up as Tinkerbell leaped up and down and yipped like it was his job, although people were going to need earplugs if he kept it up. Those yips were on steroids.

And was that a cat? In a dog show? The cat dressed in a dog suit was bigger than the little yipper. "Um, is that a cat?"

Dylan glanced over. "Yep! That's Alice Dalton's Maine Coon Cat, Buster."

Buster? The cat's name should be Bad Ass. He looked like he could gobble up Tinkerbell in two big bites.

Angelique had a flashback to Dr. Suess' *Go Dog Go*, like she was on the top of a tree at a big dog party. If she'd been wearing a hat, she would have asked Dylan if she liked it.

As she watched, Tim and Chester took their places behind Buster and in front of Tinkerbell, who immediately commenced dancing. His yips had turned into screeches, much to Chester and Buster's dismay.

Between the Doberman and the Maine Coon Cat, the cat was the bigger threat to Tinkerbell.

Go figure.

Oh and lookee there. Nurse Tracy and her dog Cookie, cutting in front of the miniature pinscher so she could stand next to Tim and Chester.

Where was a damn gator when you needed one?

And oh wasn't Nurse Tracy oh so cute? Smiling, laughing at everything Tim had to say, touching his arm, petting his dog—

There was just so much hate and so little time.

Although, Tim didn't look like he objected too much to Tracy's attentions.

He'd lost some weight. He really looked tired; he must be having nightmares again.

Maybe she'd waited too long to listen to him. Maybe he'd gotten tired of waiting.

He told her he still loved her and wanted her back, but could she trust that? Nurse Tracy looked like a solid Plan B. She guessed that she'd find out after the dog show.

Angelique took a deep breath and rubbed a hand over her heart. She had to move forward no matter what.

"Are you all set to check out the dogs?" Dylan smiled at her.

And right now that meant peeking at the pooches.

"You bet."

****

Tim desperately wished for a set of earplugs. Tinkerbell wouldn't stop jumping and barking and was managing to make all the other dogs crazy. Chester, usually so obedient, was having trouble keeping still.

If God was good, the parade and competition would be over soon.

Like yesterday.

Then there was Tracy, sporting her Chatty Cathy side. He'd never had very much to do with her. He barely ever saw her as she worked in the Lobster Cove Emergency Room and he had yet to go there. He'd seen her around, sure, especially back in the high school days when she'd hung out with Julia Stewart, now the high school principal, and their friend Edie. He'd remembered a quiet, serious person. Shy, even.

Boy, was he wrong.

In between "umm-hmmming" absently to things

Tracy babbled on about, he snuck glances at Angelique. She was very studiously ignoring him. At least he thought she was.

He hoped she was.

Color him pitiful.

Actually, please, God, color him invisible, which he'd absolutely embrace right now, to get his ears some relief from both Tracy and Tinkerbell.

Betts Quinn wandered up to the microphone. "Ladies and gentlemen, it's time for the dog parade! Thanks to each and every dog owner for taking part in this special part of our afternoon." She beamed. "The fur babies look adorable! Let's bring them up to the stage!" Stepping away from the microphone, she motioned for the first dog to move forward.

A pit bull dressed like a pirate. A poodle dressed like a leprechaun. A dachshund dressed as Darth Vader.

A couple of teens with three dogs as the Three Stooges, aka: Larry, Moe, and Curley.

Heh. A beagle dressed up as a World War One flying ace. Obvious, but cute.

Speaking of cute, Angelique looked wicked cute up there smiling at the dogs and clapping when they did tricks.

He loved her so much. He adored her and come hell or high water, he'd convince her to forgive him and marry him.

Maybe his brand spankin' new therapist was right. Maybe he did deserve a second chance at life and to grab with both hands all the love that came his way. He'd finally broken down and talked to a professional. He hated to admit that it might be helping.

So, speaking of maybe, maybe he should just take a

big ass chance and ask her to marry him right then and there when he and Chester got onto the stage.

After he groveled first, of course. Jeff had assured him that the groveling was the key to success. If it helped him to win back Angelique, he'd be the best groveler who ever groveled.

And standing in line with a Doberman dressed in a battery-operated tiara, a rabid miniature pinscher, and a flirting challenged woman dragging around a dog in a chocolate chip cookie suit counted as groveling in Tim's book.

He felt two doggie arms wrap themselves around his leg. Looking down, he groaned.

He did not need a miniature pinscher humping his leg. Shaking it, he managed to knock the demon dog loose.

"Sorry," the woman with Tinkerbell told him. "He's a little exciteable."

Ya think? "It's okay." He shrugged. "There's lots to be excited about today."

The woman beamed. "Yes there is! And little Jackson here just loves to dress up and get all the attention." She picked little Jackson up and crooned in a baby voice, "Aren't you a good boy, puppy? Aren't you just the best boy?"

Jackson looked Tim right in the eyes and growled at him. Obviously, it had been love at first sight for Jackson and Tim's leg and the little monster took exception to Tim's less than enthusiastic reaction.

Putting up with that dog definitely counted as major league groveling, to Tim's way of thinking.

Cookie, the girl, came running up to him, her face smeared with cranberry-blueberry ice cream. "Uncle

Tim! Don't forget to press the button on Chester's tiara so the lights come on and the song plays!"

"Why don't you stick around and help me?" He had no idea where the button was, other than it was on the tiara.

"Okey doke!" She scratched Chester behind his ears. "I'm gonna make sure you win, boy!"

"Oh, isn't she just adorable!" Tracy cooed at Cookie. "Aren't you cute?"

Cookie nodded but her face was filled with suspicion. "Yes, I am." Obviously loyal to Angelique, she sniffed and looked away, dismissing Tracy and her dog with a haughty glance. In that moment, she looked remarkably like her mother Katie, Entitled Queen of All She Surveyed.

For once, that was a good thing.

Looking out over the grounds, Tim noticed a small cadre of photographers wandering around taking pictures. Most of them were local media, no big deal, but he thought he recognized a couple of guys from Portland, Manchester, and worst of all, *The Boston Globe*.

He squinted. Were there some guys from *People*? Hadn't they done enough damage?

His protective instinct kicked in with a vengeance. He'd make sure they didn't bother Angelique.

"Can I hold Chester's leash, Uncle Tim?"

"Sure." He handed it to her without a second thought. The first thing she did was push the button on Chester's tiara so it blinked and jangled Happy Birthday.

Kill him now.

He heard Angelique laugh and turned in time to see

her toss her head back. He remembered the dark silken curls of her hair spilled down her back. He remembered wrapping his hands in the glossy fall of hair, so soft and smelling of roses and exotic spices. He missed it, though her blonde pixie look was cute, but as far as he was concerned, very temporary.

Very, very temporary.

He had to get her back. Living the rest of his life without her was not an option. She was the best thing that had ever happened to him.

He looked down at his ballerina dog who was patiently enduring Cookie's endless chatter and primping. It occurred to him that a body could put up with a lot when it came to true love.

****

Angelique's stomach jumped as Tim, with Chester and Cookie in tow, inched closer. She'd never gotten the warm fuzzies around children, but Cookie had wrapped herself all around Angelique's heart, something she never expected. And seeing Tim with the little girl stirred up all kinds of estrogen-fueled fantasies.

Her fingers twitched with the urge to rub her abdomen, right where she'd hold and nurture Tim's baby.

Then she shook her head. What the hell was wrong with her?

He might not want to get back together with her. He may have already moved on. Maybe he'd realized he didn't really love her, that he just loved the idea of her.

That he only loved the fact that he could take pictures of her.

If he felt that way then she was better off without him, *bien sûr*. Her throat clogged with misery.

The woman with the cat in a dog suit dragged her beast behind her. The cat yowled and hissed, the sound ungodly. Angelique didn't know much about animals but she did know that cats did not do well on leashes. Or dressed up in costumes. No way was she getting near that.

A small dog who looked like a Doberman who'd been shrunk and dressed like Tinkerbell screeched, pulled out of his owner's grasp, and made a break for it while still attached to his harness. He bee-lined it to the cat and shoved his nose up her butt. Buster the cat shrieked and hissed, leaped up, fur raised, claws out, and landed directly onto Cookie the dog's back.

Cookie took exception and attacked the cat, knocking the cat's mommy out of the way and barreling into Angelique, pushing her down on her hiney.

Angelique threw her hands over her head to protect herself from various claws and teeth. The idiot deejay decided to start the music early with a rousing rendition of "Who Let the Dogs Out".

Might as well add insult to injury, right?

No, wrong. Oh so very made of wrong.

She struggled up onto her elbows only to get pushed backwards by an over-enthusiastic Chester who dragged Cookie the girl behind him, as she seemed to be the one at the other end of the leash.

Screaming her little lungs out.

Chester drooled on Angelique's face as he barked his Dobie-sized bark in her ear. He blew hot, gross, doggy breath as he gave her slurpy doggy kisses. His big muddy paws pushed on her shoulders, tearing the lace inlays on her new ivory silk cami.

Damn. She'd saved a month for that.

One minute she was pinned by 110 pounds of enthusiastic dog, the next Tim had grabbed the dog by the collar and tried to haul him off her.

"Are you okay?" he yelled, clenching his teeth with the effort to lift Chester with one hand and corral Cookie with the other.

"Hey! That's Angelique Durand!" Photographers rushed over to the stage, camera poised to shoot.

"Fuck that." Tim snarled and let both Chester and Cookie go. Fortunately, Jeff had gotten into the breach and grabbed his screaming child.

Chester, giddy with his newfound freedom, raced away as fast as he could, probably on the tail of that hapless cat.

Tim jumped off the stage, fists flying. "You asshole!" He pushed the guy and knocked him back a couple of steps then grabbed the camera and threw it to the ground.

The rest of the media swarmed around like sharks in a feeding frenzy.

Angelique, freed from Chester, struggled to her feet. Breathless, she took a step and broke the stiletto heel off her shoe and twisted her ankle. "Ow!"

Tim turned back to her. "Are you okay?"

Tears sprang to her eyes, but she nodded gamely.

He bounded up onto the platform, scooped her up in his arms like she was Scarlett O'Hara and he was Rhett Butler. "Let's get out of here."

He didn't have to tell her twice.

Chapter Forty-Six

"Damn, they disappeared! Where would they go?" A photographer looked around, his head practically spinning like Linda Blair's.

Betts Quinn eyed him coolly. "I hear tell that Angie works at the Sea Crest Inn. They might have run there."

The guy from *The Boston Globe* pulled out his smart phone and thumbed over the keyboard. "Sea Crest Inn?" He grinned. "Got it."

He ran across the lawn to the parking lot, the rest of his brethren following close on his heels.

Betts pulled her own cellphone out and tapped in a number. "Hello? Birdie? It's me. A bunch of paparazzi are on their way to the Inn to find Angie and Tim."

She listened. "Yes, I know they're not there. Here's what I want you to do. Send those damn reporters to someplace else Angie and Tim aren't. Make it someplace else they probably won't find them. Got it?" She smiled as she listened. "Excellent."

Betts clicked off her phone and put it back in her pocket.

"You're an evil woman, you know that, right?" Dylan grinned. "I always liked that about you."

Betts nodded. "It's a dirty job but somebody has to do it."

****

"Excuse me, young man, but I'm going to have to ask you to leave right away, or else I'll have to call the Garda." Birdie McCorkle stood on the veranda in front of the Sea Crest Inn, a formidable sentinel with her arms crossed underneath her impressive breasts. "You're disturbing our guests."

"We're looking for Angelique Durand and T.L. Baldwin and we got a tip that they're here."

Birdie frowned and turned her accent up to eleven. "It's too late that you are. You just missed them. I thought I heard them say they were headed to Mariner's Fish Fry."

"Where's that?"

"Go back to Main Street and take a right at the long narrow road to the harbor. You can't miss it."

"Thanks, lady."

Birdie waited until they were out of hearing distance then jogged back into the lobby, to the front desk. She pulled the landline phone's receiver. "Hallo, Katelyn? It's Birdie McCorkle. Here's what I need you to do."

****

"Who are you looking for?" Katelyn Sullivan furrowed her brow, looking for all the world like she was scouring her brain for a memory. "I don't know any Angelique Durand."

"Short blonde hair, scar on her cheek," a photographer said.

"Scar? Oh, you must mean Angie Doucette. She and Tim were here but they didn't stay long. They told me they wanted to check out something at the Venus Gallery."

"Venus Gallery? Where's that?"

307

"Sounds like a sex club," one of the other photographers said, looking hopeful.

Katelyn shook her head. "Oh no, it's an art gallery on Maple Ave. They're open longer today than usual because of a new exhibit being installed."

The photographers left in a clump, all of them trying to get through the door at the same time. Katelyn laughed and picked up the phone. "Abigail, it's Katelyn Sullivan from Mariner's. A bunch of paparazzi are on their way to the Gallery, looking for Angie and Tim Baldwin." She rolled her eyes while she listened. "I know they're not there. I want you to send them somewhere else they're not going to be." She grinned. "That's right. I knew we could count on you."

****

"Look mister, we've been to the Sea Crest Inn, Mariner's Fish Fry, the Venus Gallery, Murphy's Bar, and the Sang Freud Coffee House, where some waitress named Melanie told us to come here. Are Angelique Durand and T. L. Baldwin here?"

Sal, owner of Sal's Pizza, which was part of the local bowling alley Lobster Lanes, stroked his chin as he thought. "Could still be here. Or maybe they went on out to The Red Club, right on the outskirts of town on Second Street. You're welcome to stay and look around, in case they're still here."

"The Red Club."

"Oh yeah. Real friendly place. They ought to make you feel right at home."

Sal and the customer he was serving watched the motley crew stroll out of the bowling alley. "Sal, you realize that you sent them—"

"To a BDSM club? Ayuh, I did." He rapped his

knuckles against the counter. "Oughtta keep 'em busy."

****

"I'm sorry. I've signed confidentiality agreements with my guests. I can't tell you who's here and who isn't." Jessie Michaels, owner of the Red Club said.

"What is this? Some kind of secret society or something?"

Another photographer, who'd already figured out the lay of the land said, "Or something."

"I'm going to need you to leave right now," Jessie said in tones that meant she was way beyond serious.

"We won't take pictures inside, I promise."

"I don't believe you and you won't get inside no way, no how." Jessie raised her eyebrows. "Please go away and leave my guests in peace."

"Is something wrong, Jessie?" Caleb Drake, dressed in the leather uniform of his Dungeon Master position came out to stand next to Jessie. Without a shirt, he looked mad, bad, and dangerous to know.

Was probably all that leather covering the rest of his body.

Maybe the whip he held in his right hand. He looked like he knew how to use it.

"Nothing I can't handle." Jessie tossed her hair over her shoulder. "You need to leave before I call the police," she told the assembled crowd.

"You heard the lady," Caleb growled. "Get out of here."

The paparazzi, grumbling mightily, moved back the pre-requisite number of feet away from the Red Club.

"I think they're in there," one pap said to another one.

"Oh yeah. Me too. Imagine the bucks we can get for pictures of Angelique Durand leaving a bondage club."

The boys settled in for the night, visions of dollar signs dancing in their heads.

Chapter Forty-Seven

"Where are we going?" Angelique limped alongside Tim. She'd taken off her shoes after he'd deposited her in his car.

"Here." Tim stopped. "No one will think to look for us here."

She looked around. "This is a cemetery."

"That is correct. This is the Lobster Cove cemetery." He grinned at her. "The best place we can hide."

Sun washed down over the well-manicured grass plots, the pristine white marble grave markers decorated with rafts of summer flowers and tiny American flags that fluttered wildly in the sea breeze.

"It's morbid," she murmured, her Cajun superstition and fear of the spooky kicking into high gear.

"It's private." He opened the huge metal gate and ushered her in, then closed the gate behind them. "And it's broad daylight. No one will even think to look for us here."

Her skin started to itch. "I suppose it could be."

"What? Are you afraid of ghosts?"

"No," she lied.

"Don't be scared, Sparky. I've got a particle accelerator in my pocket, and I know how to use it."

She slanted her eyes. "I've heard it called all kinds

311

of things before, but never that."

"Hey, baby, don't you know? I got me a veritable proton pack."

"Of course you do." Sighing, she stopped in her tracks. "Really. Why are we here?"

"I wanted to get you where we won't be interrupted, and where you can't run away from me so easy." He reached out and pushed a lock of her hair off her face. "You've got to hear me out."

Her ears buzzed. She didn't exactly expect to have this conversation in the Lobster Cove cemetery. She bit her lower lip. Any glossy shine of color that had been there earlier in the day she'd already chewed off, and she felt at a loss.

No lipstick, no control. Sizzling red lipstick was only one weapon in her arsenal, but it was a damn good one.

He was right, though. They did have a lot to talk about. "Go ahead."

He took a deep breath. "What I did to you was selfish. And you were right. At first, when I didn't know you, it was all about getting my ability to take pictures back, the ability to get that just-perfect shot. But the more I got to know you?" He shook his head as he took her hands. "I saw the beautiful woman, both inside and out. You let me in and let me see your vulnerability. Your sweetness. Your strength." He looked at the ground. "You're a very strong woman, Angelique. Don't let anyone tell you that you aren't." He brought her hands up to his mouth and brushed his lips across her knuckles.

Oh, he was saying all the right things, all the things she'd dreamed he'd say. She wanted to trust him.

She had, however, believed pretty words and trusted the wrong people in the past. "You had to know how horrible those pictures would make me feel."

He hung his head. "I admit that at first, taking those candids of you were all about the rush of having my power back. I rationalized it by telling myself I could bring you around to my point of view."

Ouch. Yet she'd asked for honesty. "At the expense of my power."

"And I truly hate that I did that to you. I should have been up front and asked if you'd pose for me."

She shook her head. "I wouldn't have."

"Yeah, I figured that. I should have tried to talk you into it, trust my Iraq work to convince you how I saw you. That I wouldn't exploit you."

"But you didn't."

He nodded. "But I didn't. And I'm so sorry." He looked out to sea. "Like I told you, I'm going to a counselor, for, you know. The PTSD. I've been a couple of times."

"That's good." She licked her lips. "I'm glad."

"I'm doing it for you."

Alarm skittered up her spine. "Oh, Tim. Don't do it for me. Do it for you."

His smile was rueful. "My therapist says the same thing. But here's the other thing. You deserve a whole man, a man who can give you the best life possible. The man who can make all your dreams come true, without you worrying if he's going to fall apart every time a car engine backfires."

Tears swam in her eyes. "Tim, I—"

"I can be that man for you."

She shook her head. "I want you to beat your

313

demons for you, not for me. Lord knows, I'm not totally together. I'm damaged, just like you."

"I need you. You have no idea how much. I haven't been able to eat, sleep, anything without you. If you forgive me and stay with me, I will move heaven and earth to make it up to you, to make you happy. Please tell me it's not too late."

Was it too late? Were they too far gone for each other?

How could she possibly know?

****

She'd been silent for too long. It couldn't mean anything good.

"There's another reason to bring you here," he said, desperation riding him hard. He let go of one hand and pulled her by the other. Dragging her from one family plot to another, he finally stopped in front of one with a stone border around the large plot with the name Sinclair styled on all the gravestones enclosed within. Some of the stones were old and well-aged by the weather. "Here." He stepped over the stone border and pulled her in with him, then pointed. "Look there. There's Rab and Lisbeth Sinclair. Rab was the town blacksmith and loved Lisbeth from afar for practically all his life."

He looked at Angelique and willed her to understand. "She finally understood and reciprocated his love and here they are. Together for eternity." He spread his arms. "An actual monument to their love and the life they made with each other."

"What? How do you know this?"

"Local legend. Everyone around here grows up knowing the story of Rab and Lisbeth Sinclair."

He had to make her see. "Just look around and you'll find others just like them. Honest men and women who took a chance on each other and their happily ever afters."

She turned her head this way and that, clearly lost.

"How about this? I'm pretty sure we've lost the reporters. How about I take you to the beach where I first fell in love with you?"

She took a couple of deep breaths then looked at him. "You know the place? The exact moment?"

"Yeah, I do."

She wouldn't meet his eyes.

Damn.

As he led her out of the cemetery he tried not to think about how even though he'd spoken of love, of his sincere devotion to her, she had not uttered one word of love for him.

She was listening to him. He assured himself that was the important thing.

Chapter Forty-Eight

"Looks like they haven't set up camp here yet," Tim said as he pulled into his driveway, turned off the ignition, and pulled up the hand brake.

Angelique breathed a sigh of relief and nodded. "*Merci au bon Dieu* for small favors."

They'd taken a side trip to Jeff's place to fetch Chester. Fortunately, Jeff had managed to grab the dog and take him home while she and Tim hid away from the paparazzi. Beth also had the foresight to pick up Angelique's bag.

"Come in with me?" Tim unlatched his seat belt.

"Yes." Her heart beat a little bit faster.

He carried her to his front door since she still didn't have any shoes on. After setting her down to open the door, he picked her up again and carried her inside. "Let's go to the beach."

She nodded. He took her to the beach and set her down on the cool sand.

"I'd seen you before, during Jeff and Beth's wedding reception at the Yacht Club. You were walking on the beach. I thought you were an angel sent to tempt me with your hair tangling in the breeze, with the amazingness of your body." He reached out and tucked an errant blonde curl behind her ear. "Then I got home and you were here, right next door. I didn't think. I just started taking pictures. I never intended to do it more than the once, but I couldn't stop. I know it was wrong," he shook his head, "so wrong, but you gave me back something more essential to me than breathing. Please forgive me."

Angelique searched his face trying to see the truth. She wanted to believe, she wanted to forgive and fall into his arms. But there was one more thing she had to see. "Can I see the pictures?"

"Are you sure you want to see them?"

"Yes."

"Okay. I'll bring them down."

She sat and stared out at the foaming waves while she waited for Tim to come back. The bubbling surf imitated the churning going on in her stomach.

She continued to sit on his beach stairs.

He told her the pictures he'd taken were beautiful. That he saw something she didn't see.

How she hoped he was right.

He dropped and sat on the steps next to her. "Here. If you don't like them, I'll burn them and destroy every trace they ever existed. I'll never take another photograph in my life."

Her hands trembled as she took the book.

"Do you want me to open it for you?"

"No." She shook her head. This, she had to do for herself. She lifted the cover.

And didn't believe what she saw.

Yes, the pictures were of her, but only because she remembered the events he'd caught. The woman was someone she had never met.

That woman smiled freely, laughed without reservation, danced with abandon along the waves. She twirled and spun. She knelt beside a child and watched a crab or some such on a sand bar at low tide.

None of the pictures showed a damaged woman with a scar. They showed a woman with a lot of life to give and to live.

They showed the love the man held for the woman he was taking the pictures of.

Tears welled in her eyes as she turned to look at him. "I don't know who this person is."

He smiled a smile so gentle and with so much love. "She's you. The woman I love. The woman I respect. The woman I can't live without."

"I will disappoint you. I always disappoint people in the end."

"You will never disappoint me." He stood and helped her up. "You can't."

He swung her into his arms, carried her inside, and up the stairs to his bedroom, where he laid her on his bed like she was made of spun sugar and twice as sweet and fragile. "I love you."

"I love you." Oh, her heart was so full it broke in two to hold all the love she had for him.

They made love, all soft kisses and gentle touches, poignant and full of promises. Every whisper, every caress was a benediction. Then, in the aftermath, they fell asleep wrapped in each other's arms, bones melted together in peaceful, sated happiness.

****

Angelique awoke to the sound of her phone blowing up. She leaned over the side of the bed feeling around for her purse. Fumbling, she located it and slid her cell on.

"Angelique! Finally! What's going on there?" Lucien demanded.

"Um," She shook her head. She was still sleepy and in a love coma. "You woke me up."

"I bet. Go online and check out TMZ then call me back. Immediately." *Plbbbbt*, he was gone.

She frowned.

"What is it?" Tim's voice was lower and gruffer than usual due to the early hour.

"Lucien called. He wants me to go online and check out TMZ."

"Let me get my laptop."

He did and they fired it up.

"Oh. My. God." Angelique pressed her fingers against her mouth. "All those scumballs are camped outside the Red Club waiting for us to come out."

"No wonder Lucien got a little bit bent." Tim chuckled.

She swatted his arm.

"Ow!"

"This isn't funny! It isn't funny at all!" She all but cried it.

"I've got an idea. We're going to give those bottom feeders a story they won't forget." He hopped out of bed. "Call your brother; tell him we've got everything under control. In fact, tell him to stay tuned to the live feed." He squinted at her. "You do still trust me to take care of you?"

"From Lucien?" Angelique knew better. "I imagine he's already on his way here to rescue me from whips and chains in a dungeon."

"Just call him and tell him to stay put. I've got it all under control."

She sighed. "I hope you know what you're doing."

"Oh yeah," he assured her. "Just trust me."

"Well, from your mouth to God's ears."

"You just watch me, Sparky. Just watch me."

****

Angelique recognized the road out of town heading to the Red Club. Really, who knew that the small, roll-up-the-sidewalks-at-nine-o'clock Lobster Cove would have such a thing.

Not that she was a prude. There was a BDSM club on every corner in New Orleans. She might have even gone to one a time or two, not that she'd ever admit, publically, to it.

A girl had to have a few secrets, right?

Tim pulled his Mercedes up to a curb about two blocks away from the club. "Let's walk."

"Walk?"

"Yeah, you know that thing you do when you put one foot in front of the other in order to get from place to place?"

"Don't be an idiot."

"Can't help it. It's my parents' cross to bear." He chuckled and made her ache to kick him in the shins. "I want them to see us coming from a place that is not the club. A place where we couldn't have snuck out the back door or in the laundry bins, whatever. They're going to see we were never there. Here's the thing." He looked a little unsure of himself. "I do want you on board with this."

"Ooooo-kay." She really didn't like the sound of this.

"It's going to mean facing the press. They're going to take our picture."

"They are?"

"I'm counting on it." He practically rubbed his

hands in glee. "As long as you're okay with it. It'll be good, I promise. Do you trust me?"

She remembered his pictures of her. "I trust you."

He laughed. "Then stick with me, Sparky."

"Why do they think we're hiding out in there? Like I've got nothing against the Red Club, but why do they think we're there?"

"I've got my theory about that, too." He grabbed her hand. "C'mon."

Well, it wasn't like he was giving her a choice about it.

He slowed their pace down to a stroll as they reached the phalanx of photographers. "Looking for someone? Or maybe two someones?" he called out.

Just like in a cartoon, all heads turned with an audible snap to look at them. It took the sharks a beat, but they recovered fast and started shooting.

She noticed several townspeople on the edges of the crowd: Betts Quinn and Birdie McCorkle from The Sea Crest Inn, Katelyn Sullivan from Mariner's Fish Fry, the ladies from the Venus Gallery, David Hu from Murphy's Bar, Melanie Owens from Sang Freud, and Sal from Lobster Lanes. Last, but not least, Jessie Michaels and Caleb Drake stepped out of the front doors of the Red Club, which Jessie owned and where Caleb was the dungeon master.

She was pretty sure the rest of the greater Lobster Cove community had gathered around. You had to love a small town.

Tim grinned like the very devil. "I'm glad you're all here," he gestured to the crowd of photographers. "Even you."

Every single photographer put his camera up over

his right eye and placed his finger on the click button.

Tim held up his hand. "Not so fast. No pictures unless it's okay with my lady." He turned and studied her face. "Are you okay with this?"

What? Hadn't he already asked her that? "Okay with what?"

"Okay with getting your picture taken. With me right next to you. Because unless you're totally good with it, no picture."

He had this odd, hopeful gleam in his eye.

"I…I told you I was." She felt a little lightheaded.

"I won't let them hurt you."

She looked around at all the people on the street in front of the Red Club. Everyone grinned at her expectantly, like their next breaths depended on her decision. She sighed. "I know."

He closed his eyes for a brief second then took her hand and brushed his lips over her fingers. The cameras whirred as he dropped to one knee in front of her, his hand still holding onto hers. "Angelique Durand, I love you with my whole heart and soul. I don't deserve you, but I promise you to do my damndest to make you happy for the rest of your life if you'll marry me." Pulling a ring box out of his pants pocket, he opened it and held it up for her to see.

Angelique felt tears running down her face as she gazed at one of the biggest diamonds she'd ever seen. Her breath caught in her throat, and she had to swallow around the lump it made.

Marry Tim? She looked down at his hopeful face and felt the last piece of her heart click into place; a piece she hadn't even known she missed, making it whole.

"Yes," she whispered. "Oh yes."

He closed his eyes and swayed like he couldn't count on his legs keeping him from falling over. "You're sure?"

"Absolutely. I've never been more sure of anything else in my life."

The crowd went crazy, clapping, whooping,

He slipped the diamond on her finger, stood, and kissed the bejeezus out of her. After coming up for air, he rested his forehead on hers. He swallowed hard. "Are you sure?"

"I've never been more sure about anything else in my entire life."

"Thank God," he murmured. "I can't even begin to imagine my life without you in it."

"Thank God you won't have to." She looked at all the people standing around and doing the heavy looking on. "Can we go home now? It's a little crowded around here."

"You got it, Sparky. Let's go.

Epilogue

"Can I get you anything, Sparky? Glass of champagne or something?"

Angelique opened her eyes. She'd nearly fallen asleep on the port bench of the cockpit of the twenty-eight foot sailboat they'd rented for their honeymoon.

She glanced down at her ring and admired the way the sunlight sent different colored beams in several directions. She would have married him without a ring, but since he'd gotten her such a huge one, she might as well enjoy it.

"Or something." She lifted her face for a kiss. He obliged.

She loved that about him.

She loved, in fact, everything about him.

He leaned down to kiss her. Nothing in her life had been sweeter.

"I don't know. It's a rare day that you turn down champagne." He tilted his head to one side. "You barely touched it yesterday at the wedding toast."

She decided the time was right to share the news that she'd been clutching tightly to her heart for the past week. "Champagne isn't good for the baby."

He crouched in front of her on legs that were less than reliable. "A baby."

She took his hand and placed it on her stomach. "*Oui.* A baby. Our baby."

He fell back on his butt with a thud. "You're sure," he whispered.

"*Oui*. We'll be a real family." Something she'd been absolutely sure she didn't want a year ago. Now she couldn't believe how excited and blessed she felt.

He nearly choked. "The two of us together already made a family."

Her blood froze. "You're not happy about the baby?"

He took her chin in his hand. "I'm happy about the baby. I'm beyond happy about the baby." He gave her a hard kiss on her mouth. "Just a few months ago I only wanted to be left alone. I wanted the world to go away." He laughed. "Then you moved in next door and you gave me my life back. I adore you, Angelique Durand Baldwin. No one else will ever love you better or longer."

"I'm counting on that, *cher*." She kissed him. "I'm counting on it.

A word about the author…

Doreen has wanted to be a writer her whole life but took a detour into being an opera singer and choral conductor. She realized that maybe she should spend more time writing when creating the backstories for her operatic characters was more fun than actually singing them. Plus her romance-lovin' heart couldn't take all the dead bodies littering the stage at the end of the performances. She is still an active conductor and is regularly found waving her arms around in front of singers.

www.doreenalsen.com

www.ingramcontent.com/pod-product-compliance
Lightning Source LLC
Chambersburg PA
CBHW071526260626
47170CB00002B/525